A Toast to Murder

ALLYSON K. ABBOTT

WITHDRAWN

KENSINGTON BOOKS

http://www.kensingtonbooks.com

KENSINGTON BOOKS are published by

Kensington Publishing Corp.
119 West 40th Street
New York, NY 10018

All Kensington titles, imprints and distributed lines are available at special quantity discounts for bulk purchases for sales promotion, premiums, fund-raising, educational or institutional use. Special book excerpts or customized printings can also be created to fit specific needs. For details, write or phone the office of the Kensington Special Sales Manager: Kensington Publishing Corp., 119 West 40th Street, New York, NY, 10018. Attn. Special Sales Department. Phone: 1-800-221-2647.

Kensington and the K logo Reg. U.S. Pat. & TM Off.

ISBN-13: 978-1-4967-0172-5
ISBN-10: 1-4967-0172-0
First Kensington Mass Market Edition: August 2017

eISBN-13: 978-1-4967-0173-2
eISBN-10: 1-4967-0173-9
First Kensington Electronic Edition: August 2017

10 9 8 7 6 5 4 3 2 1

Printed in the United States of America

There was nothing inside the folded paper, at least nothing we could see.

I had expected to find the same calligraphic writing that had been used in most of the other letters, but this one appeared to have been written on a computer in a basic font—Times New Roman, my brain told me—and printed out by a computer printer.

Dear Ms. Dalton,

This game is getting old, but fortunately for you, I like old things. I'm also smarter than you and as long as I can continue to exhibit my greater intellect, I will continue to play. But make no bones about it, if you fail another test, someone will die, and that someone might very well be you. The stakes are huge and if you hope to avoid extinction, you may have to dig deep for the answer to this one.

I'm hoping this latest letter will light a fire under your feet, though it may also dampen your spirits. Just remember to open the door to all possibilities lest someone else's life be extinguished.

Once again, I caution you to remember the rules of our engagement. No police assistance is to be used in solving my puzzles. You are not to involve any members of the police department in any way, particularly Detective Duncan Albright. I am watching you very closely, and I assure you that any violation of the rules will be met with swift and serious consequences. You have been walking a narrow line up until now, and I suggest you be more circumspect in the future. Let the history of our time together be a lesson to you.

You have until five P.M. on Sunday December 29th to figure this one out.

Yours in skepticism,
A fading fan

I stared at the letter, my mind reeling. No one said anything for several seconds.

Then Mal finally spoke. "If there are clues in there, I'm not sure I see them."

We all exchanged looks of fear, doubt, and worry.

Books by Allyson K. Abbott

Murder on the Rocks

Murder with a Twist

In the Drink

Shots in the Dark

A Toast to Murder

Published by Kensington Publishing Corp.

For Linda Hayes
Thanks for starting me off on this magnificent journey.

Acknowledgments

I can never say enough about the key people involved with creating these books: my editor, Peter Senftleben, for his wisdom, understanding, insight, and humor; my agent, Adam Chromy, for his tireless efforts on my behalf and his unfailing belief in me and my work; and all those behind the scenes at Kensington Books who help to make my books a success. It is a pleasure and an honor to work with all of you. Thank you.

Special thanks to Paula Zamiatowski, educator extraordinaire at The Domes. You not only helped me figure out my plot points, you made it fun as we plotted multiple scenarios together. People like you make this job that much more fun for me.

And special thanks to the "Porch Wednesday" group for helping with my "research." You guys keep me laughing.

With that said, the biggest thanks of all go to my readers, because without all of you, none of this would be possible. You have brought joy into my life, and I hope that in some small way I can return the favor by bringing a small measure of joy into yours. Cheers!

Chapter 1

Lots of people enjoy New Year's Eve as a chance to party, welcome in the coming year, and make resolutions they will never keep.

I've never made a New Year's resolution, and I can't remember ever partying on the holiday, either. I've always had to work because I own a bar, and bars are the places where a lot of people end up on New Year's Eve. One person who was celebrating the occasion at my bar this year would most certainly be unable to keep any resolutions made. It's hard to keep a promise to yourself when you're dead.

My name is Mack Dalton, and my bar is called, fittingly, Mack's Bar, although it was originally named after my father. My real name is Mackenzie, and I inherited the bar—as my father no doubt intended when he gave me my name—upon his death a year ago. He was murdered, and my efforts to solve that crime and another, related one that resulted in the death of the woman he had been dating, has led to a second career of sorts for me.

It wasn't only the murders that led me down this alternate career path. Another important contributing factor was the neurological disorder I've suffered from since birth, though perhaps *suffer* is too strong a word. It isn't painful or disfiguring, and while some of its effects might be considered disabling in a way, it doesn't keep me from living a relatively normal life. The disorder is called synesthesia, and my case is an extremely rare and severe form of it. It causes one's senses to get mixed up or cross-wired so that any sense I experience—smell, for instance—is manifested through a second sense at the same time. For instance, I not only hear people's voices, I often taste them. Men's voices always come with a taste, though women's on occasion trigger a visual manifestation instead. Smells may be accompanied by a sound or sensation, and things I see are often accompanied by a smell or tactile sensation of some sort.

In addition to this mishmash of sensory experiences, my senses are also very . . . well . . . sensitive, for lack of a better term. I can see, smell, taste, feel, and hear things most people can't.

The disorder was a novelty when I was younger, one that set me aside from the other kids—and that wasn't a good thing. All I wanted was to fit in, to be perceived as normal, and it didn't take me long to figure out I was anything but. I learned, as do most kids who don't fit the narrow-minded definitions for acceptability used in childhood, to hide what made me different. And when I almost got locked away in a mental hospital for a spell during my teen years for what the doctors thought were hallucinations, I got even better at hiding my unique ability. That continued on into adulthood, until earlier this year when I met a Milwaukee detective by the name of Duncan Albright.

Duncan and I discovered how my synesthesia could help when it came to interpreting crime scenes, analyzing clues, or talking to witnesses and suspects. And after we solved a couple of crimes together, I began to feel like my synesthesia was finally making itself useful. It felt good to do something productive and helpful with it. Unfortunately, not everyone saw it the way Duncan and I did, and things got messy fast.

On this particular New Year's Eve, I was in my bar, my mind busily working at muffling and dismissing all the secondary sensory experiences I was having as a result of the many sounds, sights, and smells associated with the celebration. Bars in Wisconsin are allowed to stay open all night on New Year's Eve, and in the past Mack's Bar has done just that. But this year I decided to do something different. At ten o'clock in the evening, I closed the bar to the public and had a private party for my staff, close friends, and a few select customers who belonged to a group called the Capone Club, a gathering of interested parties who helped me solve crimes. I also invited a few people who were suspects in a deadly scheme that I hoped to put an end to. It definitely wasn't your typical party crowd.

My decision to shut my doors stemmed from several things. For one, I wanted to thank most of the invitees to this private party for their unwavering support of me. I also wanted to minimize my exposure to all the typical noise and revelry that accompanies a busy bar on New Year's Eve, because it's a nightmare for me with my synesthesia. And the final reason was that this year I did have a resolution I wanted to make, and I was going to need the help of my crime-solving friends to accomplish it.

This year, my resolution was to catch and expose the person who had been tormenting me for weeks with taunting letters that had taken me citywide on several scavenger hunts. The person, or persons—I had reason to think I was dealing with a twisted, murderous twosome—had already killed two people I knew well: Lewis Carmichael, a regular customer of mine who had also been a member of the Capone Club, and Gary Gunderson, one of my employees. Threats of more deaths—mine included—had been a standard part of this perverse game. I was tired of it and determined to put an end to it. To me, this seemed to be as good a New Year's resolution as anything else I could come up with.

I suppose resolutions aren't supposed to be easy to accomplish, and this one certainly aligned with that rule. To start with, while I had a good idea who the primary letter writer was, I had no idea who the second person might be. And to add to the challenge, there was an excellent chance that it was someone I knew, one of my friends, regular customers, or employees.

It wasn't part of my original agenda to have things come to a head the way they did on New Year's Eve, but fate and circumstance came together and laughed at my silly plan, implementing one of their own. One minute I was preparing to raise a glass in a toast to the coming year along with my invited guests, and the next I was standing at the head of the stairs leading to the basement area of my bar, staring down at a dead body. Having someone die in the bar was unnerving enough by itself, particularly since this was the third death that had occurred in or near my bar in the past year, none of them from natural causes. But the identity of this particular victim sent chills down my spine and threw a wrench into the works of my plan the likes of which I could have never anticipated.

Midnight on New Year's Eve is often marked by people shouting, fireworks, and an assortment of noisemakers . . . a general clamor of sound. But on this particular New Year's Eve, it was marked by something different: a blood-curdling scream.

Chapter 2

In order to understand how things got scary and crazy unpredictably fast, I need to backtrack a little. It all began a few weeks before the fateful New Year's Eve party, in the early part of December. On the heels of my crime-solving activities with Duncan, there had been a lot of press coverage about me. This didn't sit well with Duncan's bosses, and as a result, he was suspended and ordered not to associate with me. This might not have been a huge issue but for two things. One, I had invited Duncan into my bed as well as into my life by then, and we were in the process of exploring the potential behind our relationship. Letting go of that wasn't easy.

And two, I had discovered I liked this crime-solving stuff. I relished the chance to do something good with my synesthesia. It had been an albatross around my neck for most of my life—sometimes almost literally so. Whenever I grew nervous about exposing it, or revealing it to someone for the first time, it triggered an uncomfortable strangling sensation around my throat. When Duncan came into my life and gave my quirk a valuable use, my synesthesia started to feel more like a superpower, a strength I could be proud of and no longer needed to hide. That feeling was strangely intoxicating.

Duncan and I stayed apart during the three weeks he was suspended, waiting to see if he would lose his job. When he returned to work, we returned to our relationship, but we kept it under wraps, sneaking around like a couple of love-struck, underage teenagers. The Capone Club enabled me to continue my crime-solving activities without Duncan's help—at least no help anyone knew about other than a few, trusted members—and we probably could have gone on that way for a long time, waiting out everyone's interest in me and my involvement with the police, Duncan in particular.

But I had drawn the attention of someone else, someone other than the press and the police bigwigs. This someone was waging a letter-writing campaign of fear and terror against me, and setting deadlines that, if missed, would result in the death of someone close to me. Lewis Carmichael had been murdered before I got the first letter as proof of how serious the writer was. And when I missed a deadline recently because I misinterpreted the clues in one of the letters, my bouncer/bartender Gary Gunderson had been killed. His death was particularly bitter for me, not only because I felt responsible for it, but because Gary had once put his own life on the line to save mine.

Along with the deadlines imposed by the letters, there was another caveat: I was not to involve the police—particularly Duncan, who was mentioned by name—in the solving of the letters' clues. The only thing I was supposed to use was what one reporter referred to as my "special senses." That meant no use of modern-day forensics or police investigative techniques. Duncan and I found a way around that, too, by meeting on the sly and setting up a friend of Duncan's who also happened to be a cop working an undercover assignment as my new beau. Malachi "Mal" O'Reilly came from a construction company family, which made him the perfect candidate for infiltrating a local construction company suspected of bribery, shoddy work, and other offenses. His work hours also made him the perfect candidate for assisting me in some of my investigative efforts as I strove to solve the puzzles in each of the letters. The fact that he was a cop was initially known to only three other people in the bar besides me: Cora Kingsley, a forty-something, single, redheaded, man-eater who owned her own IT company, and the Signoriello brothers, Joe and Frank, two retired insurance salesmen in their seventies whom I have known all my life. These three people were also the closest thing I had to family now that my father was gone.

Duncan's clever idea to use Mal would have been great except for one small glitch. I found myself genuinely attracted to the man, an attraction that proved mutual. We had yet to act on it, but my mind and my heart were a muddled mess.

On the day after Christmas, Mal and I set out to follow up on the latest clues about the letter writer, which had included beer-soaked paper and a small key that one might use for a diary or a jewelry box. Written at the top of the key in nearly invisible clear nail polish was a pound or number sign, followed by the numeral 1.

It took us a while to figure out the meaning behind this clue, but we eventually decided it had something to do with Pabst beer. Since Pabst was no longer brewed in Milwaukee—though rumors were circulating that they might return—the only significant landmarks I could identify were the historic Pabst Mansion, the home commissioned by Captain Frederick Pabst in 1890, and the Pabst Theater. Since the time deadlines in previous letters had been closing times for the venues where we found the clues, we made the assumption that the same thing held true with this particular letter. Based on that, we focused our attention on the Pabst Mansion. The structure sits on what was once a small, bucolic hillside but is now in the heart of downtown Milwaukee, surrounded by commercial buildings and the Marquette University campus. Guided tours of the house are given throughout the year, but for a couple of weeks around Christmastime, the public is allowed in for self-guided, albeit supervised, tours to see a renowned and extravagant display of decorations.

Duncan had originally collected the key that had come with the letter and taken it with him to have it examined for any evidence we might have missed. He had someone in the police lab who was willing to run things for him off the books, and he told this person that his sister was being stalked and he was trying to find out who it might be. But on Christmas Day, he joined me and a few trusted others—Cora, the Signoriello brothers, Mal, and Cora's current paramour, Tiny—for a private celebration. It was during our afternoon dinner that I figured out the meaning behind the letter, and Duncan returned the key to me at that time, informing me that no other evidence had been found on it.

I opened up the bar later on Christmas, and Duncan hid away in my apartment for the duration of the evening and into the night, allowing us to share some rare but treasured time together. But in order to avoid detection in case anyone might be watching, he had slipped away in the wee hours. I awoke the next morning with his side of the bed empty and a note by my coffee machine that he'd call me later.

After showering, dressing, and grabbing a quick bite to eat, I'd headed downstairs to help my on-coming staff get the bar open by eleven. Mal had shown up shortly after I opened the doors—an arrangement we had made the day before—and the two of us headed out shortly thereafter.

So it was that I, armed with my tiny key and with Mal at my side, approached the Pabst Mansion just before noon on the day after Christmas. We pur-chased two tickets and began our tour at the stately front entrance. Given the size of the place, and the fact that I had no idea exactly what I was supposed to be looking for, I figured it could take us a couple of hours to go through it unless we got lucky early on. Complicating things was the cast I had on my left leg and the crutches I had to use to get around. I'd had a car accident on my way to the Public Market—the destination indicated by clues in the letter I had misinterpreted. That accident had broken bones in my leg and cost Gary Gunderson his life.

We entered the mansion through its massive front door and found ourselves in a huge foyer complete with its own fireplace and an old-fashioned bell service center for calling servants.

"Fascinating architecture," Mal observed, studying the intricate wood carvings in the foyer and the painted coves in the adjoining dining and music rooms.

"The architecture might be at its finest, but the décor is ostentatious," I said.

Mal shrugged. "That's the way they did things back then. If you had money, you flaunted it. And at the time, this sort of intricately carved woodwork, along with richly painted ceilings and walls, were a sign of wealth."

The house, despite its overly ornate décor, was a beautiful specimen. There were hand-carved moldings and trim in every square inch of the place, and each room had its own theme and individual architecture. The doors separating the rooms were giant slabs of wood hung with humongous hinges, and each side of them sported a different carved design to match the décor of the room it was in once the door was closed.

I managed well enough for a while, enjoying the details and historical anecdotes provided by the various guides positioned throughout the place, and observing the painstaking restorations being done by the historical preservation group that had saved the mansion from destruction in 1978. It was fortunate that the home had been bought and used as a residence for the archbishop by the Archdiocese of Milwaukee. For sixty-seven years after the Pabst family moved out, it served as home to a host of archbishops, priests, and nuns, who left most of the original details in place, though they painted over much of the décor. Removal of that paint allowed the original details to be revealed in all their original, ostentatious glory, everything from hand-painted ceiling designs to silk wall coverings. It was a slow, arduous process that was still ongoing, and I imagined the restorers must have experienced a thrill each time they exposed some of the underlying treasures.

Sensory overload is an ongoing, persistent threat for me. I've spent a lot of years and effort learning how to dampen the effects some environments have on me, and I've gotten relatively adept at it. I had to if I wanted to survive and stay sane. But there are still times when new places or experiences overwhelm me.

As detailed and ornate as everything on our tour was, I managed well enough with my vivid and effluvious synesthetic responses until we got to the captain's wife's sitting room. Apparently, Frederick Pabst's wife, Maria, had a close and fervent love affair with the color pink. Her sitting room was a pink nightmare that made me feel like I was trapped inside a bottle of Pepto-Bismol. For some reason, all that pink triggered a synesthetic overload of smells, visual manifestations, and tactile responses.

"Too much," I said, closing my eyes and rubbing at my temples. "It gives me a headache."

Mal put a hand on my shoulder. "I'm with you on this one," he said, steering me in a different direction. "Fortunately, the room is roped off, so I doubt what we're looking for is in there, unless the letter writer wants us to get arrested during this search."

"It wouldn't surprise me," I grumbled. What we were looking for, we guessed, was some kind of small box that our key would fit.

"Let's move on," Mal said. "I want to see more of this architecture."

"You shouldn't be focusing on the architecture," I said in a mildly chastising tone. I kept my voice low so I wouldn't be overheard by the other people touring along with us. "Remember why we're here."

"I know, I know," Mal admitted. "But I can't help myself. It's hard to stay focused on the task at hand."

As we made our way through the various rooms, I found those words as applicable to me as they were to Mal. Maybe more so. It was a struggle to stay focused because of the many conversations going on around us, and the voluminous, colorful arrays of Christmas décor. Every minute or so, I reminded myself of our original goal and tried to look for something the key might fit, something that didn't appear to belong, or if it did look like it belonged, something that could easily be lifted. Yes, I was resigned to becoming a thief if necessary, but I justified this decision by reminding myself I could be saving a life by stealing. And if I found the item I needed, odds were it would be something someone had slipped into the décor rather than something that originated with the house. I couldn't be sure of this, however, which is why both Mal and I were wearing bulky coats and he was carrying a large satchel. Since the house was plenty warm despite the cold outside air, this didn't make our task any less arduous. I was sweating beneath my coat, and this fact triggered reactions all its own.

We tried to take our time and be as thorough as possible, and this garnered us some odd stares from other tourists and the guides who were stationed throughout the house whenever we looked under or behind furnishings. This also made us some of the slowest-moving people, and our lingering was eyed with suspicion. We hung for a long time in Frederick's study as Mal admired the coffered ceiling with its dark, thick, oak beams framing painted German proverbs and the intricately carved, built-in cupboards, each with its own secret latch to release the door. At the start of the tour, we had been instructed not to touch things or take any photographs, but whenever I had a chance and the guides' attention was focused elsewhere, I shifted things on shelves and tugged open drawers, looking for our objective.

We struck out in the study and moved on to the second floor, where we toured bedrooms and baths. Mal got down on his hands and knees a couple of times to peek under furniture and beds while I stood by, serving as sentry. Though we tried not to be too obvious and to do our spying when other people weren't around, there was enough of a crowd going through the place to make it impossible at times.

A little over two hours later, we reached the end of the tour without finding anything that looked like something my key would work in. I felt a niggle of panic setting in.

"There's still the gift shop," I said to Mal, as a guide directed us toward an exit that led into it. "Maybe it's there."

"And if not?"

"If not, I don't know where to go or what to do next. Maybe we got it wrong again. Maybe we'll have to hit up the theater." My mind resisted as I thought about what would come next if we failed: the death of someone I knew. "It has to be at the gift shop," I said with a tone of desperate hope.

We entered the small area, which was attached to the house but was an add-on to the original structure. It had originally been built as an open-air pavilion for the World's Columbian Exposition in Chicago back in 1893, an expo where Captain Pabst, the beer baron, had had the honor of serving his beer and his beer only to the millions of attendees.

Built from polished terra-cotta and embellished with a beautiful art-glass dome, the pavilion served as a display of the Pabst family fortunes and Frederick's dominance over his beer-producing empire. Once the fair had ended, Pabst had the structure dismantled and moved to the house, where it was rebuilt to serve as a summer conservatory. At some point, walls had been added to it, turning it into an enclosed room. Compared with the other areas of the house, this portion hadn't been as lovingly and carefully restored. Peeling paint, hastily patched walls, and a general whitewash of everything set it apart.

There were two people behind the cashier desk near the entrance: a man and a woman, both of whom looked to be well into their eighties. They were busy waiting on other customers, and Mal and I settled into the queue that had formed. Mal grabbed a set of Pabst coasters so it wouldn't look too strange to be standing in line. When we finally made it up to the desk, the woman, who was sitting on a stool, looked up at me with a tired smile stamped on her age-etched face.

"May I—" She paused, and squinted at me, and I saw a hint of recognition. My heart leapt. "Are you Mackenzie Dalton?" she asked.

"I am." I smiled, trying not to look as anxious as I felt.

"I have something for you." She slid off her stool and turned around, putting her back to us. It was curved and arthritic-looking beneath the cheery red Christmas sweater she was wearing. Slowly she tottered toward some shelves on the wall behind the desk, and with an audible creak, she bent over and removed a wrapped box from the bottom shelf. She shuffled her way back to us and handed me the wrapped package. "Someone left this for you the other day," she said.

"Was it a woman?" I asked. We had good reason to suspect that the letter writer might be Suzanne Collier, the very wealthy and influential wife of Tad Amundsen, one of my regular customers and a member of the Capone Club. Tad was a trophy husband, a ridiculously handsome man who had owned a small business as a CPA before he met Suzanne. Now he provided tax, financial, and stock market services for many of Suzanne's wealthy friends and acquaintances. As such, he regularly rubbed elbows with most of Milwaukee's elite, although he had remained the same down-to-earth, easygoing, relatively humble person he had been before he married Suzanne.

The woman behind the desk shook her head. "No, it was a man, a young fellow. He said he had to leave town and knew you'd be coming here, and wanted to leave this for you. He gave me a picture of you, so I'd know you when you stopped by."

"What did he look like?" I asked her, hearing the impatient sigh of the woman in line behind me, who was undoubtedly eager to pay for her items and get out rather than listen to me interrogate the old woman.

"He was average height," the woman said. She paused, glanced at Mal standing beside me. "Shorter than him by a couple inches." She looked away, gazing off into the distance. "Brown hair, brown eyes . . . nice smile," she added, reminiscing with one of her own.

"Did he give you his name?"

The woman stared at me for a moment, brow furrowed. Then her face brightened. "Why yes— yes, he did," she said, and my heart leapt again. "It was John Smith."

My heart sank. I felt certain John Smith wasn't the man's real name. "Thank you," I said, and then Mal offered up his coasters, which the woman dutifully rang up and bagged.

As soon as we were outside, I wanted to tear the package open. Mal must have sensed my eagerness because he put a staying hand on my arm. "We need to be mindful of any evidence," he said, "even though we know there probably isn't any."

We knew this because there had been no evidence of any sort on any of the other packages or letters— no fingerprints, no fibers, nothing that wasn't supposed to be there other than a stray bit of pollen in the misinterpreted letter that may or may not have been included intentionally. The letter writer had been extremely careful.

"I don't want to go all the way back to the bar before I open it," I told him. "What if it isn't what we need? What if it's just another clue to something else here on the property?"

Mal frowned at this, thought a second or two, and nodded. "Then we'll open it in the car. I have some stuff in the trunk we can use to conserve evidence if need be."

It was a compromise, a reasonable one, I felt. Mal's car was parked several blocks away, so it meant a hike—not my favorite thing to do these days, thanks to my crutches and cast—but at least it was closer to the Pabst Mansion than my bar in the event we had to return.

The sidewalks were clear of the recent snowfall, making it easy going, but it was bitterly cold outside, with tiny but fierce tendrils of icy wind that snaked their way under our coats, down our collars, and through our pants. My cheeks were burning from the wind chill by the time we reached the car. Ironically, the stinging in my cheeks triggered waves in the air like one might see rising from the road on a very hot day. The cold on my skin made my mouth taste tart.

I settled into the passenger side of the front seat while Mal went around to the trunk and removed several paper bags, a box of latex gloves, and a roll of tape. We were wearing winter gloves already, and by the time he climbed into the driver's seat, I already had the outer wrapping on the box loosened and had slid the box out. I handed Mal the paper, and he put it inside a large brown paper bag, folding the top of the bag over.

As Mal started the car, the heater came on full blast, meaning there was likely to be some fiber or dust contamination. Mal turned the blower down, as much because it was only spewing cold air at the moment as because he was trying to minimize contamination.

The box I held was plain cardboard with no markings, the kind you can buy at any shipping or mailbox store. It was closed with a single strip of tape down the middle of both the top and the bottom, though the bottom tape was a paper type, whereas the top piece was plastic. After examining it, Mal flipped the box over, reached over to his glovebox, removed a screwdriver, and opened the box on the bottom where the two flaps of cardboard met.

"The type of tape used to seal this thing closed on top is great at picking up fibers and fingerprints, so the less we disturb it the better," he explained. He held the box out to me. "Be careful."

I was. I raised the cardboard flaps to reveal a second, smaller, white box. Gently, I removed it and turned it right side up. It had a shoe box type lid on it that wasn't taped closed, and like the outer box, it had no markings on it. I removed the lid and saw yet another, smaller box, this one made of wood. After handing the shoe box lid to Mal, who examined it closely before setting it inside the outer box, I reached in and lifted up the smaller box.

I held it over the shoe box and examined it. It was a decorative wooden box covered in a variety of geometric designs, and I was disappointed—and more than a little worried—to see there was no locking device on it. In fact, I couldn't see any obvious opening.

"It's a puzzle box," Mal said. "I got one of those years ago as a birthday gift. They're intricately carved so that the seams are virtually invisible. In order to open it, you have to figure out which parts of it move and in what direction and order."

I removed my gloves and turned the box over in my hands, studying it.

"You should keep your gloves on," Mal chastised. "There might be fingerprints."

I shot him a look of skepticism. "You know as well as I do that there won't be," I said. "Whoever is behind this has been far too careful. I need to be able to feel it without the gloves in order to figure it out. Besides, if we do get lucky and find any prints, mine can simply be eliminated, right?"

Mal frowned but said nothing more on the matter. Instead, he went back to discussing the box. "These types of boxes can be very difficult to open, depending on the number of moves involved. Some of them open with only three or four moves. Others take ten or more. Maybe we should take it back to the bar and saw it open, because it could take forever to figure . . ."

His voice tapered off as I slid a small panel on one side a half inch or so.

"Wow," Mal said with a grudging look of admiration. "That was lucky."

"Not really," I said, running my fingers lightly over the surface and then sliding another panel. "I can see and feel the subtle differences in the structure." I found a third panel and pushed it up. Turning the box over each time I moved a section, I could sense the piece that had to move next. "This is kind of fun," I said, moving two more sections. Three moves later, the box opened, revealing yet another smaller box inside. This one was metal with inlaid glass, and with a sigh of relief, I noticed it had a locking mechanism.

"You are freaking amazing," Mal said. "And a little scary," he added with a frown.

"This is easy for me," I said. I put my gloves back on and lifted out the smaller box. "This is one of those times when my extra-sensitive senses come in handy."

I fished the tiny key I'd been carrying out of my pants pocket and inserted it into the lock on the metal box. With a quarter turn, the lid sprang open, revealing a folded piece of paper inside.

"Don't take it out yet," Mal cautioned. "Let's get it back to the bar."

I nodded, familiar by now with the necessary pre-cautions we had to take to ensure we captured any trace evidence or minute clues that might be inside the box or within the folds of the paper. Granted, we had already risked any trace evidence by simply opening the boxes and by my handling of the puzzle box without gloves. But some of the clues we'd en-countered in the past had been tiny—a flower petal, a bit of pollen—and I didn't want to risk missing a clue. I closed the lid on the box and slipped the key back into my pocket. Then I nested the little box back inside the puzzle box and slid the panels back into their original positions. Once I set this in the shoe box, Mal handed me the lid. I replaced it and then handed it all to him. He put it inside the larger outer box and then handed it all back to me.

"Let's go," I said.

As Mal pulled out, I held the box in my lap, feeling

as if I was holding a ticking time bomb. To distract myself, I looked out my window and tried to focus on the passing scenery.

A few blocks from my bar, we drove past a restaurant, and I saw a familiar face among the pedestrians. "Mal, look, there's Duncan." I pointed to where he was on the opposite side of the street.

Duncan was standing on the sidewalk talking with a woman—a beautiful woman, with long dark hair, delicate features, and a tall, slender body.

"Want me to stop?" Mal asked.

"Sure."

Mal turned on his blinker to move over toward a parking spot. I rolled down my window, prepared to holler at Duncan.

"Don't call out to him," Mal cautioned. "We don't know who might be watching."

He was right, and the blast of frigid air gusting into the car made the decision to close the window an easy one. We had taken many precautions over the past few weeks to hide the fact that Duncan and I were still seeing one another, just in case the letter writer was watching. It would be stupid to blow it all on a chance encounter.

I stared at Duncan, willing him to look our way as Mal maneuvered the car into a parking spot. The woman who was with Duncan suddenly flung her arms around his neck and kissed him. It wasn't a chaste kiss either. She wrapped her hand around the back of his head, pulled his face toward her, and gave him a long, sensuous lip-lock.

I turned away quickly, feeling a stab of pain in my chest. The pain was an emotional reaction, I knew, but it felt very real, and for a moment I wondered if I might be having a heart attack. I shook my head, felt the pain dissipate, and looked across the street again. Duncan pulled away from the woman and placed both of his hands on her shoulders. He was saying something to her, and judging from the expression on her face, it was something nice. She gazed up at him all dreamy-eyed, a beatific smile on her lips. Her arms snaked around his waist, her hands lacing behind his back, and she pulled him closer. I looked away again, unable to watch anymore.

Mal hadn't seen the romantic display because he had been focused on jockeying into the parking spot. As he turned off the car's engine, I reached out and touched the hand that held the key. "Start it back up," I said.

"Why? What's wrong?"

"I changed my mind. It's too dangerous to contact him out here in the open. Let's go back to the bar."

Mal studied my face for a moment before turning to glance over at the sidewalk where Duncan had been. "Where did he go?"

I looked over at where he had been moments ago and saw that both he and the woman were gone. Where had they disappeared to? Had they gone into the restaurant? Or had they walked around the corner to the next street? "I don't know," I said with a small sense of relief.

Mal started the car up again, and after signaling and waiting for passing traffic, he pulled out. A few blocks later we were at my bar, and thanks to a bit of serendipitous timing, Mal secured a spot right out front. I placed the boxes inside one of the paper bags Mal had retrieved from his trunk and climbed out of the car. With my right hand, I wrapped my fingers around the handle of the paper bag, and then around the hand support on my crutch, and headed for the front door, the bag swinging and banging against my crutch. Mal shut the car doors—I'd left mine open—and scampered to catch up to me.

"Whoa," he said as he came up alongside of me. "Let me help."

He tried to take the bag from my hand, but I grumbled, "I got it" at him and refused to let go.

He reared back as if I'd slapped him, and I instantly regretted both my tone and my actions. "Sorry," I said. "It's just the cold. I want to get inside where it's warm."

Mal didn't try again to take the bag from me. I could tell from the way he was eyeing me that he knew something was wrong, but to his credit, he didn't ask. He held the bar door open for me and followed me inside without another word. I knew he'd say something eventually but figured he'd wait until we were somewhere private. What was I going to tell him? The truth? He and Duncan were friends. Add to that Mal's feelings for me, and it didn't exactly make him an objective listener on the subject of my relationship with Duncan. It would be easy enough to lie and say it was something else bothering me—pain in my leg, or irritation over the letter writer, anything. But I didn't like the idea of lying to Mal.

Then another thought occurred to me. He and Duncan were friends, and friends often share things about themselves. Maybe Mal knew who the woman was. Maybe he'd known Duncan was seeing someone else all along. Maybe *he* had been lying to *me* all this time by omitting this key information.

I decided a frank discussion was called for and figured I'd deal with it once we were alone. First, I needed to make sure my bar was running smoothly. It was early enough in the day that the crowd was thin. Most of the tables just inside the door were empty, but I knew there would be a handful of people—maybe more—upstairs in the Capone Club room. The day after Christmas isn't usually a super busy day, but a lot of people do go out shopping in hopes of getting first dibs on some of the after-holiday sales, and that tends to bring people into the bar. By later this afternoon and into the evening, I expected a healthy crowd.

Billy Hughes, who is usually my evening and weekend bartender—hours that work well around his law school schedule—was on duty. My regular day bartender, Pete Hanson, was home sick with a stomach bug. Since Billy was on a break from school due to the holiday, he generously offered to fill in for Pete, pulling double duty that would end up giving him a fifteen-hour shift. My newly hired bouncer, Theodore Berenson, aka Teddy Bear, who also knew how to tend bar, was willing to put in some extra hours as well. Teddy was a friend of Billy's who had recently been cut off from his extremely wealthy family because he opted to pursue an art degree instead of the MBA his shipping magnate father, Harley Berenson, wanted him to have. As a result of that, he had labeled himself the black sheep of the family, and he was desperate for employment and willing to work extra hours so he could make his own money. He was determined to prove to his father that he could survive just fine on his own, and his stubborn resolve was a definite boon for me. Teddy had prior training as a bartender, and between him and Billy, they managed the bar quite nicely. And Teddy's huge size—

six-six and about three hundred pounds—made him perfect for stepping in as a bouncer.

Both of them were behind the bar when we came in, and they acknowledged our arrival with nods as we entered.

"Hey, boss," Billy said once I was within speaking distance. "Things are slow so far."

"It will pick up later." I looked over at Teddy. "Is everything going okay with you? Are you liking the job?"

"Things are going great," Teddy said. "I love it here. Thanks again for hiring me."

"You're welcome. Let me know if you need anything."

I headed for my office with Mal on my heels. Once inside, I set the bag on my desk, shrugged off my coat while balancing on my crutches, and then fell onto my couch. "I'm not feeling all that well at the moment," I said. "Do you think we could postpone opening this until later?"

Mal eyed me with a mixture of curiosity and skepticism. Ironically, I'd spent more time with him, my fake beau, than I had with Duncan, my real one, so Mal knew me well enough at this point to know something was bothering me. I could tell he didn't buy into my trumped-up excuse, but I hoped he'd accept it anyway and leave. No such luck.

He cocked his head to one side and pinned me with his laser-blue eyes. "What's going on, Mack? You've been acting kind of weird ever since we saw Duncan."

I stared at him, once again tempted to use a lie as an excuse because I didn't want to tell him what was bothering me; it made me look like an insecure ninny. But it was what it was, so I decided to go for it. "Did you see the woman Duncan was talking to?" I asked him.

He shrugged. "I caught a glimpse, but I didn't get a good look. I was too focused on parking the car. Why?"

"Why? Because she was gorgeous."

"So are you, silly." He said this as if it was the most obvious thing in the world. "Is that what this is about? Are you feeling a little jealous?" He huffed a small, dismissive laugh. "Just because Duncan was talking to a pretty woman doesn't mean—"

"He kissed her, Mal. And not one of those friendly, old acquaintance or I'm your sister kind of kisses, either. I'm talking about a romantic kiss." I looked away from him, not wanting him to see the tears I felt forming in my eyes despite my best efforts to quell them.

"You think Duncan is seeing someone else?" Mal said.

"What would you think?"

He didn't answer right away. "I think it doesn't sound like Duncan," he said eventually. "He's a pretty straightforward guy. And I know how much he cares for you."

"That doesn't mean he can't care about someone else. Or that he hasn't grown frustrated and bored with this sneaking around relationship we've had. Hell, I've been frustrated by it. Why wouldn't he be?"

"I think you should at least give him the benefit of the doubt before you hang him," Mal said carefully. "Maybe there's a perfectly logical and innocent explanation for it."

He was right, and I knew it, but that didn't make what I had seen any easier to swallow. The two of us shifted awkwardly in the minute of silence that followed. Finally, I said, "I think I need some time to digest this, Mal."

"And the letter? Are you going to wait on that?"

The tone of disbelief—and yes, judgment—I heard in his voice made me shrink up inside. Like I said, he knew me well. He knew I wouldn't be able to stand the curiosity nagging at me. Nor would I risk the lives of any of my friends over my own broken heart.

I squeezed my eyes closed and let my head fall back against the couch. "No, I don't suppose we should wait on that," I said with resignation. I lifted my head and looked at him. "But I don't want to involve Duncan yet, either. Since he was with that woman, he's clearly not going to be available now anyway. So let's you and I do it. And I'll get Cora. Does that sound reasonable?"

"Sure," Mal said slowly after a second of thought, dragging the word out into nearly two syllables. I sensed he was carefully weighing everything I'd said, searching for some hidden meaning or trapdoor phrase, tiptoeing around my emotions.

"Good." I pushed myself up from the couch and headed for the door. "Let's go upstairs to my apartment and do it. I'll call Cora when we get there. I'm sure she's up in the Capone Club room, so it shouldn't take her long to get to us."

With that, I headed out of my office and down the hall to the door that led to my apartment. I didn't look back to see if Mal was coming with me—I didn't need to because I could hear him behind me: the gentle swish of his clothing, the soft-padded fall of his shoes, the light crinkling sound of the bag containing the boxes, the faint, rhythmic whoosh of his every exhalation. Even if I couldn't hear those things, I could feel his presence behind me like a subtle pulling force, as if he were a magnet and I were made of metal. So far, I'd fought that feeling every time I sensed it, as if to give in to the pull of that magnet would be crossing a bridge that would burn behind me.

But after what I saw between Duncan and the woman on the street, I was beginning to rethink my caution. Maybe it was time to burn some bridges.

Chapter 3

I was breathless by the time I reached my apartment, and I wasn't sure if it was from my exertions, my emotions, or some combination of the two. Once I reached my dining room table, which had become an evidence-processing center of late, I took out my phone and sent a text to Cora. As expected, she answered me seconds later, and also as expected, she was in the Capone Club room. Mal dropped the box with the letter on the table and went back downstairs to await Cora's knock. I went into my father's office and grabbed several sheets of plain white printer paper we would use to help us detect any small bits of evidence that might drop from any of the boxes or the letter. By the time I carried the papers out and placed them on the table, I heard Cora and Mal conversing at the bottom of the stairs.

Cora looked excited and flushed as she entered the room carrying her ubiquitous companion—her laptop. "You found something? That's great!" she said as she settled into a chair and opened up her laptop. "Should I call Duncan to see if he can video chat with us?"

"No!" As soon as the word left my mouth, I realized that my answer was more strident than necessary. Cora shot me a look, then she gave Mal one. He simply shrugged, and Cora, looking wary, turned back to me. "So it's just us three?"

"Yes. Duncan is tied up right now, so there's no reason to try to raise him. And Mal is a cop, so it's not like we don't have representation from that quarter here." I could feel Mal's eyes on me, and I studiously ignored him. "We've done this enough times to know what we're doing and how to do it. Not to mention the fact that, so far, we haven't found a single piece of usable evidence on any of these letters, their containers, or their contents. If it is Suzanne Collier who is sending them, she has an uncanny knowledge of forensic processes."

"Perhaps she picked it up from Tad talking about the Capone Club," Cora said.

I nodded, but I also frowned. I didn't want to believe Tad was in on this with his wife, but I couldn't deny the possibility. I felt it was more likely he was as much of a pawn in this as I was, and his wife was trying to discredit me and disband the Capone Club because she thought her husband was devoting too much time and attention to both. I supposed it wasn't beyond the realm of possibilities to think she might have picked up some of her forensic knowledge simply from listening to Tad talk about the group and the cases we've been involved with.

"Can you record this, Cora?" I asked. "That way we have documentation."

"Sure. I can do it on my phone." She took it out of a pocket, tapped the face a couple of times, and then said, "Ready when you are."

Mal and I donned latex gloves, and while he held on to the bag, I took out the main box, opened it and removed the shoe box, and then took out the puzzle box. As I removed this last piece, Cora looked at it with arched brows and, in an apprehensive tone, said, "Oh, dear."

"Worry not," Mal said. "Watch her."

Once again, I examined and felt along the box's edges, managing to open it more quickly this time because the moves were preserved in my memory.

Cora smiled and shook her head. "You never cease to amaze me, Mack."

"It's just the way my world is," I said with a shrug. I set the opened box down on top of the papers and then took out the final, jeweled box. Taking the key from my pocket, I unlocked it, opened it, and took out the letter, carefully unfolding it.

There was nothing inside the folded paper, at least nothing we could see. I expected to find the same calligraphic writing on the paper that had been used in most of the other letters, but this letter appeared to have been written on a computer in a basic font—Times New Roman, my brain told me—and printed out with a computer printer of some sort.

Dear Ms. Dalton,

This game is getting old, but fortunately for you, I like old things. I'm also smarter than you, and as long as I can continue to exhibit my greater intellect, I will continue to play. But make no bones about it, if you fail another test, someone will die, and that someone might very well be you. The stakes are huge, and if you hope to avoid extinction, you may have to dig deep for the answer to this one.

*I'm hoping this latest letter will light a fire
under your feet, though it may also dampen your
spirits. Just remember to open the door to all
possibilities lest someone else's life be
extinguished.*

*Once again, I caution you to remember the rules
of our engagement. No police assistance is to be
used in solving my puzzles. You are not to involve
any members of the police department in any way,
particularly Detective Duncan Albright. I am
watching you very closely, and I assure you that
any violation of the rules will be met with swift and
serious consequences. You have been walking a
narrow line up until now, and I suggest you be
more circumspect in the future. Let the history of
our time together be a lesson to you.*

*You have until five p.m. on Sunday, December 29,
to figure this one out.*

> *Yours in skepticism,*
> *A fading fan*

I stared at the letter, my mind reeling. No one said
anything for several seconds. Then Mal finally spoke.

"If there are clues in there, I'm not sure I see them.
Is there anything unusual in the printing, Mack?"

"Not that I can see."

"The paper?" Cora asked hopefully, but I shook my
head. Just to be sure, I held it closer to my face so I
could see and smell it better. I could tell from the
smell of the ink that it was the kind used in an ink jet
printer, and said so. But that didn't help us much.

"Then we need to focus on the words," Cora said.

"Maybe there isn't a clue in here," I said, suddenly

feeling frustrated and disconsolate. "Maybe the game is over, or it's down to the final play."

We all exchanged looks of fear, doubt, and worry.

"Let's study it for a while," Mal said. "We'll take it apart one sentence at a time. If this is indeed coming to a close, we need to figure out what the endgame is supposed to be."

"It's supposed to be death," I said glumly, feeling my frustration rise. I gave Mal a pleading look. "Can't we arrest Suzanne Collier? Wouldn't that put an end to this?"

Mal grimaced. "There isn't enough evidence to arrest her—or anyone, for that matter. Particularly Suzanne Collier. Someone with that sort of money and influence can worm their way out of things even when the evidence is solid. And we're far from having that. She has enough money to post any amount of bail, assuming it's offered, and given the dearth of evidence we have here, I imagine it would be. And that's assuming the DA would even consider an arrest, which he won't, because all we have on Collier is coincidence and supposition."

"Then we'll get what we need," I said with determination. "I think the first step has to be finding out who her partner is. We know Suzanne didn't kill Lewis, so we need to figure out who could have. We need to figure out who she's been in contact with. Based on the constant reminders of how closely I'm being watched, I can't help but think that whoever is helping her is someone close to me, someone from the Capone Club, or maybe even an employee." The idea made me shudder.

"The woman at the gift shop said whoever dropped

this package off for you was a man around five-ten or so, with brown hair and brown eyes," Mal reminded me.

Cora scoffed. "Well, that certainly narrows it down," she said, her voice dripping with sarcasm.

"I know," I said. "That description fits at least four guys we know: Carter, Sam, and Greg from the Capone Club, and my day cook, Jon. Besides, in the past, un-witting accomplices have been used in the delivery of these packages, so there's no way to know if the person who delivered this one has anything to do with any of this." I could feel my sense of dread—and a growing anger—building. "Can't we get a warrant or something like that for Suzanne's phone records?" I asked.

Mal shook his head, giving me an apologetic look. "There isn't enough evidence to support one, and I can guarantee you she'd pull some high-powered lawyer out of her handbag to fight it. Besides, based on how savvy the letter writer has been so far, I doubt there is a trail like that for someone to find."

I raked a hand through my hair and sighed in irri-tation. "This is getting ridiculous," I muttered, shak-ing my head. "There has to be a way to end this."

Cora, who had stopped filming, thank goodness, had been watching this interchange between me and Mal in silence. Now she spoke. "Mack, what's up with you? Something is different. Did something happen you haven't told me about?"

I looked at her, then at Mal, who pursed his lips and shifted his gaze to the letter. I looked back at Cora and let out a perturbed sigh. "I suppose I'm not being as objective as I should be," I admitted. "I'm upset about something else." Then I told her what I'd observed between Duncan and the woman on the street. When I was done, Cora, like Mal, tried to put a different spin on things.

"Maybe it was an old friend, or even a relative. He has a sister, doesn't he?"

I gave her an exasperated look. "I'm not stupid," I said. "I know the difference between a friendly or familial kiss and a romantic one. If Duncan is kissing his sister the way he kissed this woman, we have bigger issues to deal with."

Cora frowned, but she made no further attempts to mitigate the situation. My phone rang then, cutting through an awkwardness that was practically palpable.

"It's Clay," I said, glancing at the caller ID.

Clay Sanders was a reporter who had been hounding me in the weeks following the initial revelation about my working with Duncan. I disliked and distrusted him initially because the articles he wrote, which were the first such pieces to appear anywhere, hadn't been altogether kind, and they had set off most of my publicity woes. And unlike most of the other reporters who followed his lead, Clay had been irritatingly persistent in his pursuit of me, hanging out at the bar a lot and constantly grilling my staff and customers about me. I finally decided to abide by the philosophy of keeping one's friends close and one's enemies closer, and I had invited him into the Capone Club fold recently. In exchange for letting him in, I promised him access to insider information on any cases we worked. He already had a lot of insider knowledge on the case we were working on at the time—and he proved how clever he was by informing me and Mal that he knew what Mal really did for a living. He promised not to out Mal, and over the time we investigated that last case, he proved to be a valuable and helpful resource. He also took a bullet in the gut a few days ago while we were exposing the culprit. He was currently recuperating from the emergency surgery he'd had to have as a result. Taking that bullet had upped my confidence level in him, though I was still wary of giving him my full trust.

The phone I was currently using was a burner that Mal had given me several days ago when I dropped mine in the toilet. I had my old phone on rice, hoping to dry it out, but so far it wasn't working. I supposed I'd have to buy a new one at some point, but for now the burner would do. The people who needed it had the new number, and to prove my new faith in Clay, he was included on that list.

"Hi, Clay," I said. "How are you?"

"I'm doing well," he said. "I got home from the hospital about an hour ago. Can't say I'll miss the hospital food, but I have strict instructions to keep my diet bland and soft for the next week, so I'm not sure things will be much better here. At least I get to sleep in my own bed."

"I'm glad you're doing okay. Can I bring something to you? I make a mean chicken noodle soup. Do you need someone to pick up some groceries for you?"

"No, thanks. I'm good. My coworkers have that covered quite well. But there is something else you can do for me. Can you come by my place tomorrow morning around ten?"

"Sure. What do you want me to bring?"

"Just yourself. And only yourself."

I frowned at this.

"There are some people I need you to meet," Clay added, making the mystery no clearer.

"Okay," I said warily. "Can you give me a hint what this is about?"

"I'd rather not," he said. "Just trust me, okay?"

I thought about it for a few seconds, and my gut seemed at ease with the request. "Okay," I said, making my decision. "Give me the address."

He did, and I made a mental note of it. One of the handier aspects of my synesthesia is excellent memory and recall.

Once I had disconnected the call, I explained Clay's request to Mal and Cora.

"What do you think it's about?" Mal asked.

"I don't have the vaguest idea. He said he had some people he wanted me to meet. Maybe someone else from the paper? Someone he wants to cover for him while he's recuperating?" I shrugged.

"Do you want me to go with you?" Mal asked.

"No, he was rather adamant that I come alone."

"I'm not sure I like that," Mal said with a scowl. "How much do we really know about Clay?"

"Not a lot," I admitted. "But he's proven trustworthy so far. If it would make you feel better, you can drive me there and wait in the car."

"It would."

"Good. Now that that's settled, let's get back to the letter," I said. Reluctantly, and perhaps a bit petulantly, I forced my attention back to the letter.

"Let's look for words, or themes, or clichés, or idioms that are different from the other letters," Mal suggested. "Like this phrase to *make no bones about it.*"

"Bones," Cora said thoughtfully. "A graveyard again?"

One of the previous letters had led us to a local cemetery. "Maybe," I said, unconvinced. "But I don't think whoever is behind this would use the same place twice."

"Maybe it's a different cemetery," Cora said. "There's the phrase *dig deep for the answer.*"

I considered her idea, but it still felt wrong somehow. "I don't think so," I said in a tone that made it clear I gave the idea little credence. Leaning over the table, I stared at the letter, visualizing the words, using my synesthetic synapses to search for a pattern. And then it came to me.

"*Exhibit*," I said excitedly. "I think that's the key word here. Add in *bones, dig, history, extinction* . . . what do they all suggest when you think of them with the word *exhibit*?"

Mal and Cora both looked at me, and matching smiles widened over their faces.

"The Milwaukee Public Museum," they said in unison.

Chapter 4

We sealed the letter in a plastic baggie, thereby preserving the evidence, and then sealed the various boxes inside paper bags. I carried them all into my father's office so they would be out of sight. By the time that was done, it was almost three-thirty. The museum closed at five, meaning that trip would have to wait.

"I think I'm going to call it a day," I said to no one in particular, glancing at my watch. "I'm tired and want to take a nap. Do you guys mind?"

Mal took the hint immediately and said he'd see me later, and after we made arrangements to get together tomorrow for the museum trip, he left, leaving Cora and me alone. Cora sat with her elbows on the table, staring at me with a pitying expression.

"What's that look for?" I asked.

"This thing with Duncan is really bothering you, isn't it?"

"Of course it is," I said irritably. "Wouldn't it bother you if you saw Tiny engaging in a lip-lock with some gorgeous woman you didn't know?"

"Actually, not as much as you might think." She

flashed me a crooked smile and shrugged. "Anyway, we're not talking about me and Tiny; we're talking about you and Duncan."

I looked at her and sighed. "I know I'm probably overreacting. I mean, it's not like Duncan and I have some long-standing commitment to one another. And while I assumed we were exclusive, we never actually had that discussion. So maybe I'm attaching more to the relationship than he is."

Cora raked her teeth over her lower lip and said, "What did this woman look like?"

The image popped into my head as clear as if she were standing right in front of me. "She was tall and slender, with long, brunette hair. I'm not sure about the eyes because she was too far away, but I got a sense they were dark. Her features were delicate . . . button nose, high cheekbones, a small mouth." I gave Cora an abashed look and added, "This might be a bit out there, but based on her clothing, her stature, and her general looks, I got a sense that she comes from money."

Cora turned her laptop toward me. "Look at this picture. Did she look anything like this woman?"

There on the screen was the exact image of the woman I'd seen with Duncan. "That doesn't look like her; it is her," I said. "How did you do that?"

Now it was Cora's turn to look abashed. "I have a confession to make," she said. "I did a little digging around into Duncan's background when the two of you started getting serious. Not being nosy, mind you." She paused and looked chagrined. "Okay, maybe I was being a little bit nosy, but I did it mainly because I wanted to make sure you weren't getting into something you shouldn't."

She bit her lip, a sheepish look on her face, waiting

to see what my reaction would be. I probably should have been angry, or at least miffed with her for invading my privacy, but at the moment the only thing I felt was curiosity.

"And?" I prompted.

"And this woman," she pointed at her screen, "is Duncan's ex-fiancée."

This tidbit surprised me. I don't know who I was expecting the woman to be, but ex-fiancée was definitely low on the list. "Duncan told me she left him at the altar," I said, struggling to puzzle through the facts.

"She did indeed," Cora said. "And your assessment of her was spot-on. She comes from a wealthy family in Chicago, so her runaway bride escapade made the local news. Want me to pull up the article for you?"

I shook my head. "Not now. Maybe later. What's her name?"

"Courtney Metcalfe," Cora said. "Daughter of Roger Metcalfe. Roger's grandfather, Franklin Metcalfe, was a wise fellow who invested in the stock market during the twenties and then pulled most of it out right before the 1929 crash because he didn't like the way the market was behaving. That left Franklin with a boatload of cash during the Great Depression, and he put it to use buying up land and utility companies for a fraction of what they were worth. The family has continued to invest wisely over the years, and Roger is estimated to be worth somewhere in the neighborhood of three hundred million dollars."

"Wow."

"Yeah," Cora said, nodding. "Who knew Duncan almost became the husband of a multimillionaire?"

"Maybe she thought he was after her money," I mused. "You said Courtney Metcalfe lives in Chicago?"

Cora gave me a vague, noncommittal nod. "Sort of, although she also has a residence here in Milwaukee. She's listed as the vice president of her family's company, and they own or have a stake in several Milwaukee-based businesses. So I imagine she spends a fair amount of time here."

I wondered why Duncan hadn't shared any of this information with me. How often did Courtney Metcalfe come to Milwaukee, and how long did she typically stay? Did Duncan know when she was in town? Had he been seeing her for a while? Was that why we had so little time together? Had he been with her at the same time he was dating me? His excuses for his inability to see me were almost always work-related, but now I wondered if he might have been lying to me. I thought back to my conversations with him, those talks where he gave me a reason he couldn't come by. I can typically tell if someone is lying to me because there is a change in the taste or visual manifestation I experience with the sound of their voice. Duncan's voice always tasted like chocolate, though there had been some variances in the intensity or the type of chocolate flavor depending on his mood—or maybe it was depending on mine? I tried to play back some of our past discussions about why he couldn't come by. Had there been a change in the taste of his voice during any of them? I couldn't recall any particular instances, but then I hadn't been looking for them, either. Besides, Duncan knew about my ability to pick up on lies, so it would be foolish of him to be dishonest with me.

Then again, perhaps I had been so swayed by the rich chocolate taste of his voice and my own emotions that I'd failed to notice subtle changes I should have detected. I made a mental note to be more attentive to this in the future.

I experienced a stab of jealousy that felt like a squirmy discomfort in my chest, as if there was a worm in there wriggling around. I tried to shake it off, or at least shove it away, compartmentalizing it for later scrutiny.

"Thanks, Cora," I said. "You've been very helpful, as usual."

Cora eyed me with a mix of concern and suspicion. I sensed she wasn't going to let me off that easily. "We should talk about this," she said carefully.

I smiled at her. "Yes, we should. And we will. Just not now. I'll hook up with you later, and we can talk some more."

My capitulation had come too easily, and Cora narrowed her eyes at me, her suspicion deepening. "Don't do anything crazy until we talk, okay?" she said.

"I won't."

"Promise?"

"Promise."

Cora nodded and said nothing more. She gathered up her laptop and left.

Once I was finally alone, I took a moment to gather my thoughts. This thing with Duncan had shaken me more than I'd expected, and I felt a well of emotion trying to crawl up my throat, making it feel tight. My forehead pounded with waves of pain, as if the tears I was holding back were crashing hard against the breakwater that was my skull. I shook it off—literally shaking my head like a dog shedding water—and after a moment, I felt some semblance of control and calm return.

After a few slow, bracing breaths, I felt a little better.

I spent the next hour watching mindless TV and eventually did fall asleep on my couch. When I awoke, I was surprised to see that it was nearly eight in the evening.

I went downstairs to check on the bar. As usual, my staff had things well under control, and the crowd was a good one, but manageable. After checking in with all of the employees, I considered going upstairs and poking my head in on the Capone Club. But I knew Cora would be there, Cora and her endless inquisitiveness. I adored the woman—she was like a sister to me—but at the moment, I wasn't up to the task of dodging her questions. So, instead, I asked Billy to do the closing duties for me and then headed back upstairs to the solitude of my apartment. After several more hours of TV, including one inspirational episode on the HGTV channel, I went to bed. It was the longest night's sleep I'd had in years.

Chapter 5

Mal texted me the next morning at a quarter to ten to let me know he was waiting for me out front. I had been up for a couple of hours and was ready to go, at least physically. Mentally, I felt a little uneasy about this meeting with Clay Sanders. What was he up to?

I headed downstairs, locked the bar door behind me—my incoming staff had keys to the front door—and as soon as I settled into Mal's car, he pulled out. We rode in silence for several minutes, and by that I mean we said nothing, though there were plenty of noises, both real and synesthetic, to keep my ears occupied. Finally, Mal said, "Penny for your thoughts."

I looked over at him and smiled. "I'm wondering what Clay is up to," I lied. Truth was, my mind was still focused on Duncan and Cora's revelations about Courtney Metcalfe, but I was working hard to tamp those thoughts down. Giving voice to them wouldn't help.

"Are you sure you don't want me to come inside with you when we get to Clay's?" Mal asked.

"Positive. I'm not sure how much trust I have in

Clay just yet, but I'm not worried about him trying to hurt me."

"Have you considered the possibility that he might be Suzanne's partner?"

I frowned, looked at Mal like he was crazy, and shook my head. "Clay is not the letter writer."

"How can you be sure?"

"I don't know . . . I just am. Call it a gut feeling."

Mal shook his head slowly. "Until we know for sure who's behind this crap, I'm not trusting anyone's gut. Keep your phone handy, and if you feel at all uncomfortable at any point, call me."

"Will do. I have you on speed dial."

Clay's house was a small, older home only a few blocks from Duncan's place. It was a one-story with burgundy shutters and colonial blue siding trimmed in white. The yard was covered with snow, but there were flowerbeds along the front wall and lining the sidewalk that, come spring, would make for an attractive lead-in to the small front porch.

Clay must have heard or seen me approaching—not hard to do since my crutches tend to make me a noisy walker—and he hollered for me to come in as soon as I reached the front door. I reached down, turned the knob, and entered.

The front door opened directly into a carpeted living room, though there was a small rectangle of vinyl flooring just inside the door that served as sort of a foyer. There was a coat rack to my right, but I ignored it. Until I knew what was going on, I wanted to keep my coat and be prepared to make a quick getaway, though speed of any sort would be hard to come by in my current condition.

Along the wall to my right beyond the coatrack was a couch. Clay was sitting at one end of it, an afghan covering his lap and legs. There were also two chairs in the room, one perpendicular to each end of the couch, both of them occupied. On the wall across from the sofa was a fireplace with a TV mounted above it. There was a fire going, a warm, crackling respite from the cold outside. A large, dented wash-tub filled with chopped wood sat on the hearth, and it made me wonder if Clay had started the fire when he got home from the hospital or if someone had done it for him. I realized then that I didn't know anything about Clay's personal life. Was he married? Did he have kids? A girlfriend? A roommate?

The two men occupying the chairs in the room didn't look like family or, for that matter, friends. Both of them appeared to be in their late forties or early fifties, and both had hard, stern expressions on their faces and stiff, rigid posturing. They were wearing business attire: suits, ties, button-down shirts, and dress shoes.

"Mack, take your coat off and have a seat," Clay said, patting the couch next to him. "I apologize for not getting up to greet you, but I'm still pretty slow when it comes to moving around."

I ignored his request to remove my coat, but I did move farther into the room. Rather than join Clay on the couch, however, I stopped and stood a few feet in front of the fireplace, facing the three men. I stared at the two older ones, shifting my focus from one to the other. The man in the chair to my left looked familiar, but I couldn't place him right away. My nerves were triggering a host of distracting synesthetic reactions. The man to my right struck no tone of recognition at all.

No one said a word for an interminable amount of time, and I found the silence unnerving. Of course, it wasn't totally silent. There were several synesthetic sounds I experienced that were triggered by the men's colognes or aftershaves. There was also a faint astringent or antiseptic scent I picked up on, and I wasn't sure if it was a synesthetic reaction or a real smell emanating from Clay.

"What is this about, Clay?" I said finally, settling my gaze on him.

Clay smiled and shook his head slightly, no doubt amused by my refusal to follow his instructions. "It's about collaboration," he said. "But first let me make some introductions." He pointed to his right—my left—and said, "This is Mark Holland, the chief of police here in Milwaukee."

Of course. As soon as Clay said the name, the memory came back to me. Holland's face had been all over the news for several weeks now in conjunction with the uproar surrounding the cases I and the Capone Club had solved. I'd steadfastly avoided watching any of the news, but since it was often on the bar TVs, I'd caught glimpses here and there. Mark Holland was the man who'd threatened Duncan with the loss of his job if he continued to work with me.

"And to my left," Clay went on, "is Anthony Dixon, Milwaukee's chief DA."

The second man's face might not have been familiar, but the name was. He was in the news all the time, not only because of crime stories and issues, but because Dixon had been shortlisted as one of the next gubernatorial candidates.

"Gentlemen, this is Mackenzie Dalton, otherwise known as Mack."

I knew neither of these men were fans of mine, and I feared Clay had set me up for an ambush. I shot him an irritated look.

"Don't be angry," Clay said with a tentative smile. "Hear me out first. I did a little campaigning for you while I was in the hospital, and these two gentlemen would like to chat with you about what you've done, how you did it, and where we go from here."

"I'm not interested," I said. I shifted my crutches and started for the door.

"I think you will be," Clay said quickly. Then his voice turned pleading. "Please, Mack, just hear what they have to say before you go running out. I think you'll find that when all is said and done, your life will be a whole lot less complicated."

"Ironic, coming from you," I said, giving Clay a wry look, "since you're responsible for a lot of my current complications." One other complication, the one with Courtney and Duncan, tried to rear its ugly head, but I shoved it back down.

"I know," Clay said. "And I'm sorry about that."

"Are you?" I asked, pinning him with my gaze. Based on the taste of his voice, that apology was less than sincere.

Clay looked abashed. "Right, I forgot you can tell when you're getting a load of horse crap." He sighed. "So, okay, I'm not particularly sorry for outing you in my articles, but when you hear what these gentlemen have in mind, I think you'll see no real harm has been done."

He couldn't be more wrong about that, but I couldn't tell him about the letter writer.

I looked over at Holland. "You've made it quite clear that you don't approve of me, my abilities, or what I've done with them lately. I didn't do it to try to make anyone look bad or to cause anyone—"

"Ms. Dalton, please," Holland interrupted loudly, holding his hand out toward me like a cop trying to stop traffic. His voice filled my mouth with the flavor of coconut. I stopped talking, and he flashed me a grateful smile. "You don't need to explain yourself to me, at least not in that regard, and you are wrong about my attitude toward you and your . . . um, abilities. I wasn't a fan in the beginning—that's true enough—but I've changed my way of thinking. Don't get me wrong. I'm still a little skeptical, but I've had a chat or two with Detective Albright about you, and now I've spoken to Clay here as well. And both of these men are people I hold in high regard. When they speak, I listen."

I recalled then how Duncan had told me a few days ago about a discussion he'd had with Holland about me, and how the man was more open-minded than he had been initially. My thoughts whirled with dozens of things to say, but I kept my mouth shut and waited.

"Your work, you and this group of yours," he went on, pausing to clear his throat and shifting his gaze from me to the floor, "you did a phenomenal job with the Ben Middleton case. You have managed to free a man who was wrongly convicted."

"Ben Middleton is free?" I asked.

Holland looked up at me. "He will be," he answered with a smile. "It's not something that happens overnight. There are rules and steps to be taken, and paperwork, of course." He rolled his eyes. "Always the paperwork. But Ben Middleton will be freed and exonerated."

"We have already informed him of the process," Dixon said, speaking for the first time. His voice was strong but mellifluous, and it tasted like melted butter. It and his chiseled good looks would serve him well on the campaign trail if he opted to take that route. "Of course, while this outcome is a very good one for

Mr. Middleton, it is a definite black mark for my office," Dixon went on. "We screwed up and screwed up bad. Depending on who you listen to, we're either a bunch of dumb hicks with our heads so far up our asses we don't have a clue what we're doing, or we're a cabal of puppeteering masterminds with a future plan to dominate the world." He paused and let out a mirthless chuckle. "Sometimes you can't win no matter what you do or how hard you try," he said. "And that's a bitter pill to swallow."

"It wasn't my intent to make anyone look bad," I said again. "All I'm interested in is seeing that justice is served . . . correctly."

"And that's all we're interested in, as well," Holland said. "But when the three Ps get involved—the press, the public, and politics—it can be difficult at times to get the job done at all, much less done right. These are hard times for police all across the country, what with all these cop-related shootings, and stories about cops going bad or using unnecessary force. It's always been a risky job, but the risk factor is definitely amped up of late." He paused, wincing slightly. "I don't want to add to that on a local level."

I looked over at Dixon, who was leaning forward, watching me intently, his hands laced together, elbows on his knees. "You want me to stop what I'm doing, don't you?" I said to him. "That's why you're here, right?"

Dixon shook his head. "Quite the contrary," he said. "We're here to talk about teaming up with you. We want you to work for us."

I opened my mouth to protest, but before I could get a word out, Holland corrected Dixon by saying, "*With* us. We want you to work with us."

I looked at Holland, my eyes narrowing. "And what, exactly, does that mean?"

"It means we want to bring you on board as a consultant. What you've managed to accomplish so far on your own speaks to the ability you have. Clay assures me you have a talent we can make use of, one that might help us prevent any more mistakes like the ones made with Ben Middleton."

This made Dixon shift uncomfortably in his seat.

"We would pay you, of course," Holland went on. "The terms can be ironed out later." He paused and leaned back in his seat. "But we're getting a bit ahead of ourselves here. First, we would like to see this ability in practice. Clay said you can demonstrate it for us."

I sighed and gave Clay a perturbed look. I was starting to feel like a circus freak show.

"We discussed having you test them the same way you tested me," Clay said. "You know, have them make three statements, one of which is false, and you tell them which ones are which. I prepped them ahead of time and had them think of some obscure things to use in these statements, things that wouldn't be found in a Google or other online search. And at their insistence, I also didn't tell you who was going to be here to make sure you couldn't do any research ahead of time."

"Clay swears you are something of a human lie detector," Holland said. "He says you can hear subtle changes in people's voices."

I looked at him and gave him a wan smile. "I do have the ability to tell when most people are lying," I said. "But it's not what I hear as much as what I taste or see in their voice." Holland's brow furrowed, and off on my periphery, I saw Dixon shift in his seat again.

"And it doesn't work with everyone," I went on. "The exceptions are rare, but they're out there."

"Okay then," Dixon said. He ran his hands over his thighs. "Let's start, shall we? Clay said we were to come up with three statements, but I think those odds are a little too easy, and I'd like to give you five statements instead."

There was a definite tone of skepticism in his voice that made the buttery taste saltier. It made me wonder if he was here voluntarily or because someone else, someone higher up, made him come.

"Suit yourself," I said.

"Okay." He reached into his pocket and took out a sheet of paper that he then unfolded. "I wrote them down," he said, holding the paper up, "so I wouldn't forget them. Ready?"

I nodded, and he began to read, in a slow, mechanical voice devoid of emotion that made me think he was trying to keep his voice as neutral as possible in an effort to trip me up.

"The first girl I ever kissed was named Carla," he began. "I had a paddle ball when I was a child, and I once hit the ball two hundred and two times in a row before I missed one. My favorite color is yellow. I slept with a teddy bear until I was thirteen years old. I burned a house down when I was five years old."

The taste of his voice didn't change during this recitation. Either everything he was telling me was true, or he was one of those people I couldn't read. Then another idea occurred to me.

"I don't know if reading the statements like that works the same way as simply stating them," I told him. "I'm not picking up on any significant differences between them."

Dixon shot Clay an I-told-you-so look.

"May I see the paper you wrote them on?" I asked him.

He considered this a moment and then handed me the paper. I eyed the statements he had written down, examining each one closely. He had written them on basic unlined paper, the same generic type of paper you could find in thousands of copiers and printers— and ironically, the same type of paper the letter writer used—using a basic blue ink pen. Each statement was written on its own line, and there was a slight downward slant to the sentences. I blurred the words and focused instead on the individual strokes Dixon had made in writing the sentences down. As I did so, I began to detect subtle differences here and there, clues that eventually spoke to me clearer than his voice had.

When I looked up I saw that everyone's eyes were on me. I smiled at Dixon and shook my head. "You men . . . you don't like to follow the rules, do you?" Dixon raised his eyebrows at me, challenging me. "Clay pulled the same thing on me," I went on. "You were supposed to give me only one false statement, but you've given me two."

Dixon flashed a tentative smile, his brow furrowing.

"You must have been quite the wizard with a paddle ball," I said to him. "Yellow is an unusual favorite color for a man, by the way, so you stand out in that regard. And I'm dying to hear the story about the house you burned down. I don't know the name of the first girl you ever kissed, but I know it wasn't Carla. And you didn't sleep with a teddy bear up until age thirteen, although . . ." I glanced back at that particular statement on the paper. "I think you did sleep with a teddy bear for several years, just not thirteen of them."

Dixon raised his eyebrows again, this time with astonishment. A blush crept over his cheeks, and I wasn't sure if it was my success in interpreting his statements or the mention of him sleeping with a teddy bear for several years that caused it.

"Wow," Dixon said with a grudging smile. "You are absolutely right. How did you know?"

"Normally, I pick up on subtle changes in a person's voice, but with you I didn't detect any. I think it was because you were reading them off the paper. It's like reading a book. Your mind processes the words, but it doesn't perceive the words you're speaking as statements about you. That's why I asked to look at your paper. Your handwriting gave it away. When you wrote those statements down, they were about you, and whenever you wrote down an untruth your hand altered the writing." I turned the paper around so he could see it and pointed to the statement about the first girl he kissed. "If I look at this sentence, I can see that the name Carla smells different than the rest of the words."

Dixon arched a brow at me. "It smells different," he repeated, deadpan.

I nodded. "It smells peppery, whereas the other words smell buttery."

Dixon rolled his eyes.

"Am I wrong about the name Carla?" I asked him.

"No," he admitted grudgingly.

I moved on. "In the line about the teddy bear, everything smells buttery until I look at the word *thirteen*. It, too, smells peppery. If the whole sentence smelled peppery, I'd think you never slept with a teddy bear at all, but only the word *thirteen* smells different. So my assumption is that you did sleep with one, just not until the age of thirteen."

"You burned down a house?" Holland said to Dixon, a complete non sequitur.

Dixon shot him an exasperated look. "For the record, I was only five at the time, and the place was vacant and run-down. I and two other kids were playing with matches on the back porch, trying to get warm. It was a windy day and before we knew it, the fire had spread across the floor and started climbing up a wall. We tried to put it out, and when we couldn't, we ran."

"And the teddy bear?" Clay asked, sounding and looking amused. "What's the truth there? Did you sleep with it until you were twenty-one?"

Holland and Dixon both chuckled.

"I slept with it well into grade school," Dixon admitted with a frown. "Fourth grade, I think. Then one night my father came into my room, took it away, and told me it was time to grow up and be a man." Dixon paused, gazing off into the past, his expression bittersweet. After a few seconds, he shook it off and returned to the present. "I cried myself to sleep for weeks after that," he told us. "Eventually, I learned to sleep without it. I don't know what my father did with it, but I never saw that teddy bear again."

"Okay, my turn," Holland said, rubbing his hands together. He looked both intrigued and excited. "Are you ready, Ms. Dalton?"

Resigned to my freak-show status, I said, "Sure."

"Okay, I'm going to give you four statements, and I promise only one will be false. And I won't read them because I didn't write them down." He kept rubbing his hands together like an excited kid. "Here we go. My first pet was a turtle named Twinkie. My first love was a girl named DeeAnn. I used to steal candy bars from the local convenience mart near my house. And I like to read romance novels."

Dixon snorted. "Hell, Holland, could you make it

any easier for her? Romance novels?" he said with a huff of dismissive amusement. "That's a good one."

"It's true," I said.

Dixon's smirk faded, but it went out slowly, like the glow from a firefly when it hits your windshield.

"It's also true that he stole those candy bars," I went on. "And his first love really was a girl named DeeAnn. But there was no turtle named Twinkie."

Dixon looked over at Holland, who shrugged and smiled grudgingly. "She's right," he said. "That's a nifty little trick you do, Ms. Dalton."

"It's not a trick. It's just me. It's the way I'm wired."

"And how long have you been able to do this?" Dixon asked.

"All my life. It's not just the voice thing, either. I can see subtleties others can't, like I did with your handwriting. I can also pick up on scents that most people can't, and sometimes I can tell when things have been moved."

Holland said, "Yes, Duncan told me how you were able to pick up on the fact that other people had been present in an apartment when you were helping him investigate a case a while back where a homicide was made to look like a suicide. He said you also knew that a roll of toilet paper had been changed at the scene, and that was somehow key. I forget how."

"And after he told you that, you suspended him and told him he wasn't allowed to spend time with me."

A prickly silence filled the room. I saw Clay bite back a grin.

Holland cleared his throat and said, "Yes, um, well, that might have been a hasty judgment on my part. I have had time to reconsider. And given what you have done since that case . . . well . . . it seems obvious to me that you have a God-given talent we might find useful. And if you're willing to use it, we'd like to have you join forces with us."

"What about my group, the Capone Club?"

"Capone Club?" Dixon said with a sneer. "As in Al Capone?"

"Yes, as in Al Capone," I said, hearing the irritation in my own voice. "My bar had connections to Capone back in the day, and the group started right around the time we figured that out. So they adopted the name."

"What does this group do, exactly?" Holland asked.

"They help with figuring out the crimes we look into," I told him. "It's an eclectic mix of people from many different walks of life. All of them bring different types of knowledge and expertise to the table. I use my synesthesia to help interpret things and ferret out some truths, but the group has been instrumental in coming up with clues and theories that eventually led us to solving the crimes. I don't know if I could do any of it without them."

"Well, we have our own group of people who do the same thing," Dixon said, his voice heavy with sarcasm. "They're called the police."

"It's not the same thing," I said. "The police have access to a lot of information we laypeople don't, and they know investigative techniques and have evidence-processing capabilities we don't have access to. What the police don't have is the depth and breadth of knowledge and experience the Capone Club has. It's like having a stable full of experts at your beck and call. I would think that might come in handy for some of your investigations."

Holland sighed. "I understand and admire your dedication to your group, Ms. Dalton, but we don't have much use for them. We can consult with any number of experts anytime we want or need to. Your ability is the one unique thing we don't have access to, and we'd like to change that."

"I'm sorry," I told the men. "I'm a package deal. If you want me, you get the Capone Club."

Dixon let out a sigh of impatience. "Ms. Dalton, you do realize we can shut down this group of yours anytime we want, right?"

I shot him an angry look, my temper forged from both his attitude and the ache in my back, arms, and legs from standing propped up on my damned crutches for so long. "Why would you do that? And how? They aren't breaking any laws, and they're meeting in a public establishment with the owner's approval."

"Their so-called research doesn't follow the rules of evidence. Things they learn or obtain are likely to be tainted and unusable in any prosecutorial procedures that might result from their findings. I can hit them with an obstruction of justice charge."

Holland waved away Dixon's comment. "But you won't," he said, shooting Dixon a chastising look. "We're not here to threaten you or your group, Mack. We want to find a way to work together. So how about this. You become our consultant, and whatever means you use to obtain any information you give us is up to you. But if you or your group come across any witnesses or evidence that might be pertinent to a case, it needs to be passed on to us and handled appropriately. I don't want to do anything that might taint evidence we find or invalidate a statement from someone. Catching criminals is only part of the task. We also have to be able to successfully prosecute them. There are rules we need to follow with evidence, and confidences we need to maintain. We can't have your group running around the city telling everyone about an ongoing investigation. They will have to play by our rules, and those rules will be strict and unbendable. Is that a workable compromise for you?"

I considered it . . . all of it. A proposal for collaboration was not what I'd expected when I'd come here. I had been fully prepared for the men to demand I cease and desist my crime-solving activities immediately. What they were suggesting instead was both unexpected and intriguing. It would allow me to continue to use my synesthesia for something good and would eliminate the need to hide what I was doing. It could pave the way for Duncan and me to have a more open relationship. But there was a fly in this feel-good ointment, two of them in fact: the letter writer and Courtney.

"I don't like having all these other people involved," Dixon grumbled. "It's bad enough we have to work with her. Bringing in these other people is bound to compromise my cases at some point."

"What if we do criminal background checks on all of them?" Holland offered.

Dixon shook his head. "A clear background doesn't mean they won't mess up evidence at some point. It's too risky."

They were discussing this like I wasn't even in the room with them anymore. And I didn't like the idea at all. Not only did I think several of the Capone Club members would object to the cops digging around in their lives, some of them, like Cora, skirted the edges of the law at times.

"Several of my guys participate in this group," Holland said. "Tyrese Washington and Nick Kavinsky are frequent flyers. And, of course, there's Duncan Albright. Between them I think they can manage to keep the group in line and make sure anything they do falls within the safe parameters we establish."

Dixon's frown deepened, and he sank back into his chair, arms folded over his chest. He looked like a sulking child. I got a strong sense that he wasn't in favor of this at all and was being dragged into it for some reason. Not a good omen for our future working relationship. He didn't offer up any more objections, however, so Holland looked over at me and said, "So what do you say, Mack? Will you do it?"

"I'm willing to consider it," I said. "But I'd like a little time to think it over."

I had the letter writer thing to think about, and any working arrangements I set up with the police would have to wait until that issue was resolved. Unless . . . I wondered if bringing them in on it might help us resolve things quicker. Could I trust them to be quiet about it? I wasn't sure enough at this point to risk it.

"If it's money that's holding you back," Holland said, "we'll work with you the best we can. We don't have a lot of discretionary funds, but we can pull from some other areas as needed. I'm sure we can come up with something we'll both find agreeable if you give us a chance."

"Money isn't my concern," I said.

"Then what is?" Holland asked.

"I can't say just yet," I told them. "There are some other things I need to work out. So I'd like some time to do that. What you're offering sounds tempting, but if you can't extend me the time, then my answer is no."

Dixon let out a perturbed sigh.

Holland said, "Fine. How long?"

For some reason, his question annoyed me. It also piqued my curiosity. I had a feeling something else was going on here. "What's the rush?" I asked. "Why the sudden need to sew this up?"

Holland and Dixon briefly exchanged looks. It was quick and subtle, but I picked up on it and knew there was a hidden agenda of some sort.

"No rush," Dixon said, and while I knew from the taste in his voice that this was a lie, I decided not to call him out on it. He got up from his chair, walked over to the coatrack, retrieved a coat, scarf, and hat, and then said, "I look forward to hearing from you, Ms. Dalton. Have a good day."

With that, he left. Holland rose from his chair too, but instead of walking past me, he came over and extended his arm in an offer to shake. After a moment's hesitation, I propped one crutch under my arm and shook his hand.

"Take as much time as you need, Mack," he said. "I hope you'll agree to work with us." He paused, narrowing his eyes at me. "I sense you will. You want to do this, don't you?"

Now it was my turn to narrow my eyes.

Holland chuckled. "You aren't the only one who can read people, Mack, though I'll admit your talents far exceed mine. But after nearly twenty years on the force, I've learned a thing or two about how to read people, and I can tell you are interested in this collaboration. I look forward to hearing from you."

He had rendered me speechless, and I stood and watched him as he walked over and shrugged into his coat. Before leaving, he turned to me once again. "You have a lot of fans and supporters among the police in this city."

Finally finding my voice, I said, "I think it's more my coffee than me."

"Yes, I've heard your coffee is quite good. I'll have to investigate that for myself." He smiled and donned his hat, a fur-lined, aviator style with earflaps. "Thank you for coming here today to hear us out," he said once the hat was settled on his head.

"I didn't come to hear you out," I told him. "I had no idea who was going to be here. To be honest, if I had known, I don't think I would have come because I would have been expecting a hand-slapping rather than a handshake."

"Well, I'm glad we were able to pleasantly surprise you." He looked over at Clay. "Get better, my friend," he said. "And don't hesitate to ask if you need anything."

"Will do," Clay said. And with that, Holland took his leave.

I looked over at Clay, who was grinning at me. I walked over to the chair Holland had vacated, sank into it, and then said, "What the hell were you thinking, Clay?"

Chapter 6

Clay's smile faded in a flash. He looked both surprised and wounded by my words. "What's wrong?" he asked. "I thought you'd be glad to learn those guys had been swayed over to your side."

"Well, I'm not. You had no business sandbagging me like this or trying to act as some sort of mediator here. I was doing just fine on my own. The last thing I need right now are a couple of politically motivated muckety-mucks breathing down my neck."

"No one is going to be breathing down your neck, Mack," he said, eyeing me curiously. "What's going on? There's something you haven't told me about, isn't there? Something to do with Gary Gunderson's death?"

My phone buzzed then, and when I took it out of my coat pocket, I saw there was a text from Mal. *Holy crap! Those are some high-powered folks you're meeting with. Have they reamed you a new one yet?*

I sent him back a quick *I'm fine* and then pocketed the phone. "How do you know Holland?" I asked Clay. "You guys seem like more than business acquaintances."

Clay conceded my statement with a nod. "Our families have known each other for years," he said. "Chief Holland used to live next door to us when I was a kid. He and my father were good friends."

"And how did he react to your skewering of him and the police department in the articles you wrote about me?"

Clay gave me a sheepish smile. "He wasn't pleased. But we've always had an understanding that our friendship will not influence either of us when it comes to doing our jobs. That means I get to say what I want in the paper, and he won't show me any favors if I break the law, whether it be parking tickets or something more serious. And so far, it's worked." He chuckled and added, "I have the parking tickets to prove it."

"You could have told me about your relationship with him when I first invited you into the Capone Club."

Clay shrugged. "I didn't see any reason to. It wouldn't have influenced my assessment of you or the group in any way. I remained objective. Besides, when it comes to revelations, I'm not the only one who held back, am I?"

I ignored his taunt. "Why the sudden desire to bring us together? What do you get out of it?"

"The satisfaction of seeing two dynamic forces come together to fight crime in our lovely city?"

"Come on, Clay. Quit reciting superhero rhetoric. There has to be something in this for you."

He studied me for a moment, chewing on his lower lip. "Yeah, okay, there is something in it for me. What you can do is phenomenal, and it has the potential to lead to some killer stories—pun intended. And I want the exclusive on it all. I want to be part of what you do, to witness it, and write about it."

"I don't want to be in the news, Clay. I thought you'd figured that out by now."

"I can tell you aren't doing what you do for the notoriety or any type of recognition. But you have to realize that what you're doing is groundbreaking and newsworthy."

"No!" I said, a bit more harshly than I meant to.

Clay narrowed his eyes at me. "What's going on, Mack? I know there's something else you're involved with that you haven't told me about. Why are you and Malachi so intent on visiting odd places around town? And why is Duncan Albright sneaking into your place at all hours of the day and night?"

I opened my mouth to deny this, but before I could utter a word, Clay held up a hand and said, "Don't even try to deny it or to convince me that you and Mal are an item. You may be fond of Mal, but you're not really dating him. You don't look at him the right way or touch him as often as you should. It's unfortunate for him, because I suspect his feelings for you are real and run deep. But clearly you and Duncan are still an item. I get why the two of you might have been carrying on a secretive affair in the beginning in order to hide it from his superiors. But clearly Holland is okay with the two of you at this point, so why the continued subterfuge?"

I stared at him, mouth agape. "Have you been spying on me?"

"I've been doing my job, Mack. I'm good at assessing situations and reading people. It's crucial to what I do for a living. And when you invited me to become a part of your group, I wanted to know what I was getting into. I'm fairly good at sniffing things out myself, just not in the same way you do. And I knew from the get-go that you were hiding something from me, holding something back. It's my job to get to the truth of the matter, to dig down past all the superficial stuff on the surface to the real dirt beneath. I haven't found out what that dirt is with you yet, but I know it's there. I figured out that you and Mal aren't really a couple, and that you and Duncan still are. What I don't get is the need for Mal. Given that he's an undercover cop, I suspect he's pretending to be your boyfriend so he can protect you. What I haven't figured out is what he's protecting you from or why Duncan can't do it at this point. But I'm betting Gary Gunderson's death has a place in this story."

I glared at Clay, too angry to say anything, my mind spinning as I tried to figure out what to do next. Clearly, I'd underestimated the man. He was far smarter and more astute than I'd given him credit for. Up until that moment, he hadn't given me a reason not to trust him, but discovering that he had been sneaking around behind my back didn't exactly help his case. What was his endgame?

He must have sensed my suspicions because he next said, "Mack, look, I admit I was skeptical about you in the beginning. But I've been won over. I'm not your enemy. I think you could be instrumental in making some great things happen in this city if you work with Holland and Dixon. And I'm willing to help you out in any way I can to make that happen. But only if you're honest with me. If you're going to continue to lie and hide things from me, then I'm going to have to do things my own way and do whatever I need to do to get to the truth."

"Are you threatening me?" I asked him angrily.

He sighed, and doing so made him wince and place

a hand over his belly near where he'd been shot. "I suppose it does sound that way," he said, rubbing his stomach. "That's not my intent. But I need to get to the truth. I'm driven that way." He flashed an apologetic smile. "I can't stop myself from digging any more than you can stop your synesthetic reactions."

Despite my irritation with him, I sensed from his voice that his concern for me and his desire to help were genuine. I also sensed that he was being truthful when he said he wouldn't be able to control his impulse to dig. "If I tell you everything, what do you intend to do with it?" I asked him.

He gave it a moment's thought and then shrugged. "I guess it would depend on what it is you tell me."

My phone buzzed, and I took it out and saw another text from Mal. *You okay? Need me to come in? Are there more visitors?*

"Is that Mal?" Clay asked.

I nodded. "He's waiting outside. He's worried about what's going on in here."

"Bring him in," Clay said, surprising me. "Let's lay the options out before him, too, and see what he thinks you should do."

I liked this idea. "Okay. I will."

I hit the speed-dial number for Mal's cell, and he answered before the first ring had finished. "You need me?" he said.

"I'm okay, but I would like you to come inside. Clay has something he wants to discuss, and I'd really like to get your input on it."

"Be right there."

I slipped the phone back into my pocket and then shrugged out of my coat. By the time I had it off, Mal was knocking at Clay's front door.

"Come on in," Clay yelled. The effort made him wince and rub his stomach again.

Mal opened the door and stepped inside.

"Have a seat," Clay said, gesturing toward the one empty chair. "Mack and I were just discussing our future together and how it's going to work."

Mal settled into the empty chair, eyeing Clay cautiously. "That sounds a little ominous," he said.

"In a way, it is," I told him. "Clay knows a lot more than we realized about what's going on. He knows that Duncan and I have continued to see one another on the sly, he knows that you and I are a front, and he suspects that your presence is so you can provide some degree of protection for me. He wants to know the whole story, and if I don't share, he's threatening to dig around and find it, and then do whatever he wants with the information."

Mal frowned at Clay. "Not cool, man," he said. "I appreciate the fact that you haven't blown my cover, and up until now you've been playing like one of the team. Mack and the others have treated you well. Now you're going to turn on them?"

Clay squirmed in his seat, though I wasn't sure if it was discomfort over what Mal had said or discomfort from his stomach wound. "Look," he said, "I have no desire to hurt Mack or any of the others."

"Why were Chief Holland and Tony Dixon here?" Mal asked. "Are you trying to shut Mack down?"

"Quite the opposite," Clay said. "I convinced the two of them that she is the real deal, and I talked them into taking her on as a consultant."

Mal looked to me for confirmation, and I nodded. "Did you agree to it?" he asked.

"More or less. I didn't tell them no. I told them I wanted some time to think about it. It has its pros and cons. I need to weigh it all out, particularly with regard to the Capone Club." I summarized the discussion that had taken place. "Assuming we work that piece out, I don't see a huge downside," I concluded. "They're going to pay me, and the extra income would be nice. Plus, it will let me continue doing what I'm doing without fear of repercussions and without having to sneak around."

There was the tiniest flinch of muscle on Mal's face, and I sensed it was because he realized that the end to sneaking around meant the end of our time together.

"My only big concern at this point," I went on, "is the other thing." I didn't need to elaborate. Mal knew I was referring to the letter writer.

"I'm on your side, Mack, I swear," Clay said. "But I need to know everything that's going on. I can help."

He had helped with our last case, so much so in fact that he was probably the key person who led me to the truth. And he had gotten shot for his efforts. That did show a certain degree of dedication, I supposed. Plus, he already knew too much. I had no doubt the man would manage to get to the whole truth soon enough on his own.

"You might as well tell him everything," Mal said, no doubt following the same train of thought I'd followed. "He already knows enough to hurt us, and I suspect it won't take him long to dig up the rest, even in his present condition."

Clay breathed a sigh of relief and smiled. "It has something to do with Gary Gunderson's murder, doesn't it?" he said. I nodded. "And is the death of that male nurse a few weeks ago related, too?"

My heart skipped a beat. The fact that Clay had made that connection was scary. "It is," I said. "That male nurse, as you called him, was named Lewis Carmichael, and he was a patron of my bar as well as a member of the Capone Club. How did you make the connection?"

"I don't believe in coincidence," Clay said. "And you've had too many deaths associated with your bar lately. The death of your father and the woman he was dating were explained once the culprit was caught. What are the chances that two additional people with relatively close ties to your bar just happened to be murdered within a short time for some random reason and by some random killers? I'm not a gambling man, but I'm betting those odds are long ones. And why are you and Mal here scurrying about town getting mysterious packages from people?"

"Oh my God," I said, my irritation surging again, "you *have* been following and spying on me."

"Sorry," Clay said, not sounding sorry at all, "but I sensed early on that something was afoot here, something more than what appeared on the surface. So I've been watching you to see what I could figure out. I confess, I haven't come up with an answer yet, but I get the sense that it's something very serious."

"Yes, I'd say multiple murders are very serious," I snapped.

"So what is it?" Clay asked. "Is there some nutcase out there who wants to challenge you and your crime-solving abilities by killing people and seeing if you can catch him?"

This was so close to the mark that I knew there was little sense in trying to keep it from him any longer. I slumped in my chair in defeat, sighed, and said, "Okay, Clay. You win. Here's what's going on."

Chapter 7

Over the next hour or so, Mal and I filled Clay in on the history of the letter writer, beginning with the very first letter and taking him through each of the clues and subsequent letters.

We explained to him how I deciphered the various clues and told him how Cora had discovered a commonality among the recipients of the packages I'd received: their connection to the university. After a second or two of hesitation, I went ahead and told him about our suspicions regarding who the culprit might be—at least the primary culprit—and all the connections we had made between her, the letters, the clue locations, and the people who delivered the clues. I considered keeping this information to myself, but given how much Clay had already figured out on his own, I knew it would only be a matter of time before he figured this part out, too. And I didn't want him to think I was still trying to keep him out of the loop by holding anything back.

We also told him our theory that Suzanne Collier wasn't working alone, and that we had no idea who the other person might be but suspected it might be someone in the Capone Club or an employee of the bar.

When all was said and done, Clay had three questions for us. One was who else besides us and Duncan knew about the letter writer. I told him that Cora, the Signoriello brothers, and Tiny knew. Clay's second question was whether or not we thought Tad was Suzanne's partner in crime.

"I don't know," I told him honestly. "But my gut says no. I think Suzanne's motivation for doing this is to make me and the Capone Club look bad, to give us a black mark so Tad won't be so drawn to us. I'm not sure if she suspects Tad of having an affair with me or someone else in the group, but I do know that she phones him constantly asking where he is and what he's doing, and Tad has said she's had him tailed."

"It doesn't sound like much of a motive," Clay said.

"I know," I agreed. "But Suzanne Collier is a very wealthy and powerful woman who is used to getting what she wants and having things done her way. Tad is a big part of that and of her image overall. But we know he didn't kill Lewis Carmichael because he was in the bar with some of the other club members at the time of that murder. We suspect Suzanne might have killed Gary herself because of some evidence we found in Gary's car."

I explained about the perfume, traces of Opium we found in Gary's vehicle and the discovery that it was the only perfume Suzanne Collier wore. "But we know she didn't kill Lewis, either," I went on. "She had an ironclad alibi, complete with pictures in the paper. So even if Tad knows and is involved somehow, someone else killed Lewis."

Clay frowned, shook his head, and shifted his position on the couch with a grimace. "Jealousy?" he said, his frown deepening. "You really think that's behind Suzanne Collier's motive for this?"

"I know it seems like a stretch," I admitted. "But Tad is a very handsome man who is eleven years younger than Suzanne—a trophy husband, if you will. She expects him to be at her beck and call, and I know he's been pushing back on that a lot lately, partly because of the time he's been putting in at the bar with the Capone Club, but also because I think he's simply growing tired of being her lackey. His resistance is bound to irritate her. She doesn't strike me as the sort of woman who takes rebellion lightly."

"Still," Clay said with a dubious look, "murder? She'd have to be crazy."

"Yes," I said. "We have reason to think she may have some serious mental health issues." I didn't elaborate, and to my surprise, Clay didn't ask me to.

A pregnant pause followed as Clay digested what we had told him so far, his brow furrowed in thought. I expected him to tell us we were overreaching and to summarily dismiss Suzanne as a suspect. But instead he said, "She won't be easy to take down. She has a lot of money, power, and connections."

Mal and I both nodded.

"You said these letters forbade you from getting help from the cops and specifically mentioned Duncan," Clay said.

I nodded. "That's right."

"What reason would Suzanne have for that? I would think she'd encourage your relationship with him if she's jealous of you and afraid you'll steal Tad from her."

I shrugged. "She'd have no reason as far as we can figure. That's another reason I'm convinced there is a second party involved."

"Then that's where we need to focus," Clay said. "Because knowing why Detective Albright was singled out might lead you to your second killer. I agree that there doesn't seem to be any reason for Suzanne Collier to care if Albright is involved, so the reason for mentioning him specifically must point to the second person's motivation."

Mal and I both nodded. We'd been down this trail of thought before. Then Clay hit me with his third question.

"Why haven't you told the others about these letters?"

This question was a tough one for me to answer. "I've considered doing so several times," I told him. "But in the end I felt like they would be safer not knowing. If they were aware of what was going on, they'd all be up in arms and working to investigate it, trying to figure things out. And I'm afraid doing that might rile the letter writer. Besides, the cops have been pretty adamant, warning them to stay out of the cases involving Gary and Lewis's deaths because they don't want anything to interfere with any evidence that might be uncovered."

"They already suspect something is going on with you, Mack," Clay said.

"I know," I said with a sigh. "It's come up in conversation already that the deaths of Gary and Lewis might be connected to me somehow. I used that talk as an opportunity to suggest to the group that perhaps they should back away from it all if they felt they were in jeopardy. Of course, no one did."

"They don't think they're in jeopardy," Clay said. "I've overheard some of the talk. They think you're the one in jeopardy."

"She is," Mal said. "Everyone is until we can put a stop to this craziness."

Clay cocked his head to the side and smiled at me. "You don't think the members of the Capone Club deserve to know they've been targeted?"

I shot Clay an irritated look. "Yes, and no." I let out a frustrated growl. "Believe me, Clay, I've been agonizing over this thing from day one. Am I making the right choice by not telling them? I have no idea. All I know is that I have to keep solving these damned riddles until we can put Suzanne and whoever she's working with behind bars."

"If Duncan is processing items for evidence unofficially, it's not going to help speed things up. You need legal, concrete evidence against Suzanne."

"That's the problem," Mal said. "So far there hasn't been any. There's been a dearth of viable evidence with these letters . . . no fingerprints, no usable DNA, no usable trace evidence other than things that have been intentionally included as part of the puzzles Mack has had to solve."

"There was one piece of evidence from the Public Market that may or may not have been accidental," I explained. "But other than that . . ." I shrugged and shook my head.

Mal added, "While the circumstantial evidence points to Suzanne Collier, we aren't one hundred percent sure it's her. And since she has a rock-solid alibi for at least one of the murders, if we can't find out who her partner is, there's no chance of pinning any of this on her."

I scoffed. "And there's the possibility that whoever is helping Suzanne is a member of the Capone Club," I said. "That's another reason I haven't been willing to tip my hand."

"I think you have to tip it," Clay said. "You're letting this person, or these people, manipulate you. You're letting them call the shots. You need to switch things up, change it around, take charge. Force whoever it is to show their hand."

"And just how am I supposed to do that?"

"I think you need to have your own version of the OK Corral. Gather all the parties together and have a showdown."

"That sounds dangerous," I said.

"No doubt it will be," Clay said. "But you have plenty of cops you can involve to provide protection. You've got Mal here, and if you're going for a show-down, there's no reason why you can't bring Duncan in. Plus, you've got a couple of cops who participate in the Capone Club: Tyrese and Nick."

I nodded slowly, giving thought to what he was saying, and debating whether or not I should tell him and Mal about my own suspicions when it came to cops, specifically Jimmy Patterson, Duncan's partner. After a moment of mental debate, I decided there was so much out on the table already that there was no need to hold back. "The problem with including any cops in this is that I fear one of them might be the person who is helping Suzanne."

Mal shot me a look of surprise, Clay merely looked intrigued.

"Who?" both men said at the same time. They looked at one another and then back at me.

"And why?" Mal asked. "Tell us what evidence you have that points to a cop, any cop, being involved in this."

"I have no evidence," I admitted. "All I have is a gut feeling, a concern."

Mal acceded my concern with a grudging nod. "I'll admit, your gut reactions are a hell of a lot stronger and more reliable than most people's. But I still want to know what's behind this particular gut feeling."

"I want to know who you're referring to," Clay said impatiently. He shifted his position on the couch, leaning forward and toward me, wincing in the process.

"It's Jimmy Patterson, Duncan's partner," I told them. "He's had it out for me from the first time I met him, and he told Duncan dozens of times that working with me was a big mistake. He thinks I'm a fraud or some type of charlatan, and he's questioned my abilities all along, just like the letter writer has. He has knowledge of police procedures, evidence collection and processing, and access to the cases. If Duncan did anything official, Jimmy would know. He also knows the people involved in the Capone Club. And his anger over Duncan working with me would explain why Duncan is mentioned specifically in the letters."

"That's about as circumstantial as you can get," Mal said with a frown, and Clay nodded his agreement.

"I know, but that doesn't mean he isn't behind it," I countered.

"Okay, okay," Mal said, pulling at this chin. "He has a motive, he has the means, but has he had the opportunity?"

"I don't know," I told him. "Since we know Suzanne isn't responsible for Lewis Carmichael's murder, that's the window of time we need to check. Is there any way to find out if Jimmy has an alibi for that period of time? I can't very well ask Duncan to look into it."

I looked at Mal, waiting for his answer. Clay looked at him too, his expression expectant.

"I suppose I could try to do some sniffing around," Mal said. "But I don't work in this precinct, so I don't have an easy way to get the information."

"We need to make a list of suspects," Clay said. "And

that means anyone who is an employee of the bar, or a member of the Capone Club, or connected to you and the Capone Club in some way. Then we need to focus on the ones who don't have an alibi for Lewis Carmichael's murder."

I thought back to what Duncan had said about Lewis's time of death and shared what he had told me. "The first letter I received was postmarked three days before I opened it. I'm not sure exactly when it arrived, because I was avoiding opening my mail back then. There were too many weird letters and reactions to all the publicity. Based on that, one could assume that Lewis was killed on the day the letter was postmarked, or before. However, the exact time of his death became apparent because he was wearing a watch, one that displayed the date on it. It was broken in the scuffle that took place—Lewis was beaten around the head and face pretty badly in addition to being stabbed—so we know he died on the day the letter was postmarked at eleven thirty-two in the evening. The one thing we aren't sure of is when his body was dumped onto the frozen riverbed beneath the Fonz statue, but given that the letter could have reached me and been read the very next day, it seems logical to assume that it happened sometime that same night."

"Meaning his body was there for three days?" Clay said.

I nodded. "Based on the time of death, we know certain people in the Capone Club couldn't have killed Lewis because they were in the bar at the time of death. That includes Cora and the Signoriello brothers, though I don't need their presence to know none of them could have done it. I trust those three with my life. Holly and Alicia were both there too, as was Tad. And Missy, Billy, Rich, and Debra were all working, so they couldn't have done it either."

"Who wasn't there, Mack?" Clay asked.

"Sam and Carter weren't there. They had been in earlier but had left by then. Dr. T wasn't there, and the two cops who participate the most, Nick and Tyrese, weren't either. Kevin Baldwin wasn't there, but Duncan said something about him having a solid alibi because he was on duty in the garbage truck, running his route, at the time of the murder. They were doing extra shifts on the garbage pickup because the snowstorm had kept them from doing their usual routes on time. Tiny—he's Cora's current boyfriend," I added for Clay's benefit since I didn't know if he knew Tiny, "also wasn't there. And of course, none of the newer members were present because they hadn't joined the club yet. That list includes Greg Nash, the Realtor, Stephen McGregor, the high school physics teacher, and Sonja West, the salon owner." I paused and arched my brows at Clay. "And then there's you, of course," I said with a sly smile.

"I do have an alibi for the time in question," he said. "In fact, my alibi just left. I was interviewing Anthony Dixon about his plans for a gubernatorial run that evening."

As soon as he said this, I wondered if Dixon's political goals might have been behind the rushed timing and Dixon's seemingly reluctant acquiescence to the working arrangement the two men had proposed today. "I suppose that will do," I said with a smile, noting that the taste of Clay's voice indicated he was telling the truth.

"Who is left among your employees?" Clay asked. I saw that he was writing, taking notes on what I was saying or perhaps making a list.

I hesitated, not wanting to entertain the possibility that any of my employees might have something to do with this. Clay must have sensed my reluctance because he looked up from whatever he was writing and said, "The sooner we can eliminate them, the better. Once we have this list established, we can start crossing names off, assuming we can definitively rule them out."

He was right, but it didn't make the task any more palatable. "Basically, my day staff: Pete, Jon, and Linda. And I suppose we have to consider Teddy Bear and Curtis Donovan. Neither of them was hired on yet at the time, so I doubt they've got anything to do with it."

"Still, we need to be thorough," Clay said, scribbling away.

"Oh, and Gary was off that night," I added with a grim smile. "Though I suppose we can safely rule him out at this point."

"So," Clay said, consulting his notes, "our list includes Jimmy, Sam, Carter, Dr. T, Tiny, Nick, and Tyrese from the older members of the club, and Greg Nash, Stephen McGregor, and Sonja West from the newer members. And we have Linda, Pete, Teddy, Curtis, and Jon from your staff."

"As for my employees," I said, "I think you can put Pete and Linda down low on the list. Pete has been working with us for years, and I can't see him doing this for any reason. And Linda is a small-built woman. Duncan told me Lewis was beaten pretty badly, and I don't think she has the size and strength to pull it off."

"She could have had help," Clay tossed out. "Or used something to beat him with."

Mal, who had remained quiet through this run of suspects, said, "We also have to consider that the second person might not be someone we know. Maybe

Suzanne hired someone to do her dirty work, and maybe that person has been coming to the bar on a regular basis, sitting among the other customers, watching everything that's gone on."

This idea was disturbing. I did a quick mental scan, looking back over the past couple of weeks to see if I could recall a newer customer who had started coming in regularly. No one came to mind. Then I had another idea.

"You know, I'm inclined to think that the second person isn't a hired gun," I told the men. Both of them raised their eyebrows to me in silent question. "Think about it. Hiring someone runs the risk of money exchanges that could be dangerous, and if the culprit was arrested, what's to stop them from ratting her out? I don't think Suzanne would risk that kind of exposure. Plus, if she did kill Gary herself, why? Either she had a personal grudge with him, which I doubt, or she had to do it in order to reassure whoever she was working with that she wouldn't turn on them. A quid pro quo kind of thing, you know? She had to get her hands just as dirty as the second person's were."

"I'm inclined to agree with you," Clay said. "Suzanne would have wanted to work with someone she knew, someone she felt she could trust."

"And doing it that way also makes it harder to pin all of this on any one person," Mal said. "They both have alibis for one of the murders."

My brain spun with possibilities, while my heart reeled over the idea that someone I knew, someone I trusted, might be out to kill me. A shiver shook me, and I shrugged back into my coat.

"I need to think about all of this," I said, getting out of my chair and grabbing my crutches. "Can you give me a copy of that list you just made, Clay?"

"Hold on, and you can have the original," he said. He then took out his cell phone and snapped a picture of the list. After checking to make sure it was legible, he handed the paper to me, and I tucked it into my pants pocket.

"I'm going to head back to the bar for now," I said, "but I'll be in touch. I'll let Mr. Holland and Mr. Dixon know my decision by tomorrow."

As I headed for the door, Mal got up and followed me.

Clay shifted on the couch where he sat, watching us. "Have you thought about bringing Holland in on this?" he asked.

"I did think about it," I admitted. "But I'm not comfortable with that yet. I need more time."

"I know all of this is uncomfortable for you, Mack," Clay said. "But ignoring it won't make it better. I think it's time you quit playing defense and went on the offense."

"That's easy for you to say. You don't have other people's lives depending on you."

"And you do," Clay said. "That's why you need to tell the others what's going on. Let them make their own choices regarding their safety. If you continue to keep this to yourself, you can't win. Sooner or later the group will find out, either because someone else will die or because you'll figure out who the culprits are. And when the group finds out what's been going on, they're going to be ticked off. They're probably going to be angry anyway, but at least by telling them now you might be able to mitigate the damages. They trust you, Mack, and by keeping this from them you're betraying that trust."

I whirled on Clay, my building anger and frustration reaching explosive levels. "You don't think I know that?" I snapped at him. "Do you think this has been easy for me? I've agonized over this ever since that first letter came. Maybe I haven't handled things perfectly, but I've done what I thought was best. If that means the group ends up hating me, I'll deal with it when the time comes. In the meantime, until you've walked a mile or two in my shoes, it might be better if you kept your advice to yourself."

With that, I opened the door and hobbled out with what little indignation my crutching gait allowed me.

Chapter 8

Mal chased after me, though given my slow pace with the crutches it wasn't hard for him to keep up. "Mack, slow down. There are ice patches on the sidewalks. The last thing you need right now is to hit one of those and break your other leg."

I did as he said, slowing my pace and keeping a watchful eye on the ground. Besides, the car was only a few feet away. As soon as I reached the door, I yanked it open and maneuvered myself into the seat. I tossed my crutches into the back and waited for Mal to get in on the driver's side. He settled in and remained silent, starting the engine, and pulling out onto the street. We rode in silence for several minutes before I finally aired the thoughts churning in my head.

"I'm beginning to think inviting Clay into this group was a huge mistake. I should have listened to you, Cora, and Duncan. All of you warned me."

"Why are you feeling like it was a mistake now? A day or so ago, you were talking about how much help he has been."

"He was a help," I admitted, "and he paid a dear price for his assistance, both physically and emotionally. But that was before he overstepped his bounds. Talking to Holland and Dixon, and then sandbagging me like this were uncalled for. And I don't appreciate him second-guessing everything I've done up until now."

"You may not appreciate it, but I happen to agree with him."

I turned and shot him a look of disbelief. "You agree with what? Everything he's done and said? Just the part with Holland and Dixon? Or the part about telling the Capone Club members that their lives are in danger?"

Mal gave me a rueful look. "All of it."

I gaped at him, feeling disbelief and hurt. "If that's true, why haven't you said something?"

"For the very reason you gave Clay. I haven't walked in your shoes. I don't know what it feels like to have that sort of responsibility on my shoulders."

"I assume you're referring to me telling the Capone Club members about the letter writer. But what about the other stuff? What about this business with Holland and Dixon? Do you approve of that, too?"

"I do. I've seen the sort of stress you've been under lately between trying to work without stepping on anyone's toes and carrying the burden of this letter-writer stuff. And I've also seen how much satisfaction you get from doing what you do. I saw the look on your face when Ben Middleton's sister came by to tell you how grateful and happy she, Ben, and the rest of the family were for everything you had done. This crime stuff feeds some inner need you have, and because of that I think you should keep doing what you're doing." He paused and gave me a tired, knowing smile. "Face it, Mack, you *want* to keep doing it. And with the support of people like Holland and Dixon, you *can* keep doing it, minus much of the stress you've had to deal with recently." He paused a moment and then added, "I do have some caveats, however. I think you need to think carefully about how you want it all to work, and lay that out in clear terms to them. There are a lot of things to consider: the money, how involved you are, the types of cases you're involved in, how public your involvement will be, and when this new working relationship will begin. That's just for starters."

I sighed. "I don't know anything about Holland or Dixon . . . what their personalities are like, what they'll expect from me, or what their temperaments are like. How do I know if I want to work with them, or even if I can work with them? What if I agree to their offer and then discover that I hate working with them or they hate working with me?"

After a moment of silence, Mal said, "Maybe you can continue to work with Duncan primarily."

I winced and quickly turned to look out my side window so Mal wouldn't see my reaction. Mention of working with Duncan brought back the scene in front of the restaurant this morning and all the pain that came with it. "I'm not sure I want to work with anyone," I said into the window. "I've enjoyed doing what I've done on my own or with the help of the Capone Club."

"Then tell Holland and Dixon no," Mal said.

I smiled, sighed, and shook my head. "No, you're right. I want to keep doing what I'm doing, and on some level I need it. Even Holland could see that. Besides, I pretty much implied that I'm going to accept their offer but wanted a little time to think over the details." Mal said nothing, and I turned to look out the windshield again. "I think I'll put a time limit on it. I'll give it . . . I don't know . . . maybe six months? We'll see how it goes, and if I don't want to continue it after that time, I won't."

"That seems reasonable," Mal said.

We had arrived back at the bar, and Mal was circling the block looking for a parking space. When he didn't find one close by, he pulled up in front of the bar and stopped. "You get out here," he said. "I'll go park and then meet you inside."

I started to open the door, but before I got out I turned to him. "Do you really think I should tell the members of the Capone Club about the letter writer?"

"I think it would've been better if you had told them back when it all started," Mal said. "At this point, I'm not sure. Let's think on it, and maybe run it by Duncan and the others who know. Let's see what they think."

I gave him an appreciative smile and started to say something more. But then an annoyed driver behind us who wanted to get by honked his horn. So I hauled my crutches and myself out of the car and shut the door.

Chapter 9

Mal pulled away, and the car behind him followed. They disappeared around the corner, and as I turned to head inside, another car pulled up where Mal had just been. Both the passenger and driver's doors opened, and as the car idled, Billy got out on the driver's side while his girlfriend and fiancée, Whitney, exited from the passenger side. Whitney Sampson was a stunningly beautiful woman: tall and slender with legs that went on forever, mahogany-colored skin, eyes black as coal, and cheekbones that were high and sharp, giving her face a classic, timeless beauty. She came from a well-to-do family that had a strong business and political history in Milwaukee going back several generations, and her aristocratic background was evident in her clothes and in the way she walked, talked, and held herself. Like Billy, she was interested in law, or so I assumed since that was the line of work she had chosen. Given her background and career choice, she seemed like a perfect match for Billy, and the two of them together were a stunningly gorgeous couple. But their personalities were polar opposites. Where Whitney was typically standoffish, dismissive, and arrogant at times, Billy was always gregarious, congenial, and easygoing. I had a hard time envisioning the two of them making a go of it for any length of time.

Billy came around the idling car and gave Whitney a kiss. It looked as if he was aiming for her lips, but she turned her face at the last second with an expression of impatient tolerance, and his kiss landed on her cheek instead.

"Do you know what time you'll be done?" Whitney asked him in a tired, irritated-sounding voice.

"The usual," Billy said amiably, ignoring her snub. He saw me then, and a big smile broke out on his face. "Mack," he said. "You remember Whitney?"

"Of course," I said. She was the sort of woman one didn't forget easily. I hobbled my way toward her, stopping a foot or so away and extending one hand, my crutch tucked beneath my arm.

Whitney turned to look at me, and an expression of disdain flashed across her face. It was there and gone so quickly, I almost wondered if I'd imagined it. If it wasn't for the fact that I'd seen that same expression on her face several times before, I likely would have dismissed it as a figment of my imagination. Whitney extended her hand, a polite expression now firmly in place on her face.

"My car broke down," Billy said. "It's in the shop, so Whitney drove me here today."

"I suggested he get a rental car," Whitney said, a hint of disappointment in her tone. "Or just buy a new one to replace that old heap he drives, but he said either option was a ridiculous expenditure of money."

"It is," Billy said. "My budget can't handle it right now."

Whitney rolled her eyes. "But *my* budget can," she said in a weary voice.

Whitney had finished law school and joined a prestigious firm downtown last year. Her salary, on top of her family money, meant she could probably buy Billy a new car outright. But Billy clung stubbornly to his independent ways, refusing to take advantage of Whitney's money or her family's status, determined to make his own way.

I knew from talking with Billy in the past that this clash of cultures and Billy's determined efforts to stand on his own two feet were ongoing issues between him and Whitney. Unlike Whitney, Billy didn't come from money. He was financing his education through a combination of scholarships, school loans, and the money he made working at my bar. It was a matter of pride for him to acquire his education on his own.

Whitney, on the other hand, not only had lots of money at her disposal, she was as class-conscious as they came. She'd made it clear in the past that she was not happy with Billy's job, that she considered it and my bar—and by association me, I supposed—beneath him. Billy, however, loved what he did and had said on multiple occasions that he intended to stay with his bartending duties until he graduated from law school. Whitney's continued efforts to shame him into a better job had thus far been unsuccessful. In fact, he'd even hinted a few times about how he might like to pull the occasional shift behind the bar after he finished law school as a way to unwind. This inevitably led to puns and jokes about Billy taking the bar exam, stuff we'd all heard dozens of times but still laughed at with pleasant tolerance.

"I was going to take the bus," Billy said with a boyish grin and a shrug. "But Whitney insisted that she drive me."

"The bus is so . . . pedestrian," Whitney said, uttering the word *pedestrian* as if it tasted rank and disgusting. She glanced up at the façade of my building. "Sort of like this job," she added.

I might have been offended had I been focused on what she was saying, but I wasn't. Instead, I was focused on the faint scent I picked up after I shook her hand and the sound of saxophone music that came with it. It was a smell I'd encountered elsewhere recently.

"Whitney," I said, "I love the smell of your perfume. What is it?"

"Opium," she said. "It's my favorite, and the only scent I ever wear."

"It's quite nice." I forced a smile, but it must not have looked convincing.

"Are you feeling ill, Mack?" Billy asked. "You look a little pale."

"Billy is right," Whitney said, mustering up an expression of feigned concern. "Your face is the color of paste."

"I'm fine," I said with a dismissive wave of one hand. "We redheads tend toward the pale, you know, and being cooped up inside for most of the winter doesn't help. I just need a cup of coffee, maybe with a shot of whiskey in it," I added with a wink. "Can I offer you a drink on the house, Whitney?"

As expected, Whitney looked horrified at the suggestion. It wasn't that she didn't drink; I knew from talking with Billy that she did. Rather it was the idea of going into the bar—my bar—that put her off, either because the establishment wasn't up to her standards or she didn't want to encourage Billy by seeming to approve of the place. I suspected it was both.

"That's very kind of you," Whitney said. "But I'm afraid I'll have to pass. I have another engagement I need to get to." She dismissed me then, shifting her gaze to Billy. "If you can't get a ride home at the end of your shift, call me." The tone in her voice made it clear that, if he did call her, it would be a great imposition.

"I can drive him home," I said. "I'm up at that hour anyway, so it's no problem."

"That would be wonderful, if you're sure you don't mind," Whitney said. This time her smile looked more genuine. "We girls do need our beauty sleep, you know."

"It's not a problem at all," I said. "I'm happy to do it. Billy is the best bartender I have."

Whitney looked momentarily puzzled by this statement. "What is it that makes him the best?" she asked.

My answer to that question was probably driven by some mean streak inside me, some part of my personality that I don't like to admit is there. "Well, he's fast, efficient, and knows his mixology. Plus, just look at him. The women all love him. He brings them in by the droves."

Mal, who must've found a parking place, came walking up the sidewalk. He nodded at Billy and then looked at Whitney. At the moment, Whitney's face looked like a thundercloud—no doubt because of what I'd just said—and I saw Mal's brow draw down with a mix of curiosity and concern.

Mal had never met Whitney, so I did the introductions. Whitney quickly resurrected her charming personality for Mal and even flirted with him a little by tilting her head and giving him a coquettish smile.

Fortunately, Billy brought an end to this awkward

gathering by glancing at his watch and then saying, "I'd best get to work before I'm late." His long-legged stride got him to the door in two steps, and he disappeared inside.

"Always good to see you, Whitney," I lied, with what I hoped was a convincing smile.

"Nice to meet you," Mal said.

Whitney nodded at us, spun on her heel, and headed back to her car. We, in turn, headed inside the bar. I heard Whitney peel away before the bar door closed behind me. I didn't need any special senses to tell me the woman was irritated and angry. Oddly, I found this highly satisfying.

I headed straight for my office, with Mal behind me, and as soon as we were inside and the door was closed, I turned to him with a worried look.

"Uh-oh," he said. "What's wrong?"

I reached up and stuck my gloved hand beneath his nose. "Smell that. Do you recognize it?"

Mal looked a bit taken aback, and he shook his head in confusion. "I'm not sure what it is you want me to smell," he said. "I detect a faint scent of some sort of perfume. Is that what you mean?"

"It is," I said. "That's the smell of Opium."

I watched Mal's face as he processed this information and figured out what had me upset. "Whitney?" he asked.

I nodded grimly.

"Interesting," Mal said, pulling at his chin. "I don't know anything about the woman. Does she have any motive?"

"Pretty much the same motive Suzanne Collier has," I told him. "She's engaged to Billy and hates the fact that he works here. Her family is well-to-do, and she's very class-conscious. She considers this place, Billy's job, me . . . hell, this whole section of town as beneath her. She has made her disdain known every time I've seen her."

Mal thought about this for a moment, his brow drawn down in a concerned V. "So she's a snob," he said. "It's a big leap from that to becoming a murderer."

"I know, I know." I sighed and shook my head. "But I don't think we can ignore the possibility. At the very least, I should have Cora look into her, see how many things she might have in common with our victims and the recipients of the packages. And I should probably get Duncan to see if she has an alibi for the time when Lewis Carmichael was killed."

"I suppose so," Mal said, but he didn't sound concerned.

I shrugged off my coat and tossed it over the arm of the couch. Then I dug my cell phone out of the pocket and called Cora. "Cora, it's Mack. Can you come down to my office?"

Not surprisingly, she was upstairs in the Capone Club room. "Of course. Be there in two shakes."

By the time Cora arrived, I was settled in the chair behind my desk, and Mal was out at the bar getting us some drinks. Cora came in carrying her laptop, which functioned as a fifth appendage for her.

"What's up?" she asked, setting the laptop down on my desk and settling into the chair across from me.

"Lots of stuff," I told her, rolling my eyes. "It's been quite a day so far. I'm not even sure where to begin."

"Start with your visit to Clay," Cora prompted as Mal came in carrying two glasses of wine. He set one down in front of me and the other in front of Cora.

"You didn't get anything for yourself?" I asked him. He shook his head. "I'd rather wait until later."

"So what did Clay want?" Cora asked, clearly impatient.

I filled her in on the surprise guests who had been at Clay's house and then summarized my discussion with them.

"That's an interesting turn of events," Cora said when I was done. "It could certainly make life a lot easier for you."

"Perhaps," I agreed, "but it could also complicate things. Too many cooks in the kitchen, you know?"

"Indeed I do," Cora said. "Obviously, I would rather not have those guys knowing the sort of stuff I do for you since I sometimes skirt the law, but you can probably find a way to do what they want without involving me, don't you think?" Before I could answer her, she continued on. "I can see where this could be a big benefit for you. It would make things easier all around if you plan to continue with this crime-solving stuff. Plus, it sounds as if it could be a new source of income for you, too."

"I'm less interested in the monetary aspects than I am the overall dynamic," I said. "But I agree, it will make things easier. And I promise you I won't give away any of your trade secrets. Anything you do for me stays strictly between us." I paused, realizing that wasn't entirely true. "Well, it will be strictly between me, you, Duncan, Mal, and the Signoriello brothers," I clarified.

Cora grinned. "Yeah, I've kind of let that cat out of the bag already," she admitted. "But I don't want to make things difficult for myself or my company, so I'd prefer to operate a bit more surreptitiously from here on out, assuming you decide to go ahead with this."

"I'm going to tell them yes, but I'll set a time limit on it for now," I told her. "I think it will be smarter to do it for a trial period to see how it goes. I don't want to lock myself into something I'm going to hate."

Cora nodded sagely. "It will definitely eliminate some

of the pressure between you and Duncan," she said carefully, shooting Mal a quick sideways glance. She then grabbed her Chardonnay and sipped it, studying our reactions over the rim of the glass.

I didn't know what my own facial expressions might have given away because I was looking at Mal to gauge his. He shifted uncomfortably where he stood and stared down at his feet. Something inside my chest shifted a little with this display of obvious discomfort from him, and I had a sudden, strong urge to get up, walk over to him, and hug him. I did none of those things, however. Instead, I looked back at Cora and addressed her last comment.

"Perhaps in the long run this new arrangement will make things easy for me and Duncan, but until we solve this letter writer debacle, we'll need to keep things under wraps. Besides, after that whole business this morning with Duncan's ex-fiancée, I'm not sure where our relationship stands right now."

"When do you plan to tell Dixon and Holland your decision?" Cora asked, deftly changing the subject.

"Tomorrow. I'll sleep on it to make sure I still feel this way in the morning, and if I do, I'll call Holland straightaway."

"Okay . . . moving on," Cora said. "What else happened?"

"Billy's car broke down, so he had Whitney drive him into work. I ran into them out front just a bit ago. And I noticed something about Whitney that has me a bit rattled."

"You mean something other than her usual obnoxious, snobby, pretentious attitude?" Cora said with a sneer.

I smiled, but it faded quickly. "She was wearing

Opium," I said. "And she told me it's the only perfume she ever uses."

Cora took this in, and I watched her process the information. Several seconds ticked by. Finally, she said, "Okay, we talked about how there are probably hundreds of women in the Milwaukee area alone who wear Opium. It doesn't mean anything." She glanced over at Mal and then back at me. "Does it?"

"I don't know," I said wearily. "But when you get right down to it, she has as much motive as Suzanne Collier does. She also has money like Suzanne Collier does. I think it would be foolish of us to dismiss her before we check to see if she has any other common-alities with Suzanne Collier."

Cora nodded. "Of course." She started tapping on her laptop keyboard.

I said, "I know she has connections to the university because Billy told me she's teaching a class there next semester."

Cora nodded again, still tapping away.

"Maybe the two women are working together," Mal suggested. "It seems rather unlikely, but they do have a motive in common, and I imagine they run in a lot of the same social circles, so it's not unreasonable to think they may have crossed paths in the past and shared a conversation or two. Although I'm not sure why either of them would have put in the stipulations about you working with Duncan."

"Here's one path they've crossed together," Cora said. "Whitney Sampson and her family are support-ers of Boerner Botanical Gardens, just as Suzanne is."

One of our previous clues had involved some plant samples that would have been hard to come by at this time of the year unless someone had connections to an indoor horticultural display.

"And Whitney's law firm provides legal counsel for the university," Cora went on. "That could give her access to all kinds of information, including the names, addresses, and schedules of our package recipients."

I shook my head. "I don't know. It seems far-fetched to think that these two women would be working together in some sort of murder plot. Besides, Duncan told me that whoever attacked and killed Lewis had to have been either a very strong or a relatively large person . . . perhaps both. And neither one of these women fits that description."

"I don't know," Mal said. "Whitney appears strong and fit. She looks like someone who works out on a regular basis."

"She does belong to a gym somewhere," I said. "I've seen her carrying a gym bag and dressed in workout clothes before when she's stopped by the bar."

Cora stopped typing for a moment and gave Mal a questioning look. "Lewis wasn't a big man, but he was muscular. And from what Duncan said, whoever killed him beat him quite severely around the head and face. Do you think either of these women could have done that?"

"It depends on what Lewis was beaten with. If it was fists, I'm inclined to say no. But if it was an instrument of some sort, like a pole or a bat, then I think it's possible."

"Maybe we're looking at a team effort," Cora suggested. "Maybe there are more than two of them involved. Maybe the two women hired someone to do their dirty work."

I groaned and closed my eyes, massaging my temples. There was a small, throbbing pain in my forehead that was slowly getting bigger and stronger. "I can't begin to entertain that possibility," I moaned. "It was bad enough when we thought there might be two people.

The idea that there could be three or more makes me want to throw my hands up in defeat, pack my bags, and run off somewhere to hide for the rest of my life."

Mal walked over, placed his hands on my shoulders, and began to gently knead them. "We'll get to the bottom of it," he said. "You know, given your conversation with Holland and Dixon today, maybe it's time to take this thing to the police. While this latest clue seems reasonably tame, the one before that made it sound like the letter writer was escalating, tiring of the game and the threats. We've done as much as we can on our own; maybe it's time to bring in the big guns."

I shook my head vehemently. "No. I don't want to risk that yet. We're reasonably certain we know the meaning behind the last clue, and unless our interpretation proves to be totally wrong and we come up empty-handed at the museum, I'd rather wait and see what the next one says."

Mal sighed, and I could tell he disapproved of my decision.

I decided to change the subject. "On an unrelated matter, there's something I want to run by you. I need your construction expertise. Would you mind?"

He shrugged. "Sure."

I looked over at Cora. "Feel free to stay here in my office as long as you like. I'm going to take Mal out to the new section to show him something, and then I'll probably head upstairs to the Capone Club room."

Cora nodded and said nothing. She was focused on the screen in front of her.

"I'll also tell Billy your drinks are on the house for the night." That, at least, garnered me a smile.

Chapter 10

I hoisted myself out of my chair, grabbed my crutches, gave Mal a sideways nod of my head to indicate he should follow me, and headed out to the main area of the bar.

Billy flagged me down, and I made my way over to him. "Hey, boss," he said, "I just wanted to say I'm sorry for the comments Whitney made outside. Sometimes she gets a bit full of herself."

"She does come across as a bit of a snob at times," I said. "I have to say, you and she don't seem to be a great fit."

"She isn't always that bad," Billy said defensively. "Her parents are terrible snobs, and whenever Whitney spends time around them she tends to adopt their behavior. She's a totally different person when I get her away from them for a while."

"Don't let it worry you too much," I said. "I'm not that easily offended."

"I know you're tough," Billy said. "But I also want you to know that I don't approve of the way Whitney treated you. And I will let her know that."

"I appreciate that, but don't do it for me; do it for yourself."

Billy nodded, a sage look on his face. I started to turn away and then remembered my offer to Cora. "By the way," I said, "Cora's drinks are on the house for today."

"Gotcha, boss." Billy gave me a snappy salute, flashed me that dimpled, charming smile that made all the girls drool over him, and then went back to work.

Mal and I made our way through the main area of the bar and into the new section. For now, this area was set up with tables and chairs, and on the far side of the room was a stairway to the upper level, which housed the Capone Club room, a gaming room, a larger room that could be used for private parties, a bathroom, and a second bar area. Both the Capone Club room and the gaming room were quite popular, so the upstairs stayed fairly busy. My waitstaff complained regularly about having to run up and down the stairs, and I was none too happy myself with the climb, thanks to my crutches and cast.

I led Mal to the far back corner of the room beneath the stairs. Here there was another door, one that stayed locked, which led to the basement. Just before I bought the adjoining building to expand the bar, I discovered that my basement and the basement of this neighboring building were connected by a small tunnel. Rumor had it Al Capone had used the bar back in his day as a hiding place for his bootlegged booze. This rumor was verified when I discovered a hidden cache of old liquor in one of the basement rooms. That discovery had led to the naming of the crime-solving group and the room they met in.

I took my keys from my pocket and unlocked the basement door. Reaching inside, I flipped on the light to reveal another set of stairs leading down to the cellar. Carefully, and slowly, I made my way down with Mal behind me.

At the bottom of the stairs was a large, essentially empty storage room. I had plenty of storage on my side of the basement and hadn't yet put this side to use. In a far corner of this room were the mechanicals for this half of the building: furnace, water heater, water softener, and an air-handling unit. Above this portion of the basement was an open area with a built-up stage section on the first floor, and above that was the second-floor landing and bar area. Behind the second-floor bar area was more space that I had yet to utilize. At one time, I had thought I might install a second, smaller kitchen up there, but now I had another idea.

"Wow," Mal said looking around the room. "I've never been down here before. You have a lot of room."

"I know. I've had different ideas about what to do with it, but I haven't settled on anything yet." I pointed to a door at the back of the room, which led to an adjoining room. "In the room behind that door there is a hidden tunnel that connects the two basements. It was used by Al Capone."

Mal's eyes widened. "No kidding?"

"I swear," I said.

"That's both intriguing and spooky."

I gave him a grim smile. "You have no idea. Remind me to tell you the story about that tunnel one of these days."

I walked Mal around the room, pointing toward the ceiling in different areas and explaining to him what was above each spot. When I was done, I looked at him and said, "So here's my big question. I want to put in an elevator, one that will run from here to the first and second floors. How difficult would it be, and am I crazy for even considering the idea?"

I half expected Mal to bust out laughing and look at me like I was insane. But he didn't. He arched one eyebrow, his expression intrigued. He scanned the room and pulled at his chin. After a few seconds, he walked over toward the area of the basement that was below part of the dance floor on the first level and the vacant area behind the bar on the second level.

"This would be the place to put it," he said. "Can it be done? Absolutely. Are you crazy for thinking of it? Maybe, but to be honest, I think it's a great idea. Not only could it help your staff, it provides access to the second level for handicapped people." He gave a half-hearted shrug. "That said, it won't be cheap. It will run you around twenty grand just for the elevator itself, and that doesn't count retrofitting it in and setting up the necessary mechanicals. And it will require closing off part of your bar on the first floor during the construction."

"How long do you think it would take to do it?"

"Well, you'd have to get all the necessary permits, of course, and solicit bids from contractors, but once that's done, the actual construction part shouldn't take more than a couple of weeks."

"I can deal with that. I've already survived one major construction job, so I can get through this one just fine." I looked at the area for a second and then gave a decisive nod. "I think I'm going to go ahead with it. I can't tell you how many times I've rued the fact that I didn't put it in with the initial construction. And you're right: it does provide access for the handi-capped, which ironically, is me at the moment. Of course, I'll need to have some sort of lock or access control that keeps people from being able to get into the basement."

"That's easy enough to do when you order the actual elevator," Mal said. "Can I make a suggestion?"

"Absolutely."

"Since you're going to open up the walls anyway, why don't you put in a dumbwaiter as well as an elevator? You can connect it to that upstairs area where you were thinking of putting in a kitchen."

"That's a brilliant idea," I said, rewarding him with a big smile.

"You know, if you want to try to get the permit right away, I can do some of the preliminary construction for you now while I'm on vacation from my undercover job."

"Wow," I said. "That would be fantastic." I paused and frowned. "But I don't want to take advantage of you. I feel guilty enough as it is, given how much of your free time is spent with me."

"You're not taking advantage of me," Mal said. "If I'm going to keep an eye on you the way Duncan wants me to, I need to be here when you are as often as possible. Working on this project for you will give me something to do other than sit around and watch you, or follow you around like a little puppy dog."

That last comment made me feel a twinge of guilt. I had no idea Mal felt so helpless, useless . . . maybe even emasculated.

Mal, perhaps realizing he'd said too much, tried to soften the blow. "Plus, I like doing this sort of thing."

"Okay, I'll tell you what. I'll be happy to let you start work on it, but only if you let me pay you."

Mal shook his head and smiled. "How would it

look to everyone else if I charged my girlfriend for a construction job?"

"We don't need to let anyone else know I'm paying you. We can make it appear as if you're doing it for me as a favor, and I'll pay you under the table."

Mal shook his head again. "If you do that, then I'll have all sorts of tax issues to deal with. I don't want any of those headaches. Honestly, Mack, it would be a hell of a lot easier if you would just let me do it for you for free."

I gave him a grateful smile. "You are far too kind to me, Malachi O'Reilly."

"Believe me, the pleasure is all mine. I'm psyched now. I want to get started. In fact, if you don't have any plans to go anywhere in the next couple of hours, I'm going to go draw up a plan for the project so I can get that permit."

He did look psyched. His eyes were alight with excitement, his face had an eager expression, and he was rubbing his hands together as if with glee.

"Well, there is the museum," I reminded him.

"Oh. Right."

"But I could go there by myself," I suggested.

He shook his head. "No way." He looked so disappointed, it broke my heart. Then he said, "Well, given that today is Friday, we'll have to wait until Monday to get the permit."

I glanced at my watch. It was already going on one o'clock. "Or we could do the museum tomorrow," I suggested.

"That's cutting things awfully close," he said. "The deadline is Sunday. What if we're wrong and it's not the museum at all?"

"That still leaves us an entire day to figure it out and look somewhere else. It's late already, and the museum is a huge place. We probably won't have enough time today to cover it all anyway."

"Are you sure?"

"I am. You've got me all excited about this project now. I want to get it going."

"Okay then."

With that, we went back upstairs and returned to my office so Mal could fetch his coat. He gave me a quick buss on the cheek before he left, and as I watched him leave I saw there was a vibe in his step that hadn't been there before. He was like a little boy at Christmas who had just gotten his favorite toy truck or BB gun. His excitement was contagious, and Cora didn't miss out on the fact that Mal was revved up about something.

"What's up with Mal?" she asked me. "Did you just tell him you're throwing Duncan over for him?"

I shot Cora a chagrined smile. "No," I said in a chastising tone. "I simply talked to him about an idea I had to put an elevator in beneath the stairs to the second level. Not only did he think it was a good idea, he wants to be the one to work on it. He just left to try to draw up a plan and get the necessary permits so he can start work on it right away."

"It *is* a good idea," Cora said, nodding approvingly. "I know some of your staff members will appreciate it, and there are a few customers, like the Signoriello brothers, who will appreciate it too." She paused, and looked tellingly at my casted leg. "I imagine you'll appreciate it, as well, assuming you still have that thing on by the time it's done."

"He won't let me pay him for it," I said. "I feel uncomfortable letting him do it without some sort of compensation."

"Why don't you offer him drinks and meals on the

house?" Cora suggested. "I'm willing to bet he'll accept that."

I gave her suggestion a grudging nod of approval. "That's a good idea, Cora, and as your reward, lunch is on the house."

"Thank you very much," Cora said in an exaggeratedly polite tone.

We smiled at one another for a moment, but then that moment passed and my expression grew more serious. "Any luck in your search efforts yet?" I asked.

"Some, yes. It turns out that Whitney's family has a number of connections with the university. They also offer a scholarship, one that's in the name of Whitney's grandfather, who was an educator there back in the fifties. Whitney participates in the decision-making process for those scholarship awards; however, the scholarships are limited to people of African American descent, and none of our package recipients meet that criteria."

"I think that's how Billy met her," I said to Cora. "Now that you mention it, I seem to recall a conversation I had with him a year or so ago about how Whitney was the one who asked him out initially. She was on the review committee that interviewed him for the scholarship, and she was so taken with him that she tracked him down and asked him out."

"The fact that both women are involved with scholarship programs may simply be a coincidence," Cora said. "They both come from wealthy families, so it seems inevitable that their paths might cross in situations such as this one."

"You're right," I said, thinking. "It might be more relevant to see if there are areas involving the letter writer where the women's paths don't cross. See if you can find any connections between Whitney and the casino. We couldn't find any connections between it and Suzanne. Maybe our original assumption about it being a public place where anyone could leave a clue is correct. But on the off chance that it's not, we should check to see if Whitney has some connections to it we don't know about."

"Good idea," Cora said, tapping away at her keyboard.

"There's something else I'd like you to do, if you have the time," I said.

"Name it," Cora said, not looking up from her screen.

"I want you to see if you can find any commonalities between Suzanne, our package recipients, and Duncan's partner, Jimmy Patterson."

Cora eyed me dubiously. "That's a big can of worms you're messing with there," she said. "Even if we find some connections, proving he has anything to do with the letter writer will be practically impossible."

"I know," I said with a sigh. "But I need to do it, if for no other reason than for my peace of mind."

Cora nodded, looking very solemn.

"One other thing," I said, biting my lip. "I realize that what I'm about to ask of you could get you into a lot of trouble, so please feel free to tell me no. I don't want you to do anything you're not comfortable with."

Cora looked intrigued, perhaps even a little excited, but not worried. "You'd be surprised at my comfort level," she said. There was a wicked twinkle in her eye.

"I want you to see if there's any way you can get hold of the records involving Suzanne Collier and the shrink she supposedly was seeing. I'd really like to know if that woman has some serious psychological issues."

"That won't be easy," Cora said with a worried look. "A lot of psychiatrists are sticking to the old-school way of doing things and keeping paper charts. Even if this particular psychiatrist uses an electronic health-care record, the security on those is pretty high. They're not easy to hack."

"I understand. See what you can do."

Cora nodded.

"One more thing, and then I promise I'll leave you alone," I said.

Cora gave me a sly smile. "Spit it out."

"I'm wondering if it's time to tell the rest of the Capone Club about the letter writer. Do you think I should? And what do you think their reactions will be?"

Cora leaned back in her chair, folding her arms over her chest. "Wow," she said. "What brought this on?"

"I can't see an endgame here," I told her. "I'm afraid this letter writer is going to go on and on, and escalate with each event. I'm tired of being yanked around, and it's time to try to put an end to it. We have to determine who's behind it. Our focus on Suzanne and Whitney is part of it, but I feel certain there's another party involved. And what's more, I have a sick feeling that this party is someone close to us, someone we all know. It's time to flush that person out. I have an idea about how to do that, but I want to think on it a little longer. The first step is to tell the group the truth."

Cora nodded slowly, her brows drawn together in deep thought. "That could be very dangerous," she said finally. "Dangerous for you and everyone else."

"I know that. But I've given this a lot of thought recently, and it's time to shift this game around. I want to take charge. I want to be the one calling the shots. And the more I can do to unsettle the letter writers, the better my chances are of getting them to expose themselves."

Cora drummed her fingers on the desktop, looking troubled. "Do you think the second person is someone in the Capone Club?"

"It's a possibility," I admitted. "A strong one."

There was silence for a minute or two while Cora thought things through. "Okay," she said finally, pinning me with her gaze. "I have three questions for you. One, if you tell the club members about the letter writer, are you going to tell them about the people we suspect? Two, are you going to tell them we think there are two people involved? And three, are you going to tell them that one of those people might be a member of the group?"

"I'm still working on my plan, and I don't have everything figured out yet," I told her. "However, I'm pretty certain I'm not going to tell the group whom we suspect or that we think someone in the group might be involved. At least not yet. I don't want to color anyone else's opinion on the matter or create an environment of rampant paranoia among the group. If and when I do tell them, I need to make sure the timing is right. That's where my plan will come into play."

"Care to share this plan of yours?" Cora asked.

"I will," I told her. "When the time is right and I have it better planned out. For now, I'm going to continue to play along as we have."

"Sounds like there's lots of drama on the horizon," Cora said, rubbing her hands together. "I'd best get my work done."

"When you do get done with all of that, I'd like for the two of us to sit down and look at each member of the Capone Club who is still on the suspect list. I want to dissect their lives, look for possible motives, determine who we can rule out." I fished the list Clay had given me earlier out of my pocket and went over to my copier. Once I had a copy of it, I gave it to Cora and put the original back in my pocket. "These are the people who don't have an alibi as of yet for the time when Lewis was killed. So work on these names."

"This will be fun," Cora said, scanning the list. "I'm clearing my calendar for the next two weeks."

Chapter 11

I left Cora in my office doing what she does best and made my way upstairs to the Capone Club room. But I was only halfway up the stairs when my cell phone rang and I saw it was Duncan. I hesitated, unsure if I wanted to answer the call. I looked around to see if there was anyone close by who might over-hear, thinking that might give me an excuse to ignore the call. But there was no one within hearing distance, and just before the call would have flipped over to voice mail, I answered it.

"Hello?"

"Hey, Mack," Duncan's voice said, filling my mouth with the taste of fizzy, dark chocolate. The fizziness always came through when I spoke to him over the phone. "What are you doing?"

"Not much at the moment," I said. "I was just on my way upstairs to see what's going on in the Capone Club room."

"Any chance I can steal you away for a little while?" Duncan asked. "I have the rest of the day free. I thought maybe we could spend it together."

I squeezed my eyes closed, my thoughts ripped

apart by indecision. On the one hand, I was eager to have some time with Duncan alone. But on the other, there was that little scene I had witnessed earlier between him and his ex-fiancée. I supposed I would need to get to the bottom of that, and his relationship with her, sooner rather than later. An uninterrupted period of alone time seemed like the perfect opportunity to do that.

"That sounds doable," I said. "How and where would you like to get together?"

As soon as I said this, I regretted it. I knew the two of us needed to have a discussion that might get difficult, and if that happened I preferred to be on my home ground. Fortunately, Duncan played into my hands.

"I can be at your back door in ten minutes," he said. "In disguise, of course," he added.

"I'll be there. The usual knock?" We had agreed upon a particular knock several liaisons ago so that I would have no doubt it was Duncan on the other side of the door.

"You got it." And just like that, he was gone. No good-bye, no see you soon . . . just a sudden cessation of the faint buzzing sound I always hear on any type of telephone call. I turned myself around and headed back downstairs. In order to disengage the alarm to the alley door Duncan used, I had to go back into my office. As soon as I entered, Cora looked up at me in surprise.

"Something up?" she asked.

I nodded and headed for the alarm panel. "Duncan will be here in a few minutes. I need to turn off the alarm to the alley door."

"Have you talked to him since . . . well . . . since the thing you saw?"

I shook my head. After turning off the alarm, I turned around to face her. "I'm going to ask him about it when he gets here."

Cora arched her eyebrows at me. "That could get interesting," she said in a tentative but curious tone. "Try not to jump to any conclusions before he has a chance to explain himself."

"I will," I said a bit irritably. "Though I have a hard time understanding how he'll be able to explain leaving my bed early in the morning and engaging in a lip-lock with his ex-fiancée a few hours later. Not to mention the fact that he hasn't bothered to tell me that his ex-fiancée is in town or that he still has contact with her."

"Maybe they're just friends," Cora suggested.

"If that were true, why didn't he tell me about her?"

Cora had no answer for that.

"Why does he feel like he needs to hide her from me?"

Cora opened her mouth as if she had an answer for that question, but before she could speak I continued.

"I've asked him several times about what happened on his wedding day, because he's mentioned more than once that he was left at the altar. But every time I've asked, he's just blown me off. Now I think I'm beginning to understand why."

Cora looked at me for a moment, a collage of ever-changing expressions on her face. I'm sure she wanted to say something, but she looked hesitant and indecisive. In the end, all she said was, "I'll be here if you need me."

I glanced at my watch. "He should be here in a few minutes. Would you mind waiting about fifteen minutes and then turning the alarm back on for me?"

"Happy to do it," Cora said.

With that, I left my office and went down to the end of the hallway by the alley door. I unlocked the door to my apartment and opened it, propping it with my body. Having it open would obscure most of the exit doorway from anyone who happened to enter the hallway at the other end. That would make it easier for Duncan to slip in and head upstairs without being seen.

I didn't have long to wait. About five minutes later, I heard our secret knock. I leaned over and pushed on the door, using one of my crutches to keep my apartment door propped open. Duncan opened the alley door, slipped inside, and was standing in the foyer at the base of my apartment stairs a second later. I watched long enough to make sure the alley door closed all the way and then joined him.

As soon as my apartment door closed, Duncan wrapped me in his arms and pulled me to him. The action was a little too reminiscent of the scene I had witnessed earlier, and I felt myself rebelling and pushing away from him.

"Uh-oh," Duncan said, looking down at me with a concerned expression. "What's wrong?"

"We need to talk," I said. I wriggled out from beneath his arms and started up the stairs. I'd gotten better at climbing them with my crutches over the past week or two, but I was still slow. I could feel the intensity of Duncan's gaze behind me as I went and wished I had let him go first.

"Mack," Duncan said when I reached the landing at the top of the stairs, "hold on."

I stopped where I was and turned to face him.

"What the hell is going on?" he said. "Has something

happened to someone that I don't know about? Is it something about the letter writer?"

I shook my head. "No, it's none of those things, though I do have an update for you. I need to talk to you about us, about our relationship."

"Oh," he said with a tone of resignation. "Is this about Mal? Have you finally decided to toss me over for him?"

"This has nothing to do with Mal." No sooner had the words left my lips then I started to wonder if they were true. "Let's go sit down in the kitchen. I could use a cup of coffee. Would you like one?"

"Sure," Duncan said, sounding worried.

He followed me into the kitchen and sat at the table while I went about setting up the coffeepot. As I busied myself with the coffee, I filled him in on our visit to the Pabst Mansion and what we had found there. Once I had the coffee set up and brewing, I hobbled into my father's office, got the note that had been the latest clue, and brought it out to him.

He read it and then said, "I agree with your interpretation. The museum seems like the logical choice. When are you going?"

"Mal and I are going first thing tomorrow."

"Okay," he said, pushing the letter aside. "Now tell me what's really on your mind. What do we need to discuss about our relationship?"

I braced myself and then went into it. "I've asked you before to tell me what happened with your previous relationship. You told me you were left at the altar, but you've never elaborated beyond that."

"It's not something I'm all that comfortable talking about. And I'm not sure why it matters. It's in the past."

"Is it?" I posed. "What is the current status of that relationship?"

He looked back at me, his eyes narrowing. "There isn't one," he said.

I stared at him, disappointed and a little disbelieving that he wouldn't mention the encounter from earlier or at least mention something about the current status of his relationship with the woman he once wanted to marry. I debated playing this out a little longer, giving him a chance to either come clean or hang himself some more, but decided that I wasn't in a game-playing mood.

"I saw you yesterday when Mal and I were returning from the Pabst Mansion tour. You were standing outside of a restaurant." I paused, waiting to see if he would catch on to where I was going with this line of discussion.

His eyes grew wide, and his expression morphed into one of dawning understanding. "Oh, okay. You saw me with her, didn't you? Is that what this is about?"

"I saw you with some woman. I don't know for sure who she was, but the two of you certainly looked quite chummy." I was working hard to keep the irritation and frustration I felt from coming through in my voice. I didn't want to dig myself a hole too deep to climb out of on the off chance that he had some reasonable, acceptable explanation.

"Somehow, I get the feeling you know more than you're letting on," he said carefully. "Let me guess . . . Cora helped?"

I shrugged, but I might as well have admitted to it. Duncan knew Cora's abilities better than most, and he was also familiar with her insatiable curiosity, particularly where I was concerned.

"Okay," Duncan said, leaning back in his chair. "Let me explain some things to you. To start off, Courtney Metcalfe is the woman I was engaged to, the one who stood me up at the altar, though technically I never made it to the altar. She called me the morning of our wedding, an hour before it was supposed to take place, and said she couldn't go through with it. I believe I've mentioned something about this to you before."

"You told me you were jilted at the altar, but you never went into the specifics. And somehow you never mentioned the name of your fiancée, or the fact that she comes to Milwaukee regularly, or the fact that you are apparently still seeing her. And if the kiss the two of you shared yesterday is any indication, I'd say your relationship is on pretty decent terms." I paused and shook my head in dismay. "You didn't feel the need to tell me you're still seeing your ex-fiancée or that the two of you are still quite chummy?"

I heard the sarcasm and bitterness in my voice, the acerbic tone that was my desperate attempt to cover up the hurt I was feeling.

"I haven't been seeing Courtney," Duncan said, and his voice tasted like rich milk chocolate. Nothing about it made me think he was lying. "Yesterday was the first time I've seen her since our wedding day." He paused, made a rueful face, and let out a mirthless laugh. "Technically, since I didn't see her on our wedding day, yesterday was the first time I've seen her since the day before our wedding day."

I didn't know if he, like me, was trying to hide his pain, but if he was, he was failing miserably at it. Clearly this jilting had left a scar, although the term *wound* seemed a better metaphor since it obviously wasn't healed. I could not only hear the pain in his voice, I could taste it in the bitterness of the chocolate flavor it triggered.

"You still have feelings for her, don't you?" I said.

"Yeah," Duncan snapped back. "Feelings of annoyance and resentment. And relief." He started to say something more, but then seemed to think better of it. He snapped his mouth shut, raked a hand through his hair, and sat back in his chair with a sigh. "Look," he said, "I haven't been totally honest with you. I'm not lying when I say that up until yesterday I haven't seen or spoken to Courtney since the day before our wedding. I've forgiven her for what she did—in fact, I'm somewhat grateful to her for saving us from a marriage that clearly would have failed, given what I know now—but I haven't forgotten what she did. The anger I feel today is as acute as it was eight months ago when it first happened, and I've had no desire to see or speak to Courtney since that day." He paused, shifted in his seat, and then looked away. "She, however, has made many attempts to talk to and see me over the past few months. She started calling me back in July, and since then I've had countless phone messages from her, but I haven't spoken to her, nor have I returned any of her calls. She's apologized for what she did, claiming she got stage fright at the last minute and feared we were making a big mistake. Turns out, she was right, but she no longer seems to see it that way. She has begged me to give her another chance and swears that marrying me is what she wants."

He paused and finally looked at me. "But it's not what I want, Mack. I have no feelings for her anymore other than resentment. I don't trust her, and I've seen a side of her that I never saw before the wedding. It's enough to keep me from going back. *More* than enough," he emphasized, his eyes wide.

Silence settled between us, and I studied Duncan's face, trying to determine if he was being honest with me, even though the flavor of his voice told me he was.

After a while Duncan, reached over and took my hand in his. "My feelings for you are real and genuine, Mack, but I'm sure you can understand that I'm a little gun-shy at this point. I'm not in any hurry to jump into another commitment like that. I want to take things slower, make sure I know the person I'm with. *Really* know her."

"I understand that," I said. "But if that's true, then why did you see Courtney and kiss her the way you did?"

Duncan sighed heavily. "First of all, I had no idea Courtney was going to be there. I had a message left for me at work to meet a woman at that restaurant regarding some information on a case I'm working. When I got there, Courtney met me inside. At first, I thought it was just a coincidence, but then I realized she had set the whole thing up. I started to leave, but she begged me to stay and hear her out. I didn't want to make a scene inside the restaurant, so I agreed to give her ten minutes. We sat at the bar— I refused to get a table—and I listened as she told me how she'd made this huge mistake by not showing up for the wedding, but at the time she was so paralyzed with fear and doubt that she couldn't make herself do it. She swears she loves me and wants to spend the rest of her life with me. And then she begged me to give her another chance. Basically, it's the same crap she's been saying in all the voice mails she's been leaving me over the past few months."

He paused, and I sensed he was waiting for a response from me. I didn't give him one. I simply sat in silence, staring at him, waiting for him to continue. After a moment, he did.

"I explained to her that I wasn't interested in rekindling our relationship. She kept insisting that what we had was worth fighting for, and that we should give it another chance. She offered to take things slow, feel it out, see where we ended up."

He paused, raking a hand through his hair, his expression pained. "I have no interest in doing that with her," he said. "I have no interest in being with her anymore. And I told her that. When I got up to leave, she followed me outside and kept insisting that I was lying to myself and to her. She told me she knew the heat and the love between us was still there. And then, in an apparent attempt to prove it, she grabbed me in a big bear hug and kissed me."

He paused, looking abashed. After a quick glance at me, he bowed his head and said in a low voice, "I confess that for a second or two it seemed so familiar, so normal, that I kissed her back. But it was purely a reflex, and as soon as I realized it, I pushed her away. I thought she'd be angry, but instead she just smiled at me and said she wasn't going to give up. I told her she was wasting her time and needed to move on."

He leaned back in his chair and folded his arms over his chest. "That's it," he said. "That's the whole story. The reason I didn't tell you she was calling me was because it was irrelevant. I had no intention of returning her calls and assumed she would just give up." He rolled his eyes and scoffed. "Apparently, I underestimated her tenacity."

I nodded slowly, digesting his explanation. I wasn't done grilling him yet. "I thought for some reason that your ex-fiancée lived in Chicago," I said. "I don't remember if you told me that or if it was an assumption

I made. But now Cora tells me Courtney has a house here in Milwaukee and that she spends a fair amount of time here. Were you aware of that?"

Duncan nodded. "I was, but again it seemed irrelevant."

"So you didn't feel it was relevant to let me know that your ex-fiancée was calling you regularly, begging you to take her back, and spending a fair amount of time here in Milwaukee?"

Duncan let his head roll back, and he stared at the ceiling, his arms still folded over his chest. "As far as I was concerned, it was nothing more than a nuisance." He raised his head and looked at me. "My relationship with her is over and done with. I found out some things about her after the whole wedding fiasco, and I assure you I have no interest in rekindling that relationship. I'm sorry if you feel I was being deceptive somehow, but honestly, to me it's a nonissue."

"I see," I said, nodding slowly. "Tell me something, would you feel slighted if I told you that my ex-boyfriend is hounding me to get back together?"

"Is he?" Duncan asked, frowning.

I smiled at him. "No, he's not, but I can tell from your expression and the tone in your voice that the idea bothers you. So can you understand why your situation bothers me?"

"I suppose so," Duncan said resignedly. "Sorry."

"Thank you." We shared a relieved smile. "I'm curious, does Courtney know about me?"

He shrugged. "I honestly don't know. It's not like we talk regularly or anything. Like I said, all the talking has been on her end." He paused, and his brows drew down into a frown. "Although . . ."

"What?" I asked after several seconds of silence.

"She did ask me if I had something going with that

redheaded bartender she saw in the news. I told her no. I didn't want her to start harassing you."

I bit my lip and debated asking my next question, knowing I was stepping into potentially sensitive territory. After giving it some thought, I decided to push onward, feeling it was time to fully clear the air.

"There's something else about Courtney I'd like to discuss with you, and while it might seem a bit outlandish, don't dismiss the idea outright. Give it serious consideration."

"Okay," Duncan said with a nod.

"Cora tells me that Courtney comes from a fairly wealthy family."

"She does."

"It makes me wonder if she and Suzanne Collier might have crossed paths, particularly if Courtney is spending a lot of time here in Milwaukee. Remember how we were questioning why you, specifically, were mentioned in the letters?"

I could tell from Duncan's expression that he knew where I was headed. "I know what you're thinking," he said. "But I can't see Courtney doing anything like that. Yes, she surprised me with her behavior and actions, and I admit I don't know her as well as I thought I did, but I think I know her well enough to know she wouldn't kill someone."

He might be convinced, but I was still on the fence. And I was sick and tired of being a marionette for whoever was pulling all the strings. Clay's words earlier about it being time to go on the offensive came back to me. Maybe he was right.

"I've decided it's time to try to put an end to this letter writer one way or the other," I told him. "I'm tired of being yanked around and manipulated by whoever is behind this. So I think I'm going to force

the issue and tell the members of the Capone Club
the truth about the letters."

"Are you sure you want to do that?"

"I am," I said. "It's time for me to take charge of
my own destiny, and I should let everyone else do
so, too."

"You realize some of them might be angry with you."

"Yes, but I hope they'll understand that I did what
I thought was best at the time."

"Some will understand, some may not."

"And there's a new wrinkle I should tell you about."
I then filled him in on my encounter with Whitney,
and the revelation about her use of Opium perfume.
"I have Cora looking into Whitney's connections to
the university and how many places her path crosses
with Suzanne Collier."

"So now you're thinking Whitney and Suzanne
might be working together?" There was a high note of
skepticism in his voice.

"Maybe," I said with some hesitation. "Though, to
be honest, I'm more inclined to think it's one or the
other."

"You sound like you have bones to pick with wealthy
women," Duncan said. "First, you're pairing Courtney
with Suzanne, and now Whitney? Why not consider
that it's all three of them conspiring together?"

He made it all sound utterly ridiculous, which I
supposed it probably was. But the tone in his voice,
the one that made me feel like some rank amateur,
irked me.

"If they are working together," he went on, "I'm
thinking they had to make arrangements for someone else to do the dirty work. At least part of it. I don't
think any of them has the necessary size or strength

to have inflicted the sort of wounds we found on Lewis Carmichael."

"That's assuming the wounds were inflicted with fists," I said. "What if they were wielding a weapon of some sort? Do you know what was used to beat Lewis?"

He sighed, and then nodded wearily. "It wasn't fists. The ME said it looked like some sort of object was used, something flat and heavy. But I still don't think any of the women would have had the strength to do something like that."

"Well, any one of them or the group of them certainly have the wherewithal financially to hire a hit man," I said, trying to keep the defensiveness out of my voice. "So I don't think we can rule them out, either."

Duncan leaned forward, uncrossing his arms and running his hands down his thighs. "It doesn't matter unless we can find some sort of concrete evidence that points to them. And so far, we're out of luck in that regard. And that means we have to continue to play the game. Are you sure you want to bring the whole Capone Club in on it?"

I nodded. It felt right to do it now, whereas it hadn't before. "I'm mulling over an idea, a plan I have to maybe push the letter writer's buttons and force things."

"Not sure that's a wise idea," Duncan said.

"I don't care if it's wise or not. I'm tired of being held hostage and having my friends' lives put in danger."

"What, exactly, are you planning to do?" Duncan asked. He didn't look happy.

"I don't have all the specifics figured out yet, but I'll run it by you once I do. In the meantime, it will be business as usual. Mal and I are going to the museum tomorrow, and hopefully, we'll return here with the next clue."

"Speaking of Mal, where is he?"

"He's off working on a project for me." I told Duncan about my idea regarding the elevator.

"An expensive but useful improvement," he said. "Mal will enjoy working on it. I think he misses the construction life more than he's willing to admit."

Another heavy silence settled between us, and after a bit Duncan cocked his head to one side and said, "Are we okay, Mack?"

I gave him a wan smile. "I honestly don't know. I'm not thrilled with the fact that you didn't tell me about any of this stuff with Courtney. I've been honest and upfront with you when it comes to Mal."

"I know, and all I can do is say I'm sorry, and I'll try to do better in the future, okay?"

I nodded and smiled at him. "Let's move on," I said. "Because there's something else I need to tell you about. I had a meeting earlier with Clay Sanders, and he invited a couple of other guests along who had a proposal for me."

"A proposal?" Duncan said with a curious smile. "Business or marriage?"

"Business. The other guests were your boss, Mark Holland, and the chief district attorney, Anthony Dixon. They want to work with me."

"Interesting," Duncan said. "I've had a couple of chats with Holland about you recently, and I knew he was curious about your abilities, but I had no idea he had talked with anyone else or come to any sort of decision regarding the matter."

"They're offering to hire me on as a consultant." I made finger quotes around the last word. "And they've said they'll pay me, though we haven't gotten as far as talking numbers yet. I gather they want me to assist with interrogating suspects and perhaps some of the crime-scene investigation."

I expected Duncan to be enthusiastic about this proposal, given that it was what he'd had in mind months ago, though more with me as his off-the-books personal assistant. But he looked uncertain and said, "Are you going to do it?"

I shrugged, giving him an ambivalent nod. "I don't see why not. It seems like an ideal situation. It's a way for me to bring in some extra money, and I like being able to do something constructive with my synesthesia. Despite the darkness this crime stuff has brought into my life, I find the work rewarding and enriching. I'd like to find a way to continue doing it, and working against people like Holland and Dixon doesn't make a lot of sense."

"You still seem a little hesitant."

I gave him a grudging smile. "There's the rub of having to work with other people and being forced to do things their way," I told him. "And, of course, I have mixed feelings about the publicity. Holland and Dixon want to advertise the fact that they're working with me. In fact, they want to spin the Middleton thing in a way that suggests they were working with me on that case."

Duncan nodded solemnly. "They need a way to try to save face," he said. "I warned you that might happen."

"I know, and to be honest, I don't care if they take all the credit. I'm not looking for kudos or recognition. All I want to do is use my synesthesia for something good."

"What about the Capone Club? Did they come up in the discussion at all?"

"They did. Holland and Dixon weren't quite as eager to include them. But I told him we were a package deal. So we'll see what they agree to. Before I involve the Capone Club to any great degree, I want to make sure that whoever is helping the letter writer isn't a member. And the more I look at all of the things that have happened, and how much the letter writer knows, and perhaps more importantly, all of the things the letter writer has overlooked or ignored, the more convinced I am that there's a connection to the Capone Club."

"Are you leaning toward any one person?"

"No," I said, frowning. "And that's half the battle. I can't imagine any of them betraying me in that way. Perhaps I'm too trusting or too naïve. I sincerely hope I'm wrong and that none of them are involved. But my gut is telling me someone has betrayed me and the rest of the group. It upsets me, but more than that, it makes me angry. Extremely angry. And when I find out who it is, they're going to rue the day."

Duncan smiled and arched an eyebrow at me. "Whoa," he said. "That's a side of you I haven't seen before."

I arched a brow right back at him. "And if you don't want to see it directed at you, you better clean up some things," I said in my best warning tone. "Before you and I can move on, I think you need to get this ex-fiancée crap straightened out. Even if she has nothing to do with the letter writer, she sounds like an obsessive nut job who clearly hasn't gotten the message that you're through with her. That sort of tenacity and focus can evolve into something dangerous, and I have enough stuff to worry about already. I don't need some fatal attraction thing on the side. If you're serious about being done with her, you need to make her go away for good. If you're not, you need to tell me now."

Chapter 12

Even though time alone with Duncan was a rarity, and something I typically looked forward to—not to mention something we hadn't had much of lately—I didn't feel like I could be all cozy and intimate with him after the conversation we just had. Fortunately, I didn't have to have that discussion because Cora called me seconds after I had issued Duncan the ultimatum about cleaning up his act with Courtney.

"Sorry to interrupt," she said when I answered. "I hope my timing wasn't off."

"You're fine. Did you find something?"

"I did. I have a number of connections between Whitney and Suzanne. It's not surprising given that they both come from wealthy families, tend to socialize in the same circles, and indulge in the same types of activities. But I can't connect Whitney to all of the package recipients who received scholarships, and I can't find any connection between her and the lady from the spy shop or the guy from the art store."

"I guess that's good news," I said, though I also felt a twinge of disappointment. I was hoping for some answers and a clearer direction with regard to the letter writer. And while this news did provide some answers, there was a small part of me—a part I wasn't proud of—that was hoping to discover something terrible about Whitney, something that would convince Billy to break up with her.

"But I did find a connection between Whitney and the casino," Cora added, revving my hopes back up. "It turns out her great-grandmother was Native American. And her firm represents the casino in legal matters. In fact, Whitney is their primary attorney. I checked her social media to see if I could alibi her for the time of Lewis's death, but I couldn't find anything."

"Interesting," I said. "So we can't rule out the possibility that she and Suzanne are working together."

"Not yet, anyway. Is Duncan there with you?"

"Yes."

"Do you have me on speaker?"

"No."

"Good. So it's okay if I give you some information regarding Jimmy Patterson?"

My heart skipped a beat, and it took a great deal of restraint not to look over at Duncan. I held the cell phone a little closer to my ear to make sure Duncan wouldn't be able to overhear. "Go ahead," I said. Then, for good measure, I got up from my seat and hobbled over to the coffeepot to put some extra distance between me and Duncan. I propped the phone between my ear and shoulder, and went about pouring myself another cup of coffee.

"I don't have any way to verify where Jimmy was during specific times, for the most part, without giving away the fact that I'm looking into it. However, I did find an interesting connection between him and Suzanne Collier."

"Yes?" I said, trying to sound bored and uninterested.

"He works for the family part-time during his off hours doing security."

"Really?" I felt a frisson of excitement and apprehension.

"Yes, indeed. The Colliers own several other businesses besides the art store and the restaurant that we know about. One of those businesses involves a fleet of ships, and the Colliers own several warehouses on the lakeshore. They use their own security guards on site, and Jimmy Patterson is one of them."

"That's interesting," I said, trying to sound nonchalant.

"Okay, I get that you can't discuss this much with Duncan there, correct?"

"That's right."

"I'm betting you're thinking the same thing I am: that it's not a huge leap from working for the Colliers as a security guard to doing some of Suzanne Collier's dirty work."

"Exactly." Cora had an amazing ability to anticipate or perhaps read my thoughts. "It's an interesting angle," I said into the phone. "We can discuss it some more later."

"Gotcha. You let me know when and where, and if there's anything else you want me to do along these lines."

"I will. Thanks, Cora." I disconnected the call and returned to the table, smiling at Duncan.

"What's Cora up to now?" he asked.

"She's been digging a little deeper into some of the members of the Capone Club," I told him. "I have her looking for links to Suzanne that might point a finger at someone or anything that might rule them out."

"And what did she come up with?" Duncan asked. He was eyeing me closely, and I felt uncomfortable beneath his stare. I thought fast, trying to come up with a feasible lie to tell him. And then, for whatever reason, I decided to tell him the truth. Part of my new no-holds-barred, taking-control-of-my-own-life philosophy, I guess.

"She discovered that Whitney's firm—in fact, Whitney herself—represents the casino in legal matters. She also discovered that Jimmy works for the Collier family doing security work on his off hours. Did you know that?"

Duncan frowned at me, a doubtful expression on his face. "Where is Cora getting this information?"

I told him what Cora had told me, and as I spoke, I watched him. I could tell he didn't want to believe what I was saying, but in the end I saw resignation set in. "I've hinted around at the idea of Jimmy being involved with the letter writer," I told him. "I know he doesn't like me, and I know he doesn't like you working with me. If you think about it, it makes perfect sense, including the fact that you, specifically, were mentioned in the letters."

Duncan shook his head, his brow furrowed. "Just because Jimmy is a little hesitant about what you do and is moonlighting for the Colliers doesn't mean he's a killer."

I cocked my head to the side and gave him a sympathetic look. "I know you don't want to consider the idea, but how well do you really know Jimmy? You've only been here in Milwaukee for what, eight months? Have you been working with Jimmy the entire time?"

"I have."

"And did you know he was moonlighting?"

Duncan shook his head. "But that's not surprising," he said. "The brass frowns upon us doing extra work like that. And since I'm new, Jimmy might not have felt comfortable telling me yet."

"Is Jimmy aware of any of this stuff you've done regarding the letter writer? Does he know that you're still seeing me?"

Duncan shook his head.

"He's your partner. He's the person who's supposed to have your back in a crisis. He's the person your life might depend upon. So why haven't you told him?"

"For one thing, you asked me not to. And while I trust Jimmy for the most part, your point that he and I haven't known one another very long is a valid one. Besides, I'm one of those people who feels more comfortable keeping things to myself."

"Are those the only reasons you haven't told him?"

His frown deepened. "What are you getting at?"

"I'm suggesting that perhaps your gut is telling you there's a possibility Jimmy might not be one hundred percent trustworthy."

Duncan shook his head, but it was a tentative shake, as if he wasn't thoroughly convinced. "I do think he's trustworthy," he said, but despite the words, he sounded a little tentative. "I'm just a private person."

"You mean like keeping from me the fact that your ex-fiancée has been hounding you to come back to her ever since you broke up?" The words came out in a tone that was snide and snippy. It wasn't what I intended, but my frustration with Duncan's inability to consider the possibility of Jimmy's involvement angered me.

"We're back to that now?" Duncan said in a weary tone of voice.

I stared at him, feeling my frustration build. "Yes," I snapped. "We're back to that, the fact that you've been hiding something relatively important from me ever since we met, and the fact that you refuse to open your mind to the possibility that your partner may not be what he seems."

"I didn't hide anything from you," Duncan said, his mouth tight. "I merely didn't mention something I felt was irrelevant, an annoyance I assumed would go away."

"Well, it didn't go away, did it?"

"I believe it has now," Duncan said.

"You believe it has, but you're not sure, are you?"

"I'm sure from my end, and that's all that should matter. I think you're overreacting to the situation, maybe because you're a little jealous?"

I glared at him, feeling my anger rise. As my ire increased, I saw red—literally. Everything in my field of vision was tinted with the color. "Overreacting?" I said in a tone of disbelief. "Yes, I'm feeling a little insecure about our relationship since you didn't tell me that the woman you loved enough to marry if she hadn't stood you up at the altar is now, and apparently has been, desperate to resume your relationship. If you honestly can't understand why that upsets me, then I think maybe we need to take some time apart."

"I thought we were spending quite a bit of time apart as it was," Duncan grumbled. "Perhaps that's the problem. You and I haven't seen much of one another lately, and you've been spending lots of time with Mal. If you want to get rid of me so you can date him, just say so."

"Aargh!" I clenched my fists, squeezed my eyes closed,

and made an effort to quell the anger about to burst out of me. The red deepened and swirled, like an angry, spinning pool of blood. My skin prickled. I took a deep, bracing breath, blew it out slowly, and focused on centering myself. Once the redness and the prickly sensation had subsided, and I knew I was fully in control, I opened my eyes, looking directly at Duncan. "I've been honest with you about Mal right from the start," I said in a low, even voice. "That's more than I can say for how you've treated me with regard to Courtney. I'm not interested in dumping you so I can see Mal, but I do think it would be wise if we spent some time apart."

"I think you're right," Duncan said with a sigh. He pushed himself up from the table and walked out of the kitchen.

I grabbed my crutches, hoisted myself out of my seat, and followed him. I watched as he donned his coat and hat. Under normal circumstances, he might've been able to storm out of my apartment. But there was the issue of keeping his visits secret and the need to disarm the alarm on the back-alley door. These required me to accompany him downstairs and facilitate his departure. So much for high drama.

He stood at the top of the stairs, his hands in his pockets, and said nothing. There was no need to speak at this point. I hobbled over to the top of the stairs and slowly made my way down. Once I reached the landing at the base of the stairs, I opened the door and stepped out into the back hallway of the bar. It was empty, and I looked back at Duncan.

"Hold on while I go and turn off the alarm. I'll come back and knock on the door when it's safe."

Duncan nodded but said nothing.

I crutched my way into my office, relieved to see

that Cora was no longer there, turned off the alarm, and then retraced my steps. A couple of women exited from the bathroom down the hall just as I reached the apartment door. They didn't look my way, and as soon as they disappeared around the corner into the main area of the bar, I gave a quick rap on the door. I backed up just in time to keep the door from hitting me and then held it as Duncan stepped out into the hallway and pushed open the back-alley door. For a moment, he hesitated, and I expected him to turn around and say something. But he didn't. In a flash, he was gone.

Chapter 13

I headed back into my office, turned the door alarm back on, and then settled on the couch to gather my thoughts. I certainly hadn't anticipated my time with Duncan going the way it had, and I wondered if the relationship was doomed. It seemed that no matter what we did, or how hard we tried, there were always obstacles in the way. Maybe the Fates were trying to tell me something.

The more I thought, the angrier I got. Not just about Duncan, but about this damned letter writer. I was determined to put an end to it one way or another. And slowly, my plan for doing so began to gel.

After brooding for a while, I got up and made my way out to the main area of the bar. Business was hopping, the tables filled with patrons who were still enjoying the holiday spirit with some holiday spirits. Billy was behind the bar, and Teddy Bear was back there with him.

"How are things going?" I asked no one in particular.

"Going great," Teddy answered, and Billy nodded his agreement.

"I have an idea I'd like to run by you guys, see what you think," I said. "Instead of staying open all night on New Year's Eve this year, I'm thinking of closing the bar down around ten and hosting a private party. It would be for employees and a guest, if you like, plus a few select people from our customer base, you know, people like Cora and the Signoriello brothers."

"You mean the Capone Club," Billy said archly.

"Well, yes, I suppose I do," I admitted. "But not just them. I want to open it up to family members, too. All drinks will be on the house, and the food too. I could hire someone from the outside to do the bartending and cooking. What do you think?"

"I think it's a great idea!" Billy said.

"Would you attend? And would Whitney deign to come to something like that?"

"She'd have no choice," Billy said with more confidence than I think he felt. "Lord knows, I've had to dress up and go to enough dinners and events at her request. I think it's about time she returned the favor. Besides, she owes me one." He winked at me and didn't elaborate. "But what about all the lost revenue? Can you afford to do that, Mack?"

"I'll survive." I probably shouldn't forgo the income from the only day during the year that Wisconsin bars are allowed to stay open all night long, and with the new elevator improvements, my savings account was going to take a significant hit. But I would survive it, and it was something I felt strongly I needed to do. Not only because I owed it to my staff, but because I had something else in mind for that night. Besides, I had the extra income I'd be bringing in with my consulting work with Holland and Dixon.

I looked over at Teddy with raised eyebrows. "What

do you think, Teddy? Would you stay? And would you bring someone?"

"Absolutely I would come," he said. "I'm not seeing anyone right now, but I could probably rustle up a date if I had to, though I think a party with just this group would be fun."

At that point, Debra walked up to the bar, setting her tray down, and calling out her drink orders. Billy and Teddy went to work, and I approached Debra and posed the same question to her.

"You're asking me if I would enjoy the chance to celebrate New Year's Eve like a normal person for once, rather than running my ass off all night waiting on a bunch of drunks? Hell, yeah!"

"Your husband and sons would be welcome to come, too," I told her.

She frowned at that. "Yeah, I suppose I could let them come along. Although I have to admit that the idea of having a night to myself sounds wonderful."

"We could always do that another time," I said. "In fact, I think we're overdue for a girls' night out. Let's plan one. We can go to a show and hit up some other bars so you don't feel guilty about partying at work. And I'm sure I can dig us up a designated driver. In fact, I'll bet Mal would do it."

"It's a date," Debra said with a smile. "I'll check my schedule and get back to you."

"What are you volunteering me to do now?" said a male voice off to my right. I turned and saw Mal standing there.

"I was telling Debra you'd be willing to be a designated driver for us if we did a girls' night out. Would you?"

"Absolutely," he said with an eager grin. "A car full of drunken, easy women is one of my favorite things in life." He winked at me and then at Debra, who managed to blush. "When are we doing this?"

"I don't know yet," I told him. "I'll let you know once we set a date."

"In the meantime, I have something to show you," Mal said. "Can we go into your office?"

"Sure." I reached into my pocket, pulled out my keys, and handed them to him. "Lead the way."

I gathered from the roll of paper he had tucked under his arm that he had something for me to look at regarding the elevator. Once we were inside the office and he had slipped off his coat, he unrolled the paper on my desk, and I saw that my assumption was correct.

"Here are some plans I drew up," he said, weighing down the corners of the paper with various items from my desk: a stapler, a tape dispenser, and a used mug. "I included a dumbwaiter as well because it makes sense to put one in if we're going to open the walls and do the construction necessary to create a shaft. But keep in mind that it's an option." Once he had the paper laid out flat, with the corners anchored, he removed other papers from his coat pocket. "This is a reputable company I've worked with before that manufactures and sells elevators and dumbwaiters," he said, handing me a brochure. "They have some standard models we can choose from, but they can also customize as needed. Of course, customization means more money."

I looked at his plan, which was pretty basic, and more or less what I'd had in mind all along, so I shifted my attention to the brochure.

"You can look up this company online," Mal said. "They have a lot more options and models other than what you see here. I just happened to have this brochure at home because it was the one we used for a job I helped my dad with right before I moved here." He pointed to one of the models in the brochure. "I think this one would work nicely. It's basic, but big enough to accommodate up to four people, or a wheelchair, or someone with a cart."

"It looks great," I said.

Mal handed me one more piece of paper that he had removed from his pocket. "Here's a closer idea of the cost. It's still rough, and there are always surprises with jobs like this, things like unexpected findings in the walls or electrical issues that have to be fixed in order to get past inspection. But I think it should be close."

It was a lot of money. I did a quick mental calculation of the hit I'd take to my savings and what would be left. It made me wince, but I felt it would be worth it in the long run. "I'm good with it, Mal. Thanks so much for doing all of this."

"If you're serious about this plan, I think we should turn it in and get the permits so you can get started on it sooner rather than later. Like I said earlier, I can get things started for you myself this week while I'm off duty on my undercover job."

"That works for me."

"I have just enough time to get to the planning office before they close," Mal said, rolling the papers up. "I could start on it first thing in the morning."

"Don't forget the museum."

He slapped himself on the side of his head. "That's first, of course. What time tomorrow should we head out?"

"The earlier the better," I said. "It will be late by the time I get to bed tonight because I told Billy I'd give him a ride home. Although I suppose I could ask Teddy Bear to do it."

"How does eleven-thirty sound? That gives you time to make sure everything is up and running before we leave, and time to sleep if you're up late."

"Sounds good."

"I'll see you then." He grabbed his coat and headed for my office door. "Are you okay?" he asked before leaving.

I shrugged. "Duncan was here. We had a bit of a spat."

"About that woman you saw him with?"

"That woman turned out to be his ex-fiancée, Courtney Metcalfe."

"Oh," he said with a grimace.

"He says he's not seeing her, that she tricked him into the meeting. But apparently she's been calling him for months, begging him to take her back. He claims he hasn't spoken to her before yesterday, but I'm upset that he didn't tell me about it."

"Why would he?" Mal asked.

"So if the same thing happened to you, you wouldn't tell your girlfriend about the phone calls?"

"Probably not," Mal said with an apologetic look. "Maybe it's a guy thing."

I shook my head in disbelief. "Okay then, let me run this by you. You've admitted to having feelings for me. Let's say Duncan and I broke up, and you and I started seeing one another. Would you want to know if Duncan started calling me regularly because he wanted to patch things up and get back together?"

"Only if you were having thoughts about going back to him," he said. "If you assured me that the two of us were a couple and gave me no reason to doubt you, why would I need to know? Particularly since

Duncan is a friend of mine. That would place an undue amount of stress on our friendship."

I shook my head and rolled my eyes. "You men really are from Mars," I said. "Sometimes I feel like I need an advanced college degree to understand any of you."

"Sometimes we feel the same way about you gals," Mal said with a crooked smile. "I suggest you get a good night's sleep and revisit this in the morning. That's what I'm going to do." With that, he walked back over to me, kissed me on the cheek, and left, closing my office door behind him.

I spent the next ten minutes or so lying on my couch, staring at the ceiling, and replaying the scene with Duncan over and over again in my head. Was I being ridiculous? Were my objections out of line? Was I overreacting to the situation? I didn't know the answers to any of those questions, but I knew how I felt, and I needed to stay true to myself.

In an effort to shift my focus, I removed the list Clay had given me from my pocket and studied the names on it. Some of them seemed more likely to me than others, but this was based solely on my own gut feelings . . . and perhaps a bit of desire. Some of the names were harder for me to accept than others, and I knew that wasn't a very good way to go about assessing things.

Frustrated and in need of a distraction, I stuffed the list into my desk drawer and locked it, then I went back out to the main area of the bar, thinking some busy work would be good for me. But it turned out there was little for me to do. Without my asking, Billy had already arranged with Teddy Bear to get a ride home. And the bar crowd was dying down.

Since I was now off the hook as chauffeur, I asked

Billy if he would handle the closing duties for me. He happily agreed—he always did—and I decided to retreat to my apartment. I spent the rest of the evening in bed, watching home-improvement shows until I fell asleep.

Chapter 14

I awoke the next morning just before nine o'clock. Despite all the angst in my mind when I had gone to bed the night before, I slept well and awoke feeling refreshed and ready to tackle a new day. After a quick cup of coffee, I wrapped my cast in a plastic bag and hopped in the shower. My leg itched something fierce beneath the cast, and the sensation made me see small dots scurrying about along the periphery of my vision, like a small swarm of bugs. I couldn't wait to get the thing taken off.

After getting dressed, fixing my hair, and putting on a bit of makeup, I decided to take a few minutes to scan the day's news on my laptop while I finished off my coffee. One of the first articles I came to nearly made me choke on my brew. The headline read: POLICE SEAL DEAL WITH LOCAL BAR OWNER, and there in the first sentence was my name. Apparently Chief Holland and Anthony Dixon had jumped the gun.

As I read the story, I could feel my anger growing. I was tempted to call Holland right away and tell him to go to hell, and then demand a retraction.

I managed to squelch the urge as I continued to read. The article stated that the Milwaukee Police Department was not only willing to work with me but had been working with me on several cases already. It specifically mentioned the Ben Middleton case. Chief Holland was quoted a lot. Dixon was mentioned but not quoted directly. Overall the article represented me in a reasonable light, stating simply that I had an ability to interpret certain things and certain people in a way that investigators found helpful. And because of this, they had asked me to work with them on a consulting basis. Chief Holland was quoted as saying he was excited about this new arrangement and looked forward to working with me.

The article spent a few lines discussing my "ability," which was simply described as a neurological condition that allowed me to have keener senses than the average person. This was not only a reasonably apt description, I liked the fact that my synesthesia was referred to as a condition rather than a disorder. However, the word *synesthesia* did not appear anywhere in the article.

When I reached the end of the article, I sat back in my chair, shaking my head, feeling my blood boil. I reached for my cell phone, and after looking up a number for Chief Holland on my laptop, I placed a call. A woman answered, and when I asked for Chief Holland, she asked who was calling. I told her, and she put me on hold. I expected Holland to be the next person I spoke to, but that wasn't the case. A man answered, but I knew immediately from his Southern accent that it wasn't Holland. Once again, I explained who I was and who I needed to speak to, my fingers tapping irritably on the tabletop. After a second spell on hold, I was rewarded with my quarry.

"Mack!" Holland said in a cheery, overly familiar way. "How are you this morning?"

"I'm angry," I said, my voice seething. "Where the hell do you get off publicly announcing a working relationship between us when I haven't gotten back to you?"

"Whoa!" he said. "I talked to Albright yesterday evening, and he told me you had decided to go ahead with our deal."

"I was leaning that way," I said. "But I hadn't made up my mind for sure yet."

"Are you telling me Albright lied about it?"

"No," I sighed, shaking my head in exasperation. "I did tell him that I was going to go ahead with it. But he had no right to tell you that."

"Well, I'm sorry, but he did tell me. And I was eager to get the news out."

Oh, I'm sure you were, I thought unkindly, given that the police department had taken a lot of flak over the Ben Middleton case lately. This announcement framed their shortcomings in a much more forgiving light.

"Did Duncan know you intended to announce this in the paper this morning?" I asked.

"No, he had no idea. I know a lot of people at the paper, and I had one of my contacts write the article up last night after talking to Albright. It was solely my doing."

It might be my undoing, I thought. "This has complicated things for me in ways you can't imagine," I told him.

"I'm really sorry, Mack," he said, and his voice sounded

sincere. It sucked a lot of the gusting wind from my angry sails. "I hope this faux pas hasn't prejudiced you against me or made you change your mind."

Had it? It was out there now. A retraction wouldn't do much to undo the damage. If it was handled like most other retractions, it would appear in the paper in a tiny little corner, in tiny little print, buried alongside other, more interesting stuff. No one would see it. And I had a feeling that even if the letter writer did see it, she probably wouldn't believe it anyway.

"What's done is done," I said with a resigned but impatient sigh. Though my voice sounded settled, I was anything but. By announcing in the paper that I not only had agreed to work with the cops in the future but had been working with them in the past, I was in direct violation of the rules set down by the letter writer. Duncan and Holland had put me in a position of great jeopardy without realizing it. And unfortunately, it put a lot of other people in jeopardy as well.

"Are you still willing to work with us?" Holland asked.

Yeah, if I'm still alive. Now that the cat was out of the proverbial bag, there was no reason not to work with them. "I am, but I have some conditions I would like to discuss before we strike a deal."

"Of course," Holland said. "I'm sure there are a lot of details we need to bring out, not the least of which will be the remuneration for your work. Let's get together after the first of the year. I'll have my assistant, Bruce, get in touch with you and set up a meeting. Is there anyone else you'd like to have there besides me, Tony Dixon, and yourself? Duncan Albright, for instance?"

That was an unanticipated question. "I'm not sure at this point," I said evasively. "I'll let you know when your assistant calls to set up the appointment, if that's okay."

"That will be fine. And again, I apologize for the confusion."

"Thank you. I'll talk to you soon." Without further ado, I disconnected the call. And then I dialed Duncan's number. His phone rang and flipped over to voice mail. I couldn't help but wonder if he didn't answer because he was busy or because of our discussion last night. Frankly, voice mail worked for me just fine. I left him a terse, to-the-point message mentioning the article in the paper and expressing my disappointment and anger over the fact that he had told Holland about my decision. "I'm sure you realize the ramifications this will have with the letter writer," I concluded. "If someone dies because of this, it's on your head."

I disconnected the call and immediately wished I could somehow delete my message. Blaming him for any deaths that might occur was a bit harsh. But it was too late now, and I needed to shift my focus to how to mitigate the damage. Ready or not, like it or not, my relationship with the letter writer was about to come to a head. It served to reinforce my idea about the New Year's Eve plan.

I headed downstairs to the bar to do the morning prep. The coffee was brewing, and I had an assortment of fruit set out to chop up when Debra and Pete arrived. I wondered if either of them had seen the article in the paper, but if they had, they didn't say anything about it. I noticed Debra looked tired, with dark circles under her eyes, and a lighter than usual pallor to her skin.

"Are you feeling okay?" I asked her once she had her coat off and her apron on. "You've been working a lot of extra hours lately. Maybe you should take some time off."

She gave me a wan smile and shook her head. "Believe it or not, working here is my relaxation. Things at home are a little tense right now."

"I'm sorry to hear that. If you need some time off to deal with things, all you need to do is ask."

She nodded. "I know, and I appreciate it. But right now, the best thing I can do for myself is to be here."

"Is it something with the boys?"

"No, they're both doing surprisingly well, considering they're teenagers." She made a fist and knocked on the wooden bar top.

"Is it your husband?"

She licked her lips and didn't answer right away.

"I'm sorry," I said quickly. "I didn't mean to pry."

"No, it's okay," she said. "I probably will need to talk about it at some point. But not yet. Thanks for asking, though."

"No problem. I'm having some men issues myself right now, so anytime you want to talk let me know. I'm here for you."

"Thanks, Mack."

With that, we went about our morning duties in relative silence. Pete and Debra had both been with me for a long time, and as a result, we worked well together as a team. It was like that every morning. Even though the daily tasks and duties that needed to be performed changed hands on a regular basis, it all got done with a minimum of fuss and discussion. Some mornings I made the coffee and chopped fruit, sometimes Debra did it. Restocking the beers and ice was something I typically did, but because it required a trip to the basement, Debra and Pete had taken it over since I broke my leg. Jon, my morning cook, showed up at ten-thirty and went about getting the kitchen set up. That was his domain, and we left him to it. When eleven o'clock rolled around, I unlocked the front door, and both Cora and the Signoriello brothers arrived moments later. Judging from the curious, wide-eyed looks they gave me, I guessed that they had seen the article in the paper.

Per their usual routine, the three of them settled in at a table and ordered up drinks and food. Debra fetched the drinks, and as soon as she was gone, all three of them spoke at once.

"What the heck is going on?" Joe said.

"Is this thing in the paper true?" Frank said.

"Why did you let them print that in the paper?" Cora asked.

I held up a hand to them, and they immediately settled down, waiting for my reply. I explained to them what had happened, and my conversation with chief Holland this morning. "The cat's out of the bag," I concluded. "We'll just have to figure out how to deal with it. In a way, I'm almost glad this happened, because I'm tired of letting the letter writer—or writers, as the case may be—lead me around like a dog on a leash. It's time to put an end to this, and I have an idea about how to do it."

I paused for any questions that might arise, but my rapt audience simply sat there waiting for me to continue.

"I'm going to close the bar on New Year's Eve and have a private party instead," I told them. "The party will be for employees and members of the Capone Club, along with their respective husbands, wives, girlfriends, boyfriends, or any other guests anyone wants to bring. I haven't figured out exactly how I'm going to do it yet, but I'm hoping to bring some kind of closure to this letter writer thing that night."

Cora said, "So I take it you're planning to invite Suzanne Collier. Think she'll come?"

"If I have to drag her here myself, I will," I said.

Frank massaged his temples. "This has gotten way out of hand," he said. "It's making all of us paranoid." He dropped his hand and looked at me with a serious expression. "I agree with you that it's time to bring it to an end. But you're playing with fire here, Mack."

"Frank is right," Joe said. "Clearly this person, or persons, are dangerous and not afraid to kill. While I like the idea of trying to get to the bottom of who the letter writer is once and for all, this party idea sounds like it might be a bit hazardous."

I nodded solemnly. "I realize that, but things are coming to a head now anyway after this news article this morning. It's forced my hand. I plan to invite our police members to the party as well, as much for protection as for figuring everything out. But there are no guarantees, particularly since both Tyrese and Nick are on the list of potential suspects." I looked at the two men and gave them a loving, appreciative smile. "Of course, the two of you don't need to come to the party if you don't want to. I know neither of you are the letter writer, and things could easily go bad that night. I would certainly understand if you opted to stay home."

Cora arched an eyebrow at me and clapped a hand to her chest. "What?" she said in a tone of mock hurt. "I don't get the same option? Am I on the list of suspects? Or do you just not care if I get hurt?"

I smiled at her and shook my head. "You're not on

the list of suspects, and you know I care about your welfare. But I really need you here that night. I can't force you, of course . . ."

Cora rolled her eyes and dismissed my offered escape with a wave of her hand. "You know I'll be here."

"As will we," Joe said, and Frank nodded his agreement. "Frank and I are typically in bed long before midnight, but we'll make an exception in this case."

"Throwing this party is going to be a lot of work for you," Cora said. "Not to mention expensive."

I shrugged. "True, but it will be worth it. Granted, the money I bring in on New Year's Eve is typically the most I make all year, but I can handle the loss, particularly since I now have this new source of income working as a consultant. To be honest, I've always hated being open all night on New Year's Eve. People get too rowdy, and it seems like there's always at least one big fight every year."

"I suspect that if you accomplish what you hope to, you may see a lot more than a simple fight," Frank said in an ominous tone.

Debra arrived with the food orders then, effectively shutting down our conversation for the moment. Once the sandwiches were placed in front of everyone and Debra had left, I hit them with my next issue.

"I think it's time to tell the Capone Club group about the letter writer," I said. "Some of them will be angry, no doubt, but I think it's the best thing to do at this point, given everything that's happened. That way they can make an informed decision with regard to the private party. Some of them might not want to come, and if they do they might not want to bring along a guest. My guess is that whoever is involved in this letter writer thing will want to be here, particularly once I've filled the group in on what's been going on. What do you guys think?"

"You know my thoughts on the matter," Frank said. "I felt everyone should have known all along."

His brother looked at him and shook his head slowly. "I think telling them in the beginning would've made everyone paranoid and complicated things. You were right not to tell in the beginning, but there does come a point when the truth needs to be out. And you're the only one who can make that call, Mack."

Cora gave me a half shrug and an equivocal look. "My thoughts on the matter vacillate from day to day, sometimes from hour to hour. There are times when I think we should have told them sooner and times when I think we shouldn't tell them at all. There are times when I find it reassuring to be in the know and other times when I wish I was oblivious. But overall I tend to think that informed people will make better choices and decisions."

I couldn't help but notice that Cora put the onus on *we* rather than just *me*. Her willingness to take the hit with me made me trust and adore her all the more. It's not that I didn't adore and trust the brothers— they truly were the closest thing to family I had left—but there were times when Cora understood me better than the brothers could.

"Okay," I said, with a decisive nod. "It sounds like everyone agrees that the club members should know at some point, and I feel that time is upon us. So I'm going to do it. Can you guys spread the word that I will be making an important announcement to the group tonight? Gather together as many of the members as you can and tell them I'll be there around seven."

"Are you going to tell them everything?" Frank asked.

"And are you going to expect them to keep it to themselves?" Joe asked.

"I'm going to tell them the basics," I said. "But I'm not going to point a finger at anyone, at least not yet. If we give the group enough information, maybe they'll identify a suspect or two on their own. It will be interesting to see if they come up with the same name we have. At the very least, I want them to be aware that their lives may be in danger. If that creates some paranoia, so be it. I'd rather have them be paranoid than dead."

Frank said, "Didn't the letter writer insist that you do things on your own?"

"Yeah," I said, "but the letters also said not to involve the cops, and clearly that ship has sailed with the newspaper article this morning. The fact is that the rules have changed. I'm going to ask the group to keep the details to themselves for now—I don't want this going public—but I know I can't guarantee that any of them will do so. Besides, I'm becoming more convinced with every passing day that the second letter writer is someone from the Capone Club."

This garnered several long seconds of silent contemplation.

"What about Duncan?" Cora asked. "Are you going to bring him back into the fold?"

I nodded without hesitation, realizing as I did so that he might not want to come back after our discussion yesterday. But I'd already thought this through and realized that Duncan was the one cop who knew the most about the case, other than Mal. Regardless of what I did with regard to the letter writer, Mal's true identity still needed to remain a secret. It made sense to have Duncan involved from here on out, regardless of where our personal relationship stood. Besides, I'd had a bit of a brainstorm earlier, one that would require me to set aside any difficulties I had in my personal relationship with Duncan for the time being.

"What about Mal?" Cora asked. "If you're eliminating the need to hide your continued relationship with Duncan, you're eliminating the need to pretend you have one with Mal. Are you going to explain that subterfuge to the group? Or just let you and Mal as a couple die a seemingly natural death?"

"I'm not going to do either," I said. "Until I know for sure who is involved with this letter writer thing and what their motives are, I'm going to continue downplaying my personal relationship with Duncan and have it appear as if Mal and I are a couple. Duncan will be involved—at least I hope he will—on a professional basis for now. Besides, Mal is going to continue to be around because he's going to be overseeing a new remodeling project I'm doing." Since the brothers didn't know about it yet, I filled them in on the plans regarding the elevator installation, and, not surprisingly, they agreed it would be a useful and welcome improvement.

My phone rang then, and when I looked at the caller ID, I saw it was Clay. "I need to take this," I said to the threesome. I answered the call, asked Clay to hold on, and then hobbled my way out of my chair and into my office.

"Hey, Clay," I said, once I was inside with the door closed.

"Mack, thank goodness! I was worried you wouldn't answer my call."

"Why?"

"Because of that article in the paper this morning. I was afraid you'd think I had something to do with it."

"I confess, the thought did cross my mind when I first read the piece, but then I had a chat with Holland, and he told me he had contacted someone else he knew at the paper after Duncan let it slip to him that I planned to accept his proposal. It was the perfect storm of unintentional mistakes. And damnable timing."

"It's going to make a mess of things for you, isn't it?"

"I suspect so. My efforts to keep my involvement with Duncan under wraps are futile at this point. I've decided to tell the members of the Capone Club about the letter writer later this evening and let the chips fall where they may. It goes without saying that I'm worried for their safety."

"Perhaps the knowledge, or at least the perception, that the cops have been involved all along will make whoever is behind this think twice before striking again. They may step back and reevaluate things."

"Or they may go off in a pissed-off frenzy of violence without regard for their safety or any secrecy."

"Let's hope not," Clay said. "Let me know if I can do anything to help."

"Thanks, and don't forget that you're now as much of a target as anyone else. So watch your back."

"I can take care of myself, but thanks for the reminder."

There was a knock at my office door, and I crutched around and opened it, propping the phone between my shoulder and ear. Mal stood on the other side.

"I have to go, Clay," I said, taking the phone in hand again. "Stay well and keep in touch."

"Will do."

I disconnected the call and smiled at Mal. "Ready for a trip to the museum?"

"I am. And I hope we can make it a short one because I brought along a bunch of tools so I can start working on your demolition in the basement." He rubbed his hands together eagerly. "This is the best part of any reno job. Destruction! I even got a couple of guys I know to come and help on Sunday."

I gave him a worried look. "You mean guys who work for the crooked construction company you're investigating?"

He shook his head. "Give me a little credit, Mack," he said with feigned offense. "I just rounded up a couple of undercover guys I know on the force who would love to take a sledgehammer to a wall in exchange for a free beer or two."

"Okay, I'm going to trust you on this," I said, not sure if I should. Alcohol and men bent on mass destruction with sledgehammers sounded like a dangerous combo to me. "I'll supply the beers, but I'd feel better if they had them after they're done swinging their hammers."

"Can do," Mal said with a smile.

"Listen, before we go, there's something I want to run by you." I then told him my thoughts regarding the New Year's Eve party.

"It's not a bad idea," he admitted when I was done. "There's no guarantee it will work, and there's always the potential for things to go haywire, but I think it's worth a shot."

"Mind if I give Duncan a call and run it by him before we head out to the museum?"

"Of course. Want me to wait for you outside?"

"If you don't mind," I said with a grateful smile.

"No problem. I'll be at the bar when you're ready to go."

As soon as Mal left my office, I dialed Duncan's number. His phone rang several times before flipping over to voice mail. I didn't want to go into details in a message, so I simply asked him to call me, stating that it was important that we talk. Then I hung up and went to join Mal.

Chapter 15

We headed out to the museum, with Mal driving as usual. It was a sunny day but bitterly cold, the frigid air on my face making me see heat waves again. When we arrived at the museum, we consulted a directory to determine the quickest way to get to the areas that seemed most likely to produce what we were searching for.

"Look at this," I said, pointing to an area on one of the floor's maps. "They have a special dinosaur exhibit here. The letter had references to bones, digging, extinction, and old things . . . think that might be it?"

Mal thought for a moment and shrugged. "It seems as good a place to start as any other," he said. "It's on the second floor. Let's go."

The exhibit required a separate fee, so Mal got in line to buy tickets while I sat and rested my leg. Once he had the tickets, we made our way to the escalators and rode up to the second floor. After handing our tickets over to a young woman at the entrance to the dinosaur exhibit, we headed inside.

The large, cavernous room featured a variety of

dinosaur skeletons both large and small, set up in dioramas that matched the terrain and plant life that would have been part of the dinosaur's natural habitat. The larger specimens were impressive and scary— giant reptile skeletons with vicious-looking teeth, dangerous-seeming claws designed to catch and disable or disembowel prey, and feet that appeared big enough to crush bones into dust.

We made our way around the room, circling the displays and searching for places where one might hide a note, letter, or package. There were a few benches scattered about for patrons to rest on, and we took turns sitting on all of them, settling in and then surreptitiously feeling beneath them for any packages that might have been hidden there. The room was filled with other patrons—adults and children of all ages—and with all the interactive educational displays that were set at kid height, there weren't a lot of places where one could safely conceal a package or envelope without the risk of some random person finding it.

There was a museum employee wandering about the room—a middle-aged man wearing a vest with the Milwaukee Public Museum logo on it—watching and supervising. I made eye contact with him several times, smiling and appearing as approachable and friendly as I could in case he had been given instructions to watch for me. But halfway through our tour of the exhibit, he was relieved by a different employee, and I realized how hard it would be for any one employee to be given the job of contacting me.

At several of the dioramas, Mal dropped items on the floor so he could bend down and peer beneath the edges of the exhibit areas, and I examined the interiors of each exhibit carefully, looking for any irregularities.

After an hour of this fruitless searching, we had toured all but the back of the room where the largest and most terrifying skeleton was displayed: the giganotosaurus. I found myself so horrifyingly mesmerized by the display, and the idea of being eaten by a creature like the giganotosaurus, that I kept forgetting why we were there.

Eventually, we moved beyond this last exhibit toward the very back of the room and the exit. Off to the left of the exit was a gift shop selling all manner of dinosaur-related objects, most of them geared toward kids. A woman was behind the cash register, and on the off chance that she might be the person designated to hand off a package, I wandered in to the store and browsed the shelves until she asked me if she could help me with anything.

I smiled at her and approached the counter, extending a hand in greeting. "Hi, I'm Mack Dalton," I said.

"Charlene," she said, taking my hand, but pulling hers back quickly "Did you enjoy the exhibit?"

"Very much," I said. "Except I was supposed to meet a friend here, and I haven't seen her. I don't suppose anyone left a note, or a letter, or something like that for me here?"

She frowned at this, looking even warier. "No," she said. "Wouldn't your friend just call or text you?"

Good question, and I had to think fast to come up with a plausible answer. "She's old-fashioned," I said. "She doesn't have a cell phone."

"Oh," the woman said, smiling, and nodding in a knowing manner. "I have a friend like that, too."

"Well, thanks anyway," I said, and then I turned to leave before I roused her suspicions any more. The last thing I needed was to be asked to leave the premises because of my behavior.

Mal had hung just outside the gift shop area, and when I rejoined him, I gave him a recap of my conversation with the woman. "I think this is a dead end," I said. "Maybe we need to hit up a different exhibit. Lord knows there must be old bones in dozens of other exhibits in this place."

Mal took the brochure guide from his pocket and consulted it. "From the looks of this, I'd say there are plenty. Where do we begin?"

I didn't answer him because my eyes had zeroed in on something behind him. When he looked up at me, he cocked his head to the side and said, "What is it?"

"Remember how the letter said something about lighting a fire beneath my feet and dampening my spirit? And then it said something about extinguishing a life?" Mal nodded. "Look over there."

I nodded to the wall behind him, toward a small alcove off to one side of the exit doors. There, tucked into the wall, was an emergency fire hose and extinguisher cabinet fronted by a glass door.

Mal looked at me, excitement on his face. I turned and looked back toward the gift shop; we were still in full view of Charlene. There were other patrons in the shop milling about now, and a small group of people went past us toward the exit doors. But it wasn't enough.

"I think we need a distraction," I said. "I'll create one while you go over and check out that space."

Mal nodded, and with that I hobbled back toward the gift shop. Once inside, I let one of my crutches drop. This got the attention of Charlene and one of the other shoppers. As I bent down to pick it up, I pushed my casted leg out behind me and then let myself fall onto my good knee, acting as if I'd lost my balance. I let the other crutch fly out sideways, hitting a display of small rubber dinosaurs and knocking several of them to the floor.

"Oh, darn it!" I exclaimed. Now I had the attention of everyone nearby. Several people hurried to help me while Charlene scurried over to start picking up the scattered rubberized dinosaur figures. "I'm so sorry," I said with an embarrassed laugh. "This stupid leg has turned me into such a klutz."

For the next minute or so, everyone was busy helping me back to my feet, handing me my crutches, and returning the display items to the shelves. After thanking everyone for their help and apologizing again, I left the shop area and headed for the exit doors. Mal was waiting for me on the other side.

"Anything?" I said.

He nodded, a big grin on his face. He patted his jacket pocket and said, "I found an envelope tucked in behind the extinguisher."

"Thank goodness."

"That was quite an act you pulled back there. Are you okay? You didn't hurt yourself, did you?"

"I'm fine. I took gymnastics in grade and middle school, and while I was never all that good at it, it did teach me one valuable lesson: how to fall without hurting myself."

"Well, you did a good job of it," Mal said with a smile. "I'd give you a ten."

On that high note, we made our way out of the museum and went back to the bar.

Chapter 16

Though I was anxious to see what was inside the letter, I knew we should wait until we got back to my place to open it—the whole preservation of evidence thing that was as much a part of my life these days as it was a part of any cop's life.

Cora was seated at the bar when we walked in, and I knew her presence there rather than upstairs with the rest of the Capone Club meant she was eager to catch me and give me some information. As soon as she saw me, she slid off her stool, laptop tucked under her arm, and veered onto a path to my office door, meeting me there.

"I have lots of things to tell you," she said.

Mal, who was right behind me, as usual, asked, "Want me to give you two a little time alone?"

"No need for that," I said. Then I realized I might be being presumptuous. I looked at Cora, my eyebrows raised in question. "Is there?"

She shook her head. "You both can, and probably should, hear this."

Once inside my office, Cora settled into my desk

chair, opening her laptop on top of my desk. I shrugged off my coat, as did Mal. "Before I go into my information," Cora asked, tapping some keys, "did you guys strike gold at the museum?"

"We did," I said. I looked over at Mal, who removed the envelope from inside his coat. He set it on top of my desk and then removed his coat, draping it over one arm of the couch.

The envelope was an ordinary, white, number ten, business-type one. It was sealed, but like others we had received, it came with an adhesive strip for sealing, making the likelihood of any DNA being present pretty slim. Nothing was written on the outside of the envelope.

Cora, Mal, and I exchanged looks. Nothing had to be said; we were all thinking the same thing. After several seconds of this visual standoff, I broke it by speaking up.

"I have paper over there in my printer, and a letter opener here on my desk. Or we can use my scissors. Either way, I think we should open it here and now. I have gloves for all of us right over there." I nodded with my head toward some shelves on the back wall where several boxes of gloves sat.

I half expected Mal to object right away, but he didn't. I knew Cora would go along with it because her curiosity was killing her. It took Mal a few seconds to agree, but eventually he nodded, and I jumped on that as my cue. I hobbled over to the printer, yanked out a piece of paper, and placed it on top of my desk. I looked over at Mal and made a little sideways nod toward the envelope. "Would you like to do the honors?"

Mal grabbed a pair of latex gloves from one of

the boxes on my shelves and pulled them on. He returned to the desk, reached over, and picked up my letter opener. After slipping the opener's tip under the top flap on the envelope, he neatly sliced it open. Then, after setting the opener down, he held the envelope upside down over the piece of paper I had placed on the desk and pulled the two sides apart. A folded sheet of paper that looked identical to the type on my desk and in my printer fell out. Mal lifted the envelope and peered inside to see if anything else might be clinging in there, and when he saw there wasn't, he set it aside.

Carefully, he picked up the folded paper that had fallen out of the envelope and opened it over the piece of paper on the table. We all watched carefully to see if anything fell out of the folds, and at first blush this letter appeared to be clean. Once Mal had it completely opened, I saw that it was two sheets of paper rather than one. On the top page, I saw handwriting, the words written using a form of calligraphy that appeared to match what had been in most of the previous letters. But unlike the others, this time there was no signature.

I leaned in and peered over Mal's left shoulder so I could read the letter along with him. Cora cozied up on his right.

Dear Ms. Dalton,
     If you're reading this letter, then you have proven yourself to be a most worthy adversary thus far. While I am impressed with your abilities, I'm still not convinced that what you do isn't some form of chicanery. Or perhaps you haven't been

playing by the rules I have set forth. Whichever it may be, I feel there is an end coming to our little game. My goal is to expose you for the con artist you are, and it seems that doing this will require me to ramp up the stakes. I have done so with this clue, and you will find that future clues will be much harder both in terms of content and the time allowed before your deadline. You have until five p.m. on December 31 for this one. My next victim has already been targeted. That person's life now depends upon your success.

Good luck.

There was nothing more written on this first page, and after looking at both me and Cora to see if we were done reading, Mal carefully separated the two pages and placed the first one down on the table. The second page had a short, four-line poem on it:

*Within the triplet's ova you will
find another clue,
Dig it up in time, and our game
will then ensue.
Fail and brace yourself for a
very cruel surprise,
As someone edges closer to a frightening,
untimely demise.*

In the folds of the paper there were a few faint smears of something yellowish green. Mal pointed to one of the spots. "What do you make of this, Mack?"

I made a "gimme" gesture with my gloved hands.

Mal handed over the page, and after looking at it closely, I raised it near my face, closed my eyes, and inhaled slowly and deeply through my nose. I heard a musical note—a single, low A note with a woodwind sound. I also had an odd, soft sensation on my fingertips, as if I was rubbing talc between them.

"It's something floral, but not a perfume or lotion," I said. "It's probably pollen. I not only hear something, I have this soft sensation on my fingertips that I've felt before when handling flowers." I took another whiff and shook my head. "I can't tell you the specific flower it's from, but I'm certain it's from some kind of plant."

"Anything else about the paper or the ink strike you?"

"I feel certain the ink used—at least what was used on the first page—is the same homemade ink that has been used in the other letters. The smell of the pollen is complicating things a little on the second page, but based on my overall reaction, I think it's the same ink as well. There's nothing else that leaps out at me."

"Okay," Mal said, taking the paper back from me. "Let's parse the words and see what comes up."

"Let's start with the phrase *the triplet's ova*," I said. "It seems significant."

"And I have an idea about what it might mean," Cora said. "All of the other clues have referenced places in and around Milwaukee, and I think this one does, too. I think it might be The Domes."

"The Domes?" Mal said with a questioning look.

"It's a trio of geodesic domes built in Mitchell Park," I said.

I was about to continue, but Cora interrupted and corrected me. "Technically they aren't geodesic domes because they're hive- or egg-shaped." She flashed me a smile and then looked at Mal. "It's a horticultural conservatory, and each dome has a different theme. One features a desert climate, one is tropical, and the third showcases whatever flowering plants are in season. They put on a variety of light shows and other events all year long, and during the winter months, they have a farmers' market housed in an attached greenhouse."

"That makes sense, given that the phrase *dig it up* is used," Mal said, looking at the poem. "Three horticultural domes and a greenhouse with a farmers' market is a lot of territory to cover," he added with a frown. "Any idea what part of the place we're supposed to look in?"

"I think the hint for that is in these smudges," I said, pointing to the faint green marks. "I need to figure out what they're from."

"That's going to be hard to do this time of year," Cora said. "You're going to have to go there and walk through the place to see if you can trigger a matching reaction."

I nodded, trying to think of an easier way to do it but coming up blank. "It looks like I'm in for another scavenger hunt," I grumbled. I was growing as weary of this game as the letter writer apparently was.

"I can go with you," Mal said.

"Here's something that will make things a lot easier for you," Cora said, reading something on the screen of her laptop. "Both the desert and the tropical domes are currently closed for repairs." She flashed me a happy smile. "That leaves you with only one dome to go through. If you want, I can run a list of plants that have yellow-green pollen."

I shook my head. "I suspect it will be a lengthy list, and I'd rather rely on my synesthetic responses to help me identify the source. It's not just the sight of the pollen I react to; there's the smell and feel of it, too." I looked at Mal, biting the corner of my lower lip. "I really want to touch these smudges with my bare fingers," I said. "I know that means compromising the evidence, but so far there hasn't been any evidence to compromise. Based on past experience, this letter won't be any different. And even if there are other prints on it, mine could be identified and eliminated from any that are found, right?"

Mal gave me a tentative, hesitant nod. "I suppose," he said.

I didn't wait for him to reconsider. I ripped off the glove on my right hand and then ran my index finger over the largest of the yellow-green smears. Almost instantly, I saw a green and white line with a sharp, jagged edge that arced over my field of vision.

Mal and Cora both stared at me, waiting for me to tell them what reaction, if any, I had. So I filled them in. "I think with the smell responses I can zero in on the type of plant once I'm there, but I may have to touch the pollen in them as well, to narrow it down."

Cora, who was tapping away on her keyboard nearly nonstop—sometimes without even looking at it or the computer screen—said, "The two domes that are closed do help us some, but there is a small wrench in the works that will make things a little harder for you: the farmers' market. There's the possibility that this pollen came from something being sold there rather than a plant in the open dome. So you'll probably have to visit both places."

"Maybe," I said, unconvinced. "But I'm going to

start in the open dome because the poem mentioned digging. To me that implies dirt and plants. If we strike out there, we can hit up the farmers' market."

"That makes sense, I suppose," Cora said.

"We may have a bigger problem, however," I said. "This is another letter with one more deadline, but who knows if it will remain applicable after that article in the paper this morning. If the letter writer sees that article, they're bound to get ticked off, and that might make her—assuming we're right about Suzanne Collier—go off on a whole different tangent. Or just kill someone out of spite."

Mal reached over and massaged my shoulder. "We have to hope that doesn't happen. If it does, we'll deal with it. But in the meantime, I think we should continue along with business as usual."

"I suppose," I said. "But I can't shake the feeling that this whole thing is going to blow up soon."

"Interesting choice of words," Cora said with a wry arch of one brow. "Because I found some information regarding some of our Capone Club members."

"What?" I prompted. Then I quickly added, "Hold on." I unlocked my desk drawer and fished out the list Clay had given me of possible suspects. "Let's see if we can winnow this down any," I said.

"I have a bad feeling I'm only going to make some of those names stick out more," Cora said. "To start with, your new waitress, Linda, has a brother named Henry who received a dishonorable discharge from the military and now works as a mercenary, selling his services to the highest bidder. There is some speculation, though no solid proof, that he was involved in a failed bombing attempt at a nuclear site in Washington state a couple years ago."

"I heard some rumors about that," Mal said, "but I didn't think it was a real thing."

"It was scarily real," Cora said. "The government has done a reasonably good job of keeping the details under wraps, fearing that if the public knew how close this group came to being successful, it would start a nationwide panic. But I found enough legitimate references to the incident to assure you that the attempt was very real."

Mal shuddered and raked a hand through his hair. "The Hanford nuclear site is in the tri-cities area of Richland, Kennewick, and Pasco. That's not all that far from where my family lives in Yakima."

"Okay," I said. "So Linda's brother is someone we don't want to cross paths with, but is there anything to indicate that Linda herself isn't an honest, law-abiding citizen?"

"No," Cora admitted. "But Henry is Linda's twin, and twins are often very close. And I can't find much information on her. She's new to us, and she did appear during all this letter writer business, so it's something to keep in mind."

"Okay, what else?" I asked.

Cora looked over at Mal. "How extensive of a background check does the police department do when hiring on new recruits?"

"Quite extensive," Mal said. "And just to get into the academy, you have to go through psychological testing, physical testing, and drug testing, as well as a thorough background check. Any significant criminal history, gang involvement, or membership in a group considered to be subversive is an automatic disqualification. And a lot of places will require candidates to undergo a lie detector test, even though the reliability of the test results is often questioned."

"Why do you ask?" I said. "Did you find something on Tyrese or Nick?" Since they were the two regular participants in the Capone Club, I gathered that whatever Cora had found would be related to one of these two men.

"I found something regarding Nick that is a bit worrisome, but the information is from social media, not anything official. Apparently, an ex-girlfriend of his has friended his ex-wife on Facebook."

"Nick was married?"

Cora nodded. "To one Victoria Lennon Kavinsky. They tied the knot five years ago, and it unraveled two years later. The girlfriend followed, though I'm not sure if she was in the picture before the marriage fell apart or after. Her name is Cheryl Muldoon. Apparently, Nick doesn't like his women to have a mind of their own. Cheryl and Victoria have made several comments about their shared abuser on a Facebook page set up for victims of abuse. They don't mention Nick by name, just by his initials, but I tracked down Victoria when I saw she was an ex of his and still uses her married last name."

"Interesting, but I don't see how it's particularly relevant to us and what's going on here," I said.

"Oh, come on, Mack," Cora said, looking at me with disbelief. "Don't tell me you haven't noticed that Nick has a major crush on you."

"He does?"

Cora nodded, and I looked over at Mal, seeking verification. He nodded too.

"Wow. I had no idea," I said. "I guess I've been so

distracted by everything else that's been going on that I didn't pick up on the clues."

"I noticed the dirty looks he gives me when he thinks I'm not looking," Mal said.

"There's something else about Nick that may shed some light," Cora said. "He has a bit of a gambling problem. More than a bit, actually. He's lost some big bucks, and based on what a cop makes in this town, I'm guessing a little under-the-table cash from someone looking for a henchman would be rather appealing."

"You think Nick might be Suzanne's helper?" I said.

Cora gave an ambivalent shrug.

"But he's a cop. Do you really think he'd kill someone for money?" I said, still not willing to believe. Then I realized how hypocritical I was being, given that Jimmy was high on my list.

"People do all kinds of horrible things for money," Mal said. "I've seen it time and time again. Money and love are the roots of nearly all evil."

"Do we have any idea where Nick was on the night Lewis was killed?" I asked, still looking for an out. I liked Nick—not in the way he apparently liked me— but I didn't want to believe he was a cold-blooded killer. I recalled his reactions to a murder I had helped Duncan with, the death of a young woman who was a single mother. Nick had been appalled by the senselessness of it all. Or at least he had appeared to be.

Then again, it hadn't seemed so unreasonable to the people who were directly involved with that killing, the people who had motive.

Cora said, "Nick wasn't working the night Lewis was killed, so short of asking him for an alibi, we have no way of knowing if he has one. Same thing with Tyrese. They were both off duty that evening, and I haven't been able to dig up anything that indicates where either of them might have been at the time Lewis was killed."

"So both names have to stay on the list of possibilities, along with Linda," I said, and both Cora and Mal nodded. "And Jimmy," Cora added.

I shot Mal a look.

"You mean Duncan's partner Jimmy?" he said.

I nodded, biting my lower lip, waiting for his reaction. I could tell his wheels were turning, and Cora filled him in on what we knew and why we had him on the list.

"Wow," Mal said. "Does Duncan know any of this?"

"He does now," I said.

Mal narrowed his eyes at me, a knowing expression on his face. "Let me guess. Does that have something to do with the spat you two had the other night?"

"It might have played a small role," I admitted with some chagrin. I sighed and gave Cora a foreboding look. "Do you have more?"

"I do," she said "This next one is something I came upon accidentally. Carter and I were alone in the Capone Club room earlier today for about ten minutes. We were both working on our laptops, and then Carter got a phone call from Holly on his cell. It became obvious early into it that Holly was upset about something—I don't know what—and Carter was trying to keep his end of the conversation neutral. He finally gave up, got up, and stepped out of the room into the hallway."

Cora paused, bit her lip, and gave us a sheepish look. "I got up to stretch a little, and in doing so I was able to see what was on Carter's laptop. He was writing a reply to an email from his book agent. The agent had written something to the effect that Carter's book proposal was good, but it needed something more, something to give it a bigger bite, more sensationalism for a wider audience. Carter's reply said that he was working on a unique approach to his stories, something that would be groundbreaking, challenging, evil, and twisted. And he mentioned that he hopes to get your permission to include you and what you do in his books, minimizing any police involvement."

I gave her a look of skepticism and disbelief. "Do you really think Carter would go so far as to kill people simply to get a good book deal?"

Mal scoffed. "People have been known to do worse things for lesser goals. Don't ever underestimate how low people can go."

I wasn't convinced, but I wasn't ready to cast Carter aside either. "Okay then," I said with resignation. "Carter's name stays on the list." I sighed and ran a hand through my hair. "So we haven't ruled out any of the Capone Club members at this point?"

Cora shook her head. "But I have ruled out most of your employees," she said. "I haven't been able to verify the whereabouts of your new cook, Rich Ziegler, or your new bouncer, Teddy Bear, but Jon provided me with a verifiable alibi."

I looked aghast. "You actually asked him for one?" I said with a wince.

"Not exactly," Cora said. "I made up an excuse to borrow his cell phone for a few minutes. He has a smartphone, and fortunately, the GPS was activated on it. I was able to scan through the history after I hooked it up to my laptop and see that he wasn't anywhere near the area where Lewis was killed during the critical time."

Mal let out a low whistle and shook his head, smiling. "I wish we could get away with stuff like that on the police force," he said. "It certainly would make some of our investigations a lot easier."

"I thought you could look at phone records and GPS stuff," I said.

"Oh, we can," Mal said. "But only after jumping through a gazillion hoops and making sure we have our asses covered legally. And if we can't come up with a justifiable reason to invade someone's privacy that way, we don't get to look. Sadly, ruling people out is not a justifiable reason."

"What about Curtis Donovan?" I asked Cora. "He's on my list."

"Oh, I ruled him out. He does a drag show one or two nights during the week at a place over on Second Street. He was the top bill that particular night."

"Well, at least we managed to eliminate two people," I said, staring woefully at my list.

There was a moment of silence as we all contemplated the complexity of our situation.

Cora said, "It's a pretty lengthy list."

"And it's not done yet," I said. "After today, I feel like we need to add Courtney's name. She has a strong motive, though I can't speak to her physical strength. And she certainly has a motive for excluding Duncan in the letter's instructions. She and Suzanne have likely crossed paths in the past, so maybe the two of them are working together."

Cora nodded and typed the name into her list while I penciled it onto mine.

As I set my pencil down, I stared at the list. "We have to start working our way through these names to see if we can eliminate any more of them."

"Why don't you just ask all of them if they did it?" Mal said. "Do that lie detector thing you do."

I considered what he said. "It's not a bad idea, but it seems a little aggressive. A little too in-your-face. I don't want to burn bridges with anyone in the club— or any of my employees, for that matter—if it turns out they're innocent. Though if they are innocent, they may ask me to test them." I paused, gave it a little more thought, and then shook my head. "We don't even know for sure that anyone in the club or anyone in my employ is involved."

"Should we look for more connections between these names and Suzanne Collier?" Cora asked.

Mal shook his head. "We have good reason to suspect Suzanne Collier, but let's face it, we aren't certain she's involved either."

"Then we need a way to verify that Suzanne is behind this once and for all," I said. "And I need a way to allow the people on that list to ask me to test them, question them about their guilt."

Mal narrowed his eyes at me. "Do you have something in mind?" he asked.

"I do. I think it might be time to set a little trap."

I have to admit, I liked the mischievous look in his eyes.

Chapter 17

I shared my idea with Cora and Mal, and they both agreed it seemed not only doable but logical. We discussed it for the next ten minutes or so, ironing out the details and deciding how we would implement the plan.

I glanced at my watch. "I'm supposed to meet with the club members at seven for the big announcement," I said. "Why not do it tonight?"

Cora and Mal looked at one another and then shrugged simultaneously. With the decision made, Mal and I discussed a trip to The Domes and decided we would go the following day, early enough to give us plenty of time to search and get back for Mal's destruction crew to start work in the basement.

For the next few hours, we all kept busy waiting for the big seven o'clock announcement. Cora did a little more research on The Domes and discovered that the open one had a huge poinsettia display. "I'm betting that's the source of the pollen," she said. "Unfortunately, the display is quite large and varied, so if I'm right, you have your work cut out for you."

Mal disappeared into the basement for a couple of hours to do some more planning and measuring, and to tear down some empty shelves that were on the wall he was going to remove. I worked on my year-end inventory. Several times, I checked my phone to see if I'd missed a call back from Duncan, but so far he hadn't returned my call.

Just before seven, Cora, Mal, and I regrouped in my office and went over the plan again. Then we headed upstairs.

The Capone Club room was packed, and after a quick scan of faces, I determined that the only people missing were Dr. T and Clay. Extra chairs had been dragged in from the meeting room across the hall, and once everyone was settled in, I addressed the room.

"I appreciate all of you being here," I began. "As you may have heard, I have an important announcement to make tonight, one that I perhaps should have made weeks ago. I've been second-guessing myself since this whole thing started."

I paused, examining the expressions on everyone's faces. There was some confusion, some curiosity, some wariness, and even some hints of amusement, as if a few of the folks thought this might be another game or test case I was about to present.

"A few weeks ago, I received a letter in the mail from an unknown person," I went on. "This letter was a challenge to me, an expression of disbelief in my abilities, and a demand that I prove the same. Basically, it said that I needed to figure out certain clues in the letter, and if I failed to do so, someone near to me would pay the price. It was made clear that this price would be death. In other words, if I failed, someone would die."

I paused again, watching the reactions to this information. There were some gasps, some uncomfortable sniggering, and a lot of shifting around in the chairs.

"I'm sure some of you are wondering if this letter was a joke. That was my initial impression; however, the letter included information to make it clear that it was not a joke at all. The letter made reference to the show *Happy Days* and mentioned something had been left for me to show how serious the letter writer was. That same night, Lewis Carmichael's body was found on top of the ice in the river beneath the Fonz statue."

This garnered a much larger collection of gasps, and there were a few low murmurs as people started whispering back and forth.

"I was able to solve the puzzle in that letter and others that followed. I was able to decipher clues that had been designed to test my synesthetic abilities. However, I incorrectly interpreted the clues in a recent letter, and by the time I figured out the real meaning, it was too late. You see, each of these letters also included a deadline. Shortly after that, Gary Gunderson was shot and killed by persons unknown."

Now the group was clearly restless and anxious. Glances were exchanged, profanities were uttered, and expressions had grown fearful.

"There were other caveats included in these letters," I went on. "I was forbidden to work with the police in any way as I tried to interpret the clues, and Duncan Albright was mentioned by name as someone I was not to utilize. It was made clear to me that any violation of these rules might result in the death of someone close to me. And I'm afraid that means all of you."

"We more or less guessed that whoever killed Gary was after you in some way," Carter reminded me.

"Yes, I remember. And I almost told all of you about the letter writer then. But I thought I could continue to buy some time and hoped I might be able to figure out who was behind it on my own." I paused, noting that I had the rapt attention of everyone in the room at this point. "Some of you, probably most of you, have either seen or heard about the article in this morning's paper that says I am not only going to work with the local police, but that I have been doing so for some time. This statement is an unfortunately timed one with some basis of truth to it. I was approached by the chief of police and the chief DA yesterday about working with them on a consulting basis. This request was made in part because they genuinely want to work with me and want my help with their investigative efforts in solving future crimes. But it was also made because they wanted to mitigate the damage caused by our solving of the Ben Middleton case."

"Are you going to do it?" Holly asked.

I nodded. "I gave it a lot of thought and realized that what I do . . . what we do here in this group is rewarding for me. I like being able to put my synesthesia to work and do something good with it. And working against the police and the DA's office only makes it more difficult. I intend to set down some rules and guidelines, and among those I've already mentioned to them is that I need to have the ability to continue to consult with all of you whenever I want. So, yes, I intend to go ahead with it. But I had no intention of revealing that until after this letter writer thing was resolved, for obvious reasons. The newspaper article's claim that I've been working with the police all along is most likely going to upset the letter writer. And that's why I decided it was time to tell all of you the truth."

"You think any of us could be a target," Carter said.

"I do."

Tyrese, who had been fidgeting in his chair more than anyone else, leaned forward, his expression a mix of anger and worry. "Why the hell didn't you tell us about this sooner, Mack?" he said. "We could have been looking out for some clues and watching over the members of the group, to assure their safety."

"I felt I was assuring their safety by continuing to solve the clues," I explained. "And to be honest, I thought we'd catch the guy."

"We?" Nick asked. He looked as annoyed as Tyrese did, and I couldn't help but wonder if they were upset because they were behind it all.

I nodded slowly, scanning the faces in the room. "Yes," I said. "We. I have been working with Duncan Albright on this matter since day one."

This triggered another wave of murmurs through the room. Several people—Kevin, Sonja, and Tad—seemed angry. Greg, Stephen, and Tiny looked worried, and others, like Sam, Carter, Holly, and Alicia, appeared intrigued.

"Obviously, we kept things under wraps and were careful to hide the fact that we were working together," I went on, "but now that this article in the paper has come out, there's no point in hiding it anymore."

"Do you have any idea who's behind it?" Sam asked.

"Yes, as a matter of fact we do," I said. "But we don't have any concrete proof. The person or persons behind this have been very careful not to leave any usable evidence."

"Persons?" Tyrese echoed. "Are you saying you think there's more than one?"

You could have heard a pin drop in the room after that question. Everyone's eyes and ears were focused on me.

"I think it's almost a certainty that there is more than one person involved," I said. "And that makes it doubly dangerous for all of you. I'm sorry you're in this situation."

"It's not your fault," Alicia said. "Just because someone out there has a crazy fixation on you doesn't make it your fault."

"Thanks," I said, giving her a wan smile. "But I do feel responsible to a certain degree. I had the ability to tell all of you, to warn you earlier, and I didn't. Perhaps that decision cost Gary his life. My biggest fear is that someone else in this group will be targeted, and if anyone else suffers because of this mess, I don't think I can bear it."

"Forewarned is forearmed," Carter said. "Now we all know. And we can be more careful."

"It sounds like this person has some serious psychological issues," Sam said. "They're playing a game of psychological warfare. I'd love to take a look at the letters to see if I can come up with a profile for you."

"I don't have them," I told him. "Duncan took all the letters except the most recent one to search for trace evidence."

"And did he find any?" Sam asked.

Hopeful eyes looked to me, waiting for my answer. "Unfortunately, no," I told them. Nearly everyone in the room visibly sagged.

"Maybe we should shut down the Capone Club," I

suggested. "Having all of you coming here like this seems too much like shooting fish in a barrel." I winced. "A bad analogy perhaps, but you get the drift."

I watched as the people in the room exchanged glances, murmured back and forth, and shifted some more in their seats.

"Personally, I think there is something to be gained by keeping us together," Holly said. "Not only can we keep tabs on one another that way, but as a group we may be able to help you figure this thing out, discover who's behind it."

"I agree," Carter said, and several others nodded.

"It's up to each of you to decide," I said. "I will do everything I can to mitigate the danger to any of you, but I can't promise anything. You all need to be hypervigilant and wary of your surroundings at all times. Don't take any unnecessary risks, and if you have even an iota of discomfort with a situation or person, I would suggest you seek help immediately. Try to stay in groups. Don't go out anywhere alone. And if any of you decide to leave the group because of this, I'll understand."

With that, we let the room take on a life of its own. I sat back and watched as people talked, debated, and decided how to handle things. There were a few questions to field, the most important one being whom we suspected.

"I don't want to answer that right now because we aren't sure we're right, and I don't want to point a finger at someone and be wrong. Besides, I'm not convinced that the main person behind this is the one doing the killing. I think that's the role of the second person, and we have no idea who that is."

Over the next few hours, the group moved around and eventually dissipated. During that time, either

Cora, Mal, or myself managed to isolate the people on our list of suspects, pull them aside, and tell each of them the same thing: to be extra careful because we felt certain the second person involved was a member of the Capone Club. Each person was then sworn to secrecy and made to believe they were the only person who knew.

I personally told Carter, Greg, Sonja, and Nick. Their reactions were vastly different.

Nick was the first person I hit up. When I got up to leave the room shortly after finishing my shocking revelation, using the excuse that I needed to go check on how things were going downstairs at the bar, Nick followed me out of the room and caught up with me at the top of the stairs.

"Mack," he said, "hold up a minute."

I stopped and moved to the side so I wasn't perched at the top of the stairway. I didn't think anyone would try to push me down them with all these people around, but I also realized it was smart to be safe rather than sorry.

"Why didn't you tell us sooner about this letter writing thing?" Nick asked. He reached over and placed a hand on my arm as if to steady me, but it made me nervous instead. "We could have been looking into it for you, checking for trace evidence, analyzing the letters, and . . . and . . . well . . . watching out for you." He paused, his eyes softening. "I don't want anything to happen to you."

"Thank you, Nick," I said. "I appreciate your concern. But in the beginning, I felt it would be better for me to handle it on my own. I was afraid that people in the group would go off half-cocked and make the letter writer angry, or go to the police and get them involved. And I felt like I could interpret the clues and keep the twisted little game going long enough to figure out who was behind it." I gave him a half smile and a shrug. "Besides, I had someone looking for trace evidence in analyzing the letters for me. Duncan was doing it."

Nick's look of concern turned into a scowl. "Was Duncan merely looking into the evidentiary stuff for you, or are the two of you still a couple?"

"I'm not sure where Duncan and I are on a personal level right now," I said honestly.

"Is that because of Mal? Is it serious between you two?"

I looked around to make sure no one was nearby eavesdropping. "I don't want to discuss my personal life, Nick. I want to stay focused on this situation and make sure everyone stays safe." I paused to check our surroundings again. "And there's another reason why I didn't tell the group before now. I think someone in the group may be involved."

"Involved how?" Nick asked. His grip on my arm tightened almost imperceptibly. "Are you saying you think the second person is someone from the Capone Club?"

"That's exactly what I'm saying."

I watched Nick as he watched me, the two of us staring at one another, gauging, studying, analyzing. The expression on his face was hard to read. He looked worried and concerned one second, and then mightily pissed off the next. I couldn't tell if he wanted to kiss me or shove me down the stairs. Fortunately, Sonja West came out of the Capone Club room at that point, and as she approached us, Nick finally broke eye contact with me.

"I need to get going," he said hurriedly. Then he turned and practically ran down the stairs.

I shifted my attention to Sonja, smiling warmly as she approached. "Are you doing okay, Sonja?" I asked her. "I'm sure this situation must be stressful for all of you."

"That's an understatement," she said irritably. "I'm heading home. I've really enjoyed the time I've spent here, but now I feel like it was all under a false pretense, and a dangerous one at that. I don't know how I feel about the group now. And I'm not sure if I'll be back."

"I'm truly sorry, Sonja," I said. "The group was smaller when all this started, and I really felt I had a strong enough grip on it to be able to handle things. I didn't set out to deceive or jeopardize anyone. I hope you'll reconsider and come back once everything is settled, but I certainly understand your feelings on the matter." I paused to give her a chance to respond, and also to provide a bit of drama before my next comment. "It's probably just as well anyway," I went on, "because not only am I pretty sure there are two people behind this, I also feel certain one of them is a member of the Capone Club."

Sonja's eyes grew wide, and her head reared back as if she'd been slapped. Her mouth opened, but nothing came out. After a moment, she snapped it shut, her lips pressed into a thin, grim line. Then, without further ado, she headed down the stairs at a fast clip.

I stood for a moment at the top of the stairs, digesting these two encounters and the differing reactions. I hadn't picked up on any particular warning signs from either Sonja or Nick, and the things they said to me seemed genuine. The tastes of their voices hadn't changed during our talks, but then again,

I hadn't asked either of them if they were a killer. *Perhaps I should have.*

With that macabre thought in my head, I headed downstairs to check in at the bar. I knew Billy had nothing to do with the letter writer, because his whereabouts at the time of both murders were well-documented. He had been working at my bar. Teddy Bear didn't strike me as someone I needed to be concerned about, but he had made it onto the list of suspects. Given that, I decided to have a tête-à-tête with both of them.

I asked Debra to step behind the bar for a bit to cover, and then I pulled the two men aside and asked them into my office. Once inside, I gave them a brief summary of the letter writer's history and the information I had just shared with the Capone Club, and ended with a warning to both of them to be careful.

"You can't let your guard down, even here," I told them. "There's a very good chance there are two people behind this thing, and one of them might be a member of the Capone Club. I don't know it for sure, but certain evidence points that way."

"Who do you think it is?" Teddy Bear asked.

"I don't know. I have some suspicions, but nothing concrete. And I don't want to point a finger at anyone without knowing for sure." I shot a look at Billy, who appeared troubled and a little angry. "All I can tell you right now is that you probably shouldn't trust anyone completely."

Billy narrowed his eyes at me, thunderclouds on his face. "Was Gary killed because of this letter writer?" he asked.

I nodded guiltily. "I'm afraid so. I didn't interpret one of the letters correctly in time. I eventually figured it out, but on my way there, I had my accident and ended up with this." I reached down and tapped my cast.

"So you had this letter writing thing going on, and you knew Gary died because of it, and you didn't tell the rest of us about it?"

I squeezed my eyes closed, knowing I deserved his wrath, but hating it. "I debated long and hard about informing you," I said, opening my eyes and forcing myself to meet his gaze. "But I felt that the fewer people involved, the better. I've had Duncan and Cora working on this with me, and I thought that as long as I was able to figure out the clues and keep the game going, all of you would be safe." My eyes burned with tears I was struggling to hold back. I was prepared for recriminations from everyone once they learned the truth, but Billy's look of utter betrayal hit me harder than I'd expected. "I'm truly sorry, Billy," I said. My voice cracked as I spoke his name, and my welling tears spilled over. "I did what I thought was best at the time."

Billy's expression softened almost immediately. He looked away for a moment, sighed heavily, and then looked back at me. "It's okay, Mack," he said. "I get it."

Teddy pulled at his chin, looking thoughtful. "So you think this article that appeared in the paper this morning is going to set the murderer off, right?"

I nodded, swiping at the tears tracking down my cheeks. The feel of them made me see breaking waves of water crashing over rocks.

"And you think the letter writer—or writers, as the case may be—will come after one of us?" Teddy continued.

"That's what some of the letters said," I told him. "Although more recently the writer threatened me personally, stating she was tiring of the game. So I may be the next victim."

"She?" Billy said, zeroing in on this immediately.

I realized my mistake right away and cursed under my breath, wishing I could snatch the word back. The very tenacity that would make Billy an excellent trial lawyer was also about to make my life hell. I knew he wouldn't let this go without an adequate explanation.

"We have good reasons to think Suzanne Collier might be behind it," I said, making a decision I hoped I wouldn't live to regret. Or die to regret.

"Suzanne Collier, as in the heir to the Collier fortune, Tad's wife, and one of the richest women in Milwaukee?" Billy said aghast. "*That* Suzanne Collier?"

"One and the same."

"It wouldn't surprise me," Teddy Bear said.

I shot him a questioning look.

"There are plenty of rumors about Suzanne and her level of stability, or lack thereof," he explained. "She's caused scenes at any number of events, but typically someone in her family, usually her husband or her father, either calms her down or whisks her away before things get too bad. There have been stories about things she has said and done in smaller groups, too. She's known for having a quick-fire temper, for being insanely jealous about Tad, and for frequently getting paranoid that people are out to get her or steal her money. Her ego is huge, and she's constantly trying to prove how much smarter she is than anyone else. She also has a very long memory, and if she feels you've ever done her wrong in any way, watch out. She's destroyed more than a few people."

"Destroyed how?" I asked.

"Several ways," Teddy Bear said. "She's put companies

out of business by starting untrue rumors about their business practices or the unsavory lifestyle choices of the owners; she's used her financial control to bankrupt companies and people; and she's used her powerful influence to blacklist anyone she doesn't like. All that money gives her a lot of power in this city."

"So all we have to do is avoid Suzanne?" Billy said.

"Not exactly," I told them. "If, indeed, Suzanne is the primary person behind it, she isn't working alone. We know for a fact that she didn't kill Lewis Carmichael, at least not with her own hands. That's not to say she didn't have something to do with it, just that she was somewhere else with an ironclad alibi and pictures in the paper at the time of Lewis's death. That means someone else is working with her. She has the money to hire anyone she wants, but because of certain things that have been said and done, I think whoever is helping her is someone close to me, like the members of the Capone Club."

"Or an employee?" Teddy suggested.

Billy shot him a look and then turned back to me. "Is he right? Are we all suspects?"

I shook my head and smiled reassuringly. "I've ruled out most of you based on the times of both deaths. I know you have nothing to do with it, Billy, because you were here working on both occasions. Though to be honest, I didn't need an alibi to know you couldn't have been involved."

Teddy sucked in his lower lip and stroked his beard. "I'm guessing I'm on the suspect list then?" he said.

I gave him a grim, but apologetic smile. "Can you give me an alibi for the time when Lewis Carmichael was killed?"

He shrugged. "When was it?"

I told him, and he spent several seconds tugging harder on his beard than he tugged at his memory. "I got nothing," he said finally. "I can barely remember what I ate for breakfast today, much less something that happened weeks ago."

Billy said, "Just ask him, Mack. Do your lie detector thing."

Teddy shot me a questioning look.

"You haven't told him about me?" I said to Billy.

"I told him some basics, that your senses are more heightened than most, but that was it. I didn't tell him that you're a human lie detector."

Now it was my turn to give Teddy a questioning look.

He held his hands out to his sides, palms up. "What do I have to do?"

It was interesting that these two were the first people to suggest this to me. When Mal and Cora and I discussed our plan, we guessed that the majority of the people would first ask if they were a suspect, and then ask to have me question them as a way of eliminating that suspicion. Teddy wouldn't have if Billy hadn't clued him in since he didn't know about this particular ability of mine, but at least he had asked if he was a suspect. That alone put him much lower on the list in my opinion. Innocent people were eager to try to clear their names. Guilty people weren't, because they couldn't. Neither Nick nor Sonja had asked the key questions.

Still, since I hadn't done any groundwork with Teddy, I couldn't be sure this would even work. In order to tell if someone is lying, it helps if I have a "test" lie—similar to what I had done with Holland and Dixon—to base things on. After thinking for a moment, I told Teddy to tell me three things—obscure things—two of which were true and one of which was a lie.

He thought for a moment, and then said, "Okay. One, my favorite artist is Da Vinci. Two, I stole a car once. Three, I have a terrible case of claustrophobia." He licked his lips in anticipation and then grinned at me, eyebrows raised.

"We definitely won't lock you in the pantry," I said. "And I'm eager to hear about this car you stole. Who is your favorite artist?"

Teddy's eyes grew huge. He stared at me slack-jawed for a moment, before finally shutting his mouth and shaking off his amazement. "Wow! That's some trick you have there."

"You really stole a car?" Billy said.

He nodded.

"How come I didn't come across that on your background check?" I asked him. Had Cora missed something?

"I was twelve," he said. "And I did it on a dare. I have a juvie record, but it's locked. I swear I've been a good boy ever since."

"So who is your favorite artist?" I asked.

"Monet, hands down," he said.

"And have you ever killed anyone?" I asked quickly.

"No," he shot back just as quickly, looking me straight in the eye. And then, just to add some icing to this piece of cake, he added, "I've never killed anyone or helped anyone else kill anyone."

I let a few seconds tick by. "Okay. I believe you," I said. "Now you're both in the clear."

"Then let's get back to the discussion at hand," Billy said. "If Suzanne Collier is behind this, what's her motive?"

I opened my mouth to answer, to explain that we felt her desire to keep Tad away from me and the bar was behind it, but Teddy beat me to it.

"I don't think that woman needs much of a motive," he said. "Based on the rumors I've heard, all you have to do is look at her cross-eyed. And if you look at Tad at all, she gets insanely jealous."

Billy, true to his lawyerly training, wanted more answers. "What evidence do you have against Suzanne? And do you think Tad is involved?"

I bit my lip, hesitant to get into the details. "The evidence so far is all circumstantial, but there is a lot of it," I told him. "There are enough coincidences to make me think they aren't coincidences, if you get my drift. And we know Tad didn't kill Lewis because he was here in the bar when it happened. Does he know about what Suzanne is doing, assuming we're right about her?" I asked rhetorically with a shrug. "We don't really know. But my gut says he does not."

"Well, if you're right about Suzanne, you have your work cut out for you," Billy said. With a sideways nod of his head, he added, "Like Teddy Bear here said, that woman has a lot of power in this town, and it won't be easy to bring her down."

"I know," I said with a heavy sigh. "That's why I'm continuing to play the game for now, with the hope that at some point she'll slip up and give us some real evidence. Perhaps we can find out who she's working with and get that person to turn on her."

Billy looked like he had more questions, and I had no doubt he could sit and discuss this issue with me for hours if I let him. So I glanced at my watch and said, "You guys best get back to work. It's pretty busy, and I don't think Debra can man the bar and wait on tables for very long."

Billy gave me a frustrated look, but he didn't argue.

"I'm trusting the two of you not to breathe a word of this to anyone else. No one." Both men nodded. "Give me your word," I pushed, and then one at a time they each did, with no hint of deception in their voices. I knew it wasn't a guarantee of anything more than their genuine intent to keep the promise, but they were both levelheaded and reliable men otherwise, so I felt the odds were good that they would hold true to their pledges. "Thanks, guys. Now go back to work, and send Debra in here, okay?"

They did what I asked, and when Debra came into the office, her eyes were wide with curiosity.

"What the heck is going on?" she asked. "Everyone is acting weird, the Capone Club people look like they just saw a ghost, and everyone is whispering back and forth."

I had her sit down and then filled her in on the saga of the letter writer. She listened without interruption, and when I was done, rather than looking spooked as I expected, she looked relieved.

"Any questions for me?" I asked her, worried that she hadn't grasped the gist of my message.

"Nope," she said. "I'm just happy to know I'm not getting fired."

"Fired? Why would I fire you?"

"No reason that I knew of, but you've been acting so squirrelly lately, I knew something was up. I thought maybe I was in trouble."

"Not at all. In fact, you and Billy are my two most trusted and valuable employees."

"Okay then," she said, wiping her hands along her

thighs. "Anything I can do to help you with this letter writer idiot?"

I smiled at her. "No. I'm working on it with the help of Duncan and the cops in the Capone Club. Just make sure you stay safe. From now on, I don't want any of you leaving here alone at night. Make sure you have someone with you. Okay?"

"Okay." There was a moment of silence, and then she said, "Is that it? Can I go back to work?"

Her reaction, or rather the lack of one, was a little disturbing. But then, based on some of the things she'd had to deal with as the mother of two teenaged sons, I supposed a serial killer was small potatoes.

"Yes, you can go back to work. But please don't discuss this with anyone. I've told Billy and Teddy, but I haven't spoken to Jon, Rich, Curtis, Linda, or Pete. I plan to tell all of them by morning, and the only person I'm not sure about with regard to an alibi when it comes to Lewis's death is Linda."

"Linda?" Debra said, looking skeptical. "I can't see her killing a fly. She's so meek and . . . well, mousy, for lack of a better term."

"I'm inclined to agree with you, but she has some connections that are a little iffy. Just be on the alert, okay?"

"Gotcha." She got up and headed for the door, but I called her back.

"And Debra? Thanks for picking up all the extra hours. I really appreciate it. Just be careful you don't run yourself into the ground."

"I'm fine," she said with a dismissive wave of a hand. "You stay safe, too, Mack, okay?"

"I will. And can you send Missy in here next, please?"

Missy's reaction was similar to Debra's. I got the

impression that this was just one more nuisance to her, and as a single mother of two toddlers, she had plenty of those. After I garnered a promise from her to be extra careful and not go anywhere alone, particularly when leaving the bar late at night, she went back to work.

After giving myself a few moments to prepare, I picked up the phone and continued on my mission.

Chapter 18

Over the next hour or so, I called Pete, Jon, and Curtis at home and filled each of them in on the letter writer. I wanted them to hear it from me rather than secondhand. They all took it in stride and promised to be extra cautious until the matter was resolved. Pete was the only one of them on the suspect list due to a lack of an alibi, but I'd known him for years and had no doubts about him. Given that, I didn't bait any of the men with information, and I let them know that I trusted each of them.

With that done, I went into the kitchen and told Rich. He not only didn't seem bothered by the news, he acted rather excited about it. "A real-life crime going on right here in the bar," he said. "Who knew?"

I informed him, as I had the others, that I knew he wasn't behind it, but I didn't offer up how it was I knew this. The less he knew about Cora's poking around, the better.

The only employee left was Linda, and since she wasn't working, I tried to call her. She didn't answer, and I left her a message to call me when she had a moment.

I spent a few minutes debating whether or not I should try to call Duncan again, and after some mental debate, I decided to wait and headed back upstairs to the Capone Club room. I didn't get far. Halfway across the new room addition on my way to the stairs, Greg Nash met me and asked if he could speak to me in private.

Like Sonja, Greg was a newcomer to the Capone Club. He was a local Realtor who had known Ginny Rifkin, another, highly successful local Realtor, who was also the woman my father was dating when he was killed, and the woman who later became a victim herself. Ginny's death and the subsequent resolution to her murder had made the news, along with the formation of the Capone Club. Greg, when he first showed up, had expressed an interest in participating in the crime-solving activities the group partook of as a way of honoring Ginny's memory. So far, he had been a quiet observer, not offering much in the way of expertise, thoughts, or ideas.

I led him to the far corner of the room, near the door to the basement. There was no one close by who could overhear.

"What can I do for you, Greg?"

"These letters you've been getting," he said. He began chewing nervously at his lower lip. "Something happened to me today that makes me wonder if I was intended to be the next victim of whoever is writing them."

He had my rapt attention now. "Tell me."

He glanced around nervously, still chewing on that lower lip. "I got a call this morning around eleven o'clock at the office. It was a woman on the phone.

And she said she was interested in a property I have listed out by the lake. It's a very expensive property, and when I have listings like that I try to vet people over the phone before I commit to showing it to them, to make sure they're serious buyers and not just some lookie-loo. This woman told me she didn't want to give out her name because the purchase needed to be kept private and anonymous for personal reasons she didn't want to share." He paused, looking embarrassed. After another glance around to make sure no one was eavesdropping, he continued. "I should have stuck to my guns and followed my own rules," he said. "But these high-end properties are so hard to sell, and the type of people who can afford them are often quirky and have special needs or demands. So against my better judgment, I agreed to meet her out there at two o'clock."

"Did you recognize the voice at all?"

Greg shook his head. "No, but the woman did sound . . . I don't know . . . cultured, I guess, for lack of a better term. I admit I had dollar signs in my eyes, and they might've been obscuring my better judgment. Though I have to say, if I had known this afternoon what I know now about this letter writer thing, I don't think I would've gone out there."

I felt a flush of guilt.

"The property is kind of isolated. It's vacant and protected with a gate that provides access to the house. It's bordered on both sides by fencing and large groves of poplar trees. It's on the lake, so there's a great view of the water, but this time of year, there's no one out there."

Again he paused. He licked his lips, which I noticed were looking a bit ragged from his constant chewing.

He ran a hand through his hair and shook his head in a way that made it look like a shudder.

"What happened?" I asked him.

"Fortunately, nothing," he said. "But that's because I had a bad feeling about the whole thing. I drove out to the house, and when I reached the gate, I noticed that it was ajar. Normally the gate is locked, and there is a camera and speaker unit that can be activated, and the gate lock can be released from inside the house. But there's also a number code that can be used at the gate itself if someone wants in. According to the sellers, the only people who know that number are family members and a few close friends. So seeing the gate open gave me pause. My first concern was that someone might be robbing the place, but I went ahead and drove through the gate and up to the house. It appeared to be locked and secure, and I started to get out and go inside, but something made me hesitate. I don't know . . . it was like the hair on the back of my neck was standing on end. Whatever it was, it made me stay in the car and head back down the drive to the gate. Once there, I waited for a while for the time of the appointment to come and go. When no one showed up by two-thirty, I shut the gate and left."

"I take it the woman who called you initially didn't call back?"

Greg shook his head, his chewed lips pressed into a grim line. "I phoned the local police and had them go out there with me earlier this evening so I could check the property over and make sure nothing was amiss. The house was locked up tight, and when we went inside, everything looked fine. So I chalked the whole thing up to a case of nerves triggered by the breakfast burrito I had this morning. But after hearing what you had to say, I'm not so sure now."

Neither was I. Had Greg been targeted by Suzanne? "What is the address of this property?" I asked him.

He gave it to me, and I logged it into my memory.

"I don't know what to tell you, Greg," I said. "Can I say for sure that what happened was all in your imagination, and that I think you're safe? No, I can't. But I also have no way of knowing if the threat you perceived was real."

Greg started chewing on his lips again, and he looked around the room with a wide-eyed, wary expression. "I've got some vacation time coming," he said. "I think now might be a good time to use it. I promised myself a week in the Caribbean, and this is the perfect time of year to go there."

"That might not be a bad idea," I said. "And I'm sorry I didn't tell all of you sooner. In hindsight, it's easy to see that I probably should have."

"Don't sweat it," Greg said, waving away my concerns. "I don't envy you the position you were put in, and I don't know what I would've done if I were in your shoes. But I do think that, for my own good, I need to step back from the group for a while and let this thing play out. I have no interest in being a pawn in someone else's sick and twisted game."

I nodded my understanding and reached over to give his shoulder a reassuring squeeze. "I do hope you'll come back once things settle down," I said. "And I have to confess, I'm a little jealous. I'd give anything to be able to escape to the Caribbean for a week or two along about now and leave all my troubles and worries behind. When you get there, have a big old rum drink with an umbrella in it for me."

Greg flashed me a warm, friendly smile. "Consider

it done," he said. "And don't worry, I'll be back. In the meantime, good luck with this thing, Mack. I hope you catch the bastard and he gets his just rewards."

On that note, he headed for the front door. Out of all the people I had spoken to and observed so far, he was the one I felt most comfortable dismissing. I was pretty certain he wasn't involved, because I'd heard him lie before and knew how it was reflected in his voice. It was only a white lie, but I picked up on it right away. Sonja had hit him up for a date, and he had told her he was already seeing someone. Normally his voice had a sweet, fruity taste to it, but when he'd said this to Sonja, the taste had turned so tart it nearly made me pucker. And when he'd said to me that he hoped we caught the bastard, and that the culprit would get his just rewards, his voice had maintained its sweet, fruity flavor. That left me inclined to believe in his innocence.

But I was also determined to be cautious and smart about things. So I made a mental note to have Cora follow up and make sure that Greg Nash did, indeed, head for the Caribbean.

When I got back upstairs to the Capone Club room, the group had dwindled down. Most had gone home for the night, and those who remained were the people who didn't have to get up early in the morning for any reason. This included our participating cops, Nick and Tyrese—apparently, Nick had returned after fleeing from me earlier; they both worked the night shift and would have to leave soon to start their shifts. Carter was there since he had no specific work schedule now that he was focused solely on his writing, and Stephen McGregor, who was enjoying the holiday break from his job as a physics teacher at the local high school. Sam, Cora, and Mal were also in the room.

I settled into a seat at a table next to Mal, who was sitting across from Cora. As usual, she was tapping away at the keyboard on her laptop. Carter was typing away on his too. The other four men were sitting together at a nearby table, having a lively discussion about how to approach an investigation into who the letter writer might be. On the table in front of them were a number of sheets of paper with various words and diagrams scrawled on them. All four looked up and nodded at me as I entered the room, but they didn't interrupt their discussion. I listened as I settled in, and after a moment Cora slid her laptop over to me so I could read what she had written on the screen. It was a summary of what had taken place while I was gone from the room, and what Cora had dug up with her computer research. The first item on the screen was a sentence that read: Suzanne Collier is a major contributor to Anthony Dixon's political campaign!

Like I didn't think taking down Suzanne Collier would be hard enough as it was. This was not unexpected news, but I was disappointed nonetheless.

I continued reading the rest of the screen, which was a list of names under the heading: MAL AND I SPOKE TO. Between the two of them, they had hit up all of the other suspects except for Tyrese and Carter. At the bottom of the list, she had typed: *Not one of them asked if they were suspects or suggested you test them to see if they were telling the truth.*

I nodded when I was done reading everything, and then typed something in beneath her info, asking her to check and see if Greg Nash followed through and traveled to the Caribbean, and telling her that Sonja

had apparently flown the coop and that I had cleared
Teddy. When I was done, I pushed the laptop back
over to Cora. She read what I'd typed and nodded.

I gestured toward the trio at the other table. "Have
they come up with anything feasible?"

"A lot of anger from Tyrese and Nick over the fact
that you didn't tell them sooner," Cora said, leaning
in close and speaking at just above a whisper in my
ear. "I think Stephen is looking at the whole thing like
it's some kind of adventure, and Sam is all about the
psychological profile. Carter is mostly hurt that you
didn't confide in him. Although I do believe his pain
has been tempered somewhat by his excitement over
the book potential."

I smiled at that, keeping my eyes focused on the
three men. I listened as they debated the letter
writer's request to not involve the police, the motive
behind that request, and what it might mean now that
it had been revealed that this rule had been broken.
After a moment, there was a pause in the conversation, and they turned to me to ask my thoughts on the
matter.

Tyrese said, "I get why the person behind these
letters wouldn't want you to involve the police, but
why was Duncan mentioned specifically? That seems
odd, and perhaps telling somehow."

"I agree," I said. "It could simply be that the person
was aware of my work with Duncan initially, saw us as
a team, and therefore excluded him specifically. Or it
could be that whoever's writing these letters has a
reason to want to keep me and Duncan apart."

Nick turned away suddenly, shifting uncomfortably
in his seat and running a finger around the inside of
his collar. It was unusual behavior from him, and I noticed right away. If he did have a romantic interest in

me, then he also had a strong motive for wanting Duncan out of the picture. Plus, he had the necessary forensic knowledge, not to mention access to police procedures, investigations, and files. I wondered if he had shared with the other two men the theory that someone from the Capone Club was involved. Despite my admonition to keep it to himself, I expected him to share the information with Tyrese since the two men worked as partners. As soon as I could get Tyrese alone, I would find out if that happened. If, however, Nick chose to keep that information to himself, it would make me even more suspicious toward him.

There was an intensity, a level of determination and focus in Nick that was a little disturbing. Something about him raised my hackles whenever I was near him. It might simply have been his dedication to his work and the nature of his personality. It might also have been a result of his unrequited feelings toward me. But I couldn't ignore the possibility that it could also be because the man was a twisted, demented, and clever killer. And if Cora's findings were right, he was a domestic abuser.

"Whatever the reason," Tyrese said, "it seems weird. I suppose it's unfortunate in a way that this article appeared in the paper today, but I also think it might turn out to be a good thing. You don't want to give these people too much control. You can't let them think they're in charge. A sudden revelation like this, one that will make whoever is behind these letters think they've been getting duped the entire time, is bound to rattle his or her cage. And when you rattle cages, people tend to lash out and do stupid things."

Sam said, "Or it may simply make them more determined to try to outsmart her. I suspect the person behind this is quite intelligent."

Nick glanced at his watch and nudged Tyrese. "We need to get going. Our shift starts in just over an hour."

Tyrese nodded.

"I need to hit the can before we go," Nick added. "I'll meet you downstairs." Again, Tyrese nodded, and with that Nick stood up and left the room.

Stephen McGregor got up, grabbed his coat from the back of his chair, and said, "I need to be getting home, too, before the wife gets on my case. Good night." He followed Nick out of the room.

Tyrese lingered for a minute and finished his cup of coffee—the cops came into my bar for my coffee as much, if not more, than they did for the booze—before getting up from his seat.

"It's been an interesting night," he said, taking his jacket from the back of his chair and slipping it on. "Stay safe, everyone."

As those of us who remained murmured back our own good nights, I realized Tyrese's exit would give me the perfect opportunity to get him off alone for a quick little chat. I nudged Cora with my elbow, and she understood right away. She leaned over toward Carter and started talking with him about the case. Sam listened in eagerly. I struggled up out of my chair and followed Tyrese out of the room.

The man was fast on his feet and was at the top of the stairs by the time I exited the room, forcing me to holler at him to wait up. He turned, smiling at me and looking curious. "What do you need, Mack?"

After checking to make sure no one was nearby to eavesdrop, I said, "There are some things about this case that I want to share with you confidentially. I've told the group that I think there are two people involved, but what I didn't say to the others is that I suspect one of those people may be a member of the Capone Club."

Tyrese furrowed his brow, taking an involuntary step back. He was close enough to the top of the stairs that I reached out and grabbed his arm, fearful he might fall. "What the hell?" he said. "Are you serious?"

"As a heart attack," I said with a pained smile. His surprise seemed genuine, meaning Nick hadn't shared this theory with him. "Certain things that have happened, and information the letter writer seems to know, have convinced me that whoever is behind this has some insider knowledge."

Tyrese shook his head woefully, his mouth skewing sideways as he sucked on the inside of his cheek. "What a damned mess," he said. "But that helps me understand why you didn't tell the group sooner."

"That was part of the reason," I admitted. "But I was also afraid that if I told them, someone would go off half-cocked and do something stupid that would escalate things. I wanted to keep everything in my control for as long as I could. In hindsight . . ." I shrugged, letting him draw his own conclusions.

"I get it," Tyrese said. "Don't beat yourself up over it." He sighed and looked at his watch. "I have to go, but if you need anything during the night, don't hesitate to call."

"Thanks, Tyrese."

He turned to leave but then hesitated and turned back. "You said Duncan has been working on this on the sly," he said. "Does that mean the two of you are still together on the sly?"

"That's all kind of up in the air right now," I said honestly. "Why?"

"You and Mal . . ." He gestured with a nod toward the Capone Club room. "He's a cop, isn't he?"

I was so surprised by this question that I didn't answer right away. That, in and of itself, was an answer.

"I knew it," Tyrese said with a self-satisfied grin. "Certain things the guy said and did when we went to the prison gave it away."

The fact that Tyrese now knew this wasn't good, but it didn't worry me overly much. I trusted him. He came across as honest and forthright, and not once had any of my senses picked up anything worrisome about him. In my mind, I had already crossed him off the suspect list. But I realized I might have to second-guess myself. He hadn't asked me who I suspected, nor had he asked me if he was a suspect. That seemed odd, considering he was a cop.

"You're right," I admitted. "He's working under-cover on something else and hanging out with me in his spare time, both as a protector and as a diversion to convince anyone who's watching that Duncan and I are no longer together in any way, shape, or form. Please don't give him away."

"No need to worry about that, Mack. His secret is safe with me." He glanced at his watch again. "I really do have to go. Be careful, okay?" I nodded, and with that he hurried down the stairs.

I turned around and headed back into the Capone Club room. Sam was up and saying his good-byes, and he left with a promise to be back tomorrow. Now that the only people left were Cora, Mal, and Carter, I decided we could have a chat with Carter regarding our theory.

I glanced back toward the door of the room to make sure there were no unexpected visitors popping in. Seeing that the door and the hall outside were empty, I settled into a chair and dove in.

"Carter, I want to talk to you about this letter writer thing," I began.

"Why didn't you tell me about it sooner?" he said,

the hurt clear in his voice. "I thought I was part of your insider group, one of the trusted ones."

"I figured the fewer people who knew, the better it would be," I said, neatly avoiding giving him an answer to his question. "And there's something else about it you don't know yet."

"You think someone from the club is involved, don't you?"

My eyebrows shot up, as did Cora's. Mal's might have; I wasn't looking at him when Carter dropped his bomb of a revelation.

Rather than confirm or deny Carter's statement, I hit him back with a question of my own. "What makes you say that?"

He shrugged, tapped his fingers on the tabletop, and then said, "I know you pretty well by now. You might think that's presumptuous of me, and I wouldn't blame you if you did. But I'm a good study of character. I read people well. In part, it's because I've always wanted to be a writer, and I've always been interested in what makes people tick. But I think it's a natural talent I have. It served me well as a waiter. My ability to read people and anticipate their needs earned me better than average tips."

He paused for a few seconds, and when no one spoke, he continued. "You, Mack, are a consummate caregiver. You worry far more about other people than you do about yourself. I think that stems to some degree from living your entire life in a service industry, but I also think you are kind, thoughtful, and altruistic by nature. So when you told us tonight about this harassment, and how long it had been going on, I wondered why you had waited so long to tell everyone. I assumed part of your decision was based on a desire to protect everyone in the group, but given that two people have died already, that logic seemed a bit skewed, particularly for you. So it had to have been something else that made you hesitate. After thinking about it for a bit, the only logical reason I could come up with was that you suspected someone in the group was the culprit, or one of the culprits, anyway."

He paused again and looked back and forth between the three of us. No one said a word.

"Tell me I'm wrong," Carter said.

"You're not," I told him.

"Any idea who it is?"

I shook my head. "We know who it isn't because we've been able to establish alibis for some of the members. But beyond that . . ." I shrugged.

"And I'm guessing I'm on the suspect list since no one has asked me for any alibis," Carter said.

I gave him a grudging nod.

"Well, I was here when Gary was killed," he said.

"It's not Gary's death we're looking at," Cora said. "It's Lewis's."

"Ah, I see," Carter said. His fingers were once again tapping on the tabletop, faster now than before. "I don't have an alibi for that particular time period because I was home alone. But I didn't kill Lewis, or anyone else, for that matter."

He looked me straight in the eye as he said this, and I guessed he was saying it for my benefit, allowing me to analyze his speech pattern and the taste of his voice.

My suspicion was confirmed when he then said, "Ask me anything you want, Mack. You've tested me before when we were playing games, so you know what my voice does when I'm lying."

He was right. I'd been tested by several members of the Capone Club in the past, and in each case, I was able to tell when they were lying to me. All of them squirmed a bit when I did it, and I knew that my ability to see through their lies made them uncomfortable.

As if he was reading my mind, Carter said, "Why don't you just ask everyone who is on the suspect list to see if any of them lie to you?"

"I thought about doing that," I told him. "But it isn't as easy as it seems, at least not if I want to preserve some level of comfort, trust, and friendship with the group members. To begin with, I haven't tested everyone's voice patterns—mainly the newcomers, but a couple of the older members, too. Aside from some games we played back when the group was first established and people wanted to test me, I've more or less tuned out the changes in people's voices because everyone tells white lies, and it seems like an invasion of privacy to be constantly monitoring what people say. And secondly, what question do I ask? I don't think the person writing the actual letters—at least the majority of them—is from the group, so asking that won't help. And while I have a strong suspicion about who the letter writer is, I'm not certain, so asking anyone if they are working with that person is of little value. That leaves me with Lewis's death. Do I go around and ask everyone if they killed Lewis Carmichael? Half the people would probably give me a non-answer, or laugh it off, or make some sarcastic remark. And I imagine the other half would be upset and offended."

"Not me," Carter said. "Ask me."

I stared at him.

"Come on, Mack," he insisted. "Ask me. I want to clear my name. In fact, ask me that and one or two other questions, and I'll lie in answering one of them, to give you a comparison."

His earnest expression and desperate tone told me how badly he wanted me to believe in him and his innocence. I looked over at Cora, who shrugged, then at Mal, who nodded toward Carter in a *go ahead* fashion.

"Okay, Carter, what is your mother's maiden name, what's your favorite food, and did you kill Lewis Carmichael?" The mental schism created by the incongruity of those questions being asked together literally made my head hurt.

"My mother's maiden name is my first name, Carter," he said. "My favorite food is macaroni and cheese, and no, I did not kill Lewis Carmichael."

As soon as he was done, I felt the eyes of Cora and Mal on me, watching, waiting for my response. I didn't prolong the suspense. "Okay, Carter, I believe you didn't kill Lewis," I said. "And what is your favorite food?"

Carter smiled, and I heard both Mal and Cora let out breaths of relief. "It's peaches," Carter said. "I'd give my right arm for a juicy, perfectly ripened peach."

Now it was my turn to smile. "Nice move, Carter. Now tell me the truth this time."

Carter's smile widened and looked a little impish. Cora wagged a finger at him, and Mal just shook his head and smiled.

"I just wanted to see if you were paying attention," Carter said with a wink. "And the truth is my favorite food is bacon, and that kind you use on your BLTs here is the best."

This time he was telling me the truth. "Okay then," I said. "Consider yourself exonerated. And that means you are part of the team that's going to help us catch a killer."

Chapter 19

By the time I was done filling Carter in on what we knew about the letter writer, it was nearly closing time. We called it a night, and agreed to look at it all with a fresh eye the next day. Carter and Cora left and, since it was late, Mal escorted Cora back to her office/apartment, which was only a block or so away.

I shooed all of my staff out the door at the same time, after once again eliciting promises from them to stick together on their way to their cars and to keep a watchful eye out. Mal returned from walking Cora home, and after I let him in, he made the rounds of the place to ensure that everything was locked up tight.

Linda called me back while I was doing my cleanup, and I settled in at the bar while I talked to her.

Her reaction to the news wasn't what I expected.

"So you've been messing around with this crime-solving stuff, and now you have someone who is stalking you because of it?"

"Well, yes, I guess. I—"

"What did you think would happen?" she asked

angrily. Before I could answer, she went on. "When people poke around and accuse others of crimes without any solid evidence, they're just asking for trouble. And you don't stop to think about what you're doing to the lives of the other people involved."

Clearly, she was angry. Was it because of the situation with her brother? Did she think her brother was innocent and wrongly suspected?

"Linda, I—"

"What's done is done," she said, once again interrupting me. "Let the cards fall where they may." She let out a fatalistic sigh. "I have to go, Mack. I'll see you tomorrow."

She hung up. I sat there, staring at my phone with a perplexed expression for several seconds.

Mal saw the look on my face and settled in on the barstool next to me. "What's wrong?"

I filled him in on my odd conversation with Linda.

"She sounds unstable," he said. "Maybe you should fire her."

He was probably right, but something about Linda in general made me want to wait. "I get a sense from her that she's very vulnerable. There's something in her past, something other than this thing with her brother, and I think it's had an effect on her. Let's hold off for now and see what happens."

I could tell Mal didn't approve of my plan, but he didn't argue. I got up and went behind the bar to finish my cleanup duties.

Mal watched me for a few minutes and then said, "Mack, there's something I want to talk to you about."

"What?"

"I don't feel comfortable with you staying here alone at night. The place is locked up and all, but now that this letter writer thing has blown up, I'm worried for your safety."

"I'll be okay," I said, but I didn't sound convincing to my own ear. Truth was, the whole thing had me spooked.

"You probably will be, but I'd still feel better if I was here. Let me stay over. I'm not looking for anything intimate or personal, I promise. Just let me have the couch to sleep on."

I gave it a split second of thought, and then nodded. It would make me feel more comfortable knowing he was there, and I trusted him when he said he wouldn't make it personal.

"I'm going out to my car to grab my go-bag," he said. "I'll be back in a minute. Will you lock up behind me and then let me back in?"

"Of course."

An hour later, we were upstairs in my apartment, and after a brief round of debate that bordered on argument, Mal agreed to sleep in my father's bed rather than on the couch. I convinced him in the end by insisting that I would feel like I had more privacy if he was in a room with a door that could be closed. Despite this excuse, when I finally went to bed I left my bedroom door open and was happy to see that Mal had his only partially closed.

With everything that had happened, I expected a restless night of tossing, turning, and strange dreams. But instead I slept better than I had in a long time, a heavy, restful, and dreamless sleep.

I awoke the following morning feeling content, well rested, and eager to start the day. As I sat up in bed, I caught the scent of fresh-brewed coffee and knew that Mal had gotten up ahead of me. I hit the bathroom to pee and run a brush through my hair and over my teeth, and then I headed for the kitchen. Mal was sitting at the kitchen table, dressed in a light gray T-shirt and dark gray sweatpants, his hair sticking up on the crown of his head in an Alfalfa-like cowlick. It made me smile.

"Good morning," I said.

"Good morning. How did you sleep?"

"Surprisingly well," I answered. "How about you?"

"The same. I have to say, your father's bed is quite comfortable. I hope you're truly okay with me sleeping there."

I was. "He would be glad to know someone enjoyed it," I told him. "He spent the better of a year buying that mattress, hitting up dozens of bedding and furniture stores, and lying on every mattress they had. The Princess and the Pea had nothing on my father. If there was the tiniest lump, bump, or flaw in a mattress, he could feel it. He had this thick notebook full of ratings and comments for every mattress he'd tried. He drove the store workers crazy. I know, because I went with him on these excursions a few times, on Sunday mornings when the bar was closed. He loved to shop on Sundays. While other people were in church worshipping their deity, my father was bed-hopping all over Milwaukee."

Mal chuckled. "Well, he picked a good one."

My smile faded, my mood sobering. "He only got to sleep in it for a few months," I said. "He bought it in October of last year, and then he was killed in January." I realized with a shock that the anniversary of that day was just around the corner, though the word *anniversary* sounded far too celebratory and cheerful for marking that particular occasion.

Mal's expression sobered as well. I expected him to

offer up some standard condolence phrase, but he said nothing. Instead, he got up from his seat, walked over and pulled the other chair out from the table, took hold of my hand, and steered me to the seat. I sat down and then watched him as he poured me a cup of coffee, topping it off with a dollop of heavy cream the way I like it. He set it down in front of me and then went over to the stove, where he started fixing something to eat.

I sat in comfortable silence, watching him work, enjoying the fragrant scents of vanilla, cinnamon, and butter that emanated from whatever concoction he was preparing. Before too long, I realized he was making crêpes filled with strawberries and cream. I took out my cell phone, which I had slipped into the pocket of my robe, and checked it for calls. There were none, which both relieved and disappointed me. No news was good news, I figured, when it came to my friends and patrons and the letter writer. If anything had happened, I'm sure my phone would have been lit up with messages. But some part of me was also hoping there might have been a message from Duncan.

At one point, I got up and retrieved my tablet from the living room and brought it back to the kitchen table so I could check on the daily news. Mal watched me in silence, continuing with what he was doing. By the time he set three sugar-dusted crêpes in front of me, my stomach was growling so loudly I swear people out on the street could have heard it.

"Bon appetite," he said.

"Thank you. If it tastes half as good as it smells, I'll be in heaven."

He topped off my coffee and then went back to the

stove to fix his own helping. I started scanning the newspaper.

It was a relatively quiet news day—a relief for me. No murders, no riots, in fact no real violence of any sort locally. Yet despite my relief, I felt like this was the proverbial calm before the storm. Surely the letter writer—Suzanne presumably—had seen the article about me in yesterday's paper. Even if she hadn't seen it on her own, if I was right about someone in the Capone Club being involved, whoever it was would tell her about it. It was bound to cause a reaction sooner or later, and waiting for something to happen was a bit nerve-racking.

By the time Mal had joined me at the table, I had scanned through all of the newsy part of the paper.

"Anything?" he asked.

I shook my head.

"My guys are going to come and help me with the demo this afternoon. I hope the noise won't be too disruptive to your business."

"If it is, it is," I said with a shrug. "It's only temporary, and it will be worth it in the long run."

"They'll be here at five when you open," he said, punctuating the comment with a huge forkful of crêpe. "Several of them worked all night. Undercover work isn't always a Monday through Friday, nine-to-five thing the way mine is. In the meantime, when do you want to visit The Domes?"

I glanced at the wall clock and saw it was closing in on ten o'clock. "I need to do some prep stuff downstairs so we're ready to open at five in case we don't get back before then. And I have some things I need to order and get ready for the New Year's Eve party. After that I'm free. So let's figure on leaving here around eleven-thirty, if that's okay with you."

"That's fine."

"I guess I better get dressed then," I said. I pushed the tablet aside, stabbed the last bite of crêpe on my plate, and shoved it in my mouth. After relishing my final taste of this delightful breakfast, I washed it down with a big swallow of coffee and got up from the table.

As I headed out of the kitchen, I walked over and gave Mal a kiss on top of his head, just in front of that crazy cowlick. "Thank you for breakfast," I said. "And for everything else." The kiss might have made one or both of us feel awkward, or it might have created an air of tension between us, yet it did neither.

Half an hour later, Mal and I were both dressed and downstairs in the bar. Over the next hour, I placed some orders for extra bottles of champagne, dug out some New Year's themed decorations I had in the basement, and cut up some fruit for drinks. Mal spent this time down in the basement of the new section, presumably doing something related to the elevator project.

He reappeared just before eleven-thirty, but by the time I finished what I was doing and we both got bundled up to head out, we were leaving fifteen minutes later than planned. It didn't matter; we had no specific agenda, and technically we had until Monday if the deadline in the letter could be trusted. But that article in the paper had changed everything, and I was worried that the rules to this nasty little game were about to change really fast.

Mitchell Park wasn't far away, and we pulled into the parking lot beside The Domes just before noon. Mal was huddled inside his coat as we walked toward the entrance. My crutches prevented me from huddling, and the frigid air eked its way between the layers of clothing I had on with each swinging step I took. The cold made me want to hurry inside, but I stopped at a human sundial located at the entryway to the building.

"What is this?" Mal asked.

"It's a human sundial. My father brought me here to The Domes several times when I was a kid, always on Sunday mornings, and always around the same time of day. That's because the bar didn't open until five on Sundays, and those mornings were our main free time together. I remember thinking the sundial was a scam because it always showed the same time of day whenever I saw it. Once, when I was in high school, some friends and I went to Mitchell Park, and in the late afternoon I wandered over to that sundial to try it out, to see if it really could show a different time."

"And did it?" Mal asked.

"It did." As I said this, I flashed back to that day, recalling how one of my classmates caught me being a human sundial, and teased me about it. The other kids who had been there joined in, all of them poking good-natured fun at me for a few minutes. The memory of it made me blush now the way I had then, triggering a sensation of hot sauce on my tongue.

"How does it work?" Mal asked, as I shook off the memory.

I pointed toward a rectangular metal plate embedded in the concrete that had the months of the year stamped into it, each one in its own little box. In two arcs of small, embedded metal circles above the months—one arc of circles below the other—were the numbers one through twelve, though not in perfect numerical order. One of the arcs started with the number six, the one above it with the number seven.

"Stand in the box for the current month and face north." I pointed to one of four other metal circles embedded in the sidewalk, each one with a letter stamped into it that marked the four points of the compass. "Put your arms up over your head, clasp your hands together, and your shadow will point to the current time. One set of numbers is for daylight saving time, and the other is for regular time."

Mal dutifully stood in the December box and did as instructed. And the shadow of his hands pointed straight to the twelve in one row and the one in the other. He lowered his arms and glanced at his watch. "Cool," he said, giving himself a hug and shivering against the cold, making his comment perfectly appropriate. "Can we go inside now?"

I was more than happy to oblige. When we went through the main entrance, we had to stop and pay an admission fee. Mal proffered his wallet, and I didn't object.

"There is only one dome open," the girl dispensing tickets said with an apologetic look. "But the farmers' market is in full swing, and there is a beautiful poinsettia display in the open dome, our Show Dome."

"That's okay," I assured her with a smile. We made our way into the connecting portion of the building. To our right were the entries to the two closed domes; to our left was the open Floral Show Dome. We made our way there and entered into a mini Christmas wonderland. The interior was filled with poinsettias of all colors: red, salmon, pink, white, yellow, purple, and several variegated varieties. They were displayed in strategic groupings bordering a cobbled path that wended its way through mini Christmas villages and other holiday dioramas, decorated Christmas trees, and benches that invited observers to sit back, relax, and take it all in.

Beautiful as it was, relaxation was not on the agenda

for me. My head was filled with synesthetic reactions to the piped-in holiday music, the many smells of the plants, and the elaborate visual displays.

"This isn't going to be easy," I said to Mal, squeezing my eyes closed and taking a moment to try to parse my reactions. Though I was getting better at it, deconstructing my synesthetic responses this way was new to me. In the past, I eventually learned real from synesthetic through a combination of listening to others' descriptions of things, a smidge of intuition, and a few suppressive efforts that were more of a game I played with myself. But now, with my interpretations being key to my ability to analyze something as important as a crime scene, separating my "normal" reactions— though the muddled, mixed-up experiences I had *were* my norm—from the synesthetic ones was more involved.

I recalled the specific reactions I'd had to the smell and feel of the smears on the letter. Starting with the smell, I sifted through the many musical sounds I was experiencing—some louder than others, most likely because of proximity—and tried to zero in on one that matched the sound I'd heard with the letter. All the sounds were woodwind types of notes, everything from oboes to flutes. Despite the fact that I couldn't carry a note when it came to singing, I was able to identify a single note unfailingly. I studied music in school and quickly discovered that each note came with its own color. A D-sharp is a certain shade of yellow, slightly greener than a plain D, which isn't as pale as the yellow of a D-flat. The sound I'd heard with the letter had definitely been a low A, a solid, rich, royal purple note.

Mal and I walked along the path, and I focused on the various notes. Every time I heard that low A note, we stopped, and I zeroed in on the specific plants creating the sound. Once I made sure no one was watching me, I gently prodded the insides of the flower, disturbing the pollen and then rubbing it between my fingers. Rubbing the pollen on the letter had triggered a green and white, jagged, arcing line, but by the time we were halfway around the interior of the Show Dome, I had yet to experience that same visual. I saw arcing lines, but they were smoother, or of a different color, or thicker, or straighter than the one I'd seen with the letter. Each time I touched some pollen, I had to wipe my fingers thoroughly, doing so on the inside of my coat. At one point, I even stuck them in a small pond that was part of a display. I was beginning to lose hope when we came across a collection of pink and green variegated poinsettias growing around a small diorama of a gingerbread house. This time, when I rubbed my fingers together, everything fell into place. I saw the jagged, green and white arcing line.

"This is the spot," I said to Mal, eyeing the large patch of plants. "But how are we supposed to dig in here?" I looked around us at all the other sightseers meandering inside the dome, searching for anyone who looked official. "We'll get busted and tossed out of here for sure, maybe worse."

Mal looked around too. "What choice do we have?" he asked rhetorically.

I thought back to the poem, rereading it in my mind. "The word *edge* was used," I said. "Maybe that means I'm supposed to look along the border of this particular garden." It was a reach, and we both knew it, but as Mal had said, what other choice did we have?

I sat down on the low stone wall bordering the

planting area and casually sank my hand into the dirt behind it. The soil was loose and soft, and I plunged my fingers down into it, thumb toward the wall, pinky toward the center of the planting area. I did this a number of times, moving forward a half inch or so with each subsequent plunge, hoping I might feel or strike something. Mal saw what I was doing, and he positioned himself in a way that provided me with some screening from the eyes of others nearby.

When I had explored as much of the area as I could from where I was sitting, I got up and moved to a different spot along the wall, hiding my dirt-smeared hand inside my pocket. I sat on a different section of wall, acting as if I was admiring the gingerbread house display. While I looked at the house, my hand got busy poking holes in the dirt. For once, I was glad to have my crutches to haul around. Their presence, along with my cast, made it less strange for me to be sitting on the walls. My dirt-covered hand, however, was a little less easy to explain. I figured if anyone noticed it and asked, I would say I lost my balance and fell, plunging my hand into the dirt in an effort to catch myself.

The path, and hence the wall bordering it and the patch of poinsettias we were focused on, was curved. I had started my search in the middle of the planted area, and now I had reached one end of it. So far, I'd found nothing but dirt. I looked at Mal, shook my head, and got up again, this time heading to the other end of the wall. This portion was located at an intersection of pathways, making it even more difficult to do what I was doing without drawing unwanted attention. I positioned myself a foot or so from the end of the variegated poinsettia area and once again sat on the wall.

Mal and I let a few people pass by before I started mining the dirt again. In one spot, the soil felt noticeably different, looser. My heart picked up its pace, and a second later, my fingers hit up against something solid that felt like it was covered in plastic wrap. I dug my fingers a little deeper down one side of it and felt a bottom edge. After a quick glance around to see if anyone was watching what I was doing, I grabbed it as tight as I could and pulled it loose from its grave, flinging dirt onto my lap in the process.

It was a small tin, like the kind you can buy with mints in them, covered in plastic wrap. After again glancing around to see if anyone was watching us—no one appeared to be—I handed the tin to Mal, grabbed my crutches, and struggled back to my feet.

"Let's get out of here," I said, wiggling the fingers on my dirt-encrusted hand. In my coat pocket, I had a pair of gloves that I had worn there, but I didn't want to stick my filthy hand into one of them. And because of my crutches, I couldn't hide my hand in my coat pocket either.

We followed a meandering path back to the entrance to this particular dome and then out into the main connecting area. I held my breath the entire way, half expecting someone official to stop and threaten us with expulsion or, worse, the police. How ironic that would have been.

Once we reached the main hall area, I saw a solution to my nervousness. "Can you wait while I visit the ladies' room?" I said to Mal. "I really want to wash my hand off."

"Of course."

It took me longer than I liked, but I had to dig impacted dirt from beneath my fingernails, and the soil clung with an amazing tenacity to every line in the skin of my hand. When I was done and went back out to the main area, Mal was standing near the entrance talking to a man wearing a uniform with THE DOMES printed on the shirt. My heart skipped a beat, and I hesitated, unsure if I should approach him or act like I didn't know him. Mal didn't look distressed or upset, and the man he was talking to was smiling and nodding as Mal spoke. I decided to go over to him, and when I saw Mal look at me and smile, I felt my tension ease away.

"Thanks," Mal said, shaking the man's hand as I neared. "You've been a big help."

The uniformed man smiled and said, "My pleasure," and with a brief nod toward me, he headed off.

"What was that about?" I asked Mal. "I had a bit of a panic when I saw you talking to an official. I thought we were about to be busted."

"Nah, I was just getting some information from him." We headed for the exit, and Mal kept talking as we walked. "Like the fact that the structure wasn't properly maintained some decades ago, and as a result, there has been some water and other damage. In fact, some of the glass panes in the domes have fallen in the past. That's why there was that netting bordering the inside perimeter."

I hadn't noticed any netting. I'd been too focused on my synesthetic reactions.

"The Domes probably have only about ten years of life left in them," Mal went on. "So there is this group called Friends of The Domes that's working to raise funds for a future rebuild."

"Interesting," I said, not sounding all that interested. But his next words definitely got my attention.

"And it just so happens that the Collier family is a big supporter and contributor."

I shot him a look. "Meaning Suzanne might have easy access to the place." Mal nodded. "You know, if we're right about Suzanne, and we somehow manage to convince the police of that, there are going to be a lot of causes, people, and organizations that will be ticked off at us for eliminating one of their chief financial sources."

"Hopefully, the family will continue the support."

On that thought, we continued our way back to the car. Once inside, Mal took off his winter gloves and donned a pair of latex ones instead. Once he had the new gloves on, he removed the tin from his pocket. Dirt still clung to the outside of it, meaning Mal's pocket also contained some dirt. At this point, I was tired of waiting to read the letters and felt certain there would be little or no trace evidence worth collecting. Still, Mal couldn't let go of his occupational training completely, so he had brought along some plain, brown butcher paper to lay beneath the tin when we opened it. He did so now, spreading it out on his lap with one hand while he held the tin in the other. As soon as the paper was in place, he looked at me, removed the outer plastic wrap, and opened the tin.

Tiny bits of dirt fell onto the brown paper as he revealed a small, folded piece of paper wrapped in plastic and nestled inside the tin. Mal removed it, and after examining it carefully, he found an edge on the plastic covering and began to remove it. Once he had it unwrapped, he set the plastic down on the butcher paper in a different section from the outer wrap and carefully unfolded the note that had been inside.

It was the same type of paper used in all the other notes. And once again, the letter was written in calligraphic form, though I noticed the lines weren't quite as clean as they had been in other letters. The message this time was short, terse, and to the point.

> *Ms. Dalton,*
>   *You have violated the rules of our game.*
> *There will be a price to pay.*
>   *I warned you,*
>   *An ex-fan*

I stared at the letter in disbelief, dread washing over me. I looked at Mal. "The newspaper article," I said. "Given the timing and the dates on the previous note, this one must've been changed. The clue to come to The Domes was obtained before the article appeared. I'm guessing something different was hidden in that tin before that newspaper article appeared, and then it was swapped out."

Mal nodded, his expression worried. "I have a bad feeling about this," he said. "I think things are about to get a lot more dangerous."

I felt dread with his words, but it was no more dread than I'd been feeling all along. "Two people have been murdered already," I said. "How much more dangerous can it get?"

Mal didn't answer right away. He just stared at me with a sympathetic expression overlying his look of concern. Finally, he said, "Sadly, I think it can get a lot more dangerous. And I'd be willing to bet that you are the next person on the hit list."

He looked away from me and out the windows of his

car, scanning the area around us. A chill shook me, and I was unsure if it was the cold or the situation that had triggered it. Feeling paranoid, I too looked out the windows, scanning the faces of the few people we could see.

Mal folded the letter back up, rewrapped the plastic around it, and put it back inside the tin. He then folded the tin up inside the butcher paper along with the outer wrap, taking care to make sure all the dirt and anything else that might have dropped from it was contained inside the paper. He then handed it to me, and I placed it inside a plastic evidence bag we had also brought along. I didn't seal the bag closed—it would never be usable as legitimate evidence—and stuffed it in my clean coat pocket.

Mal started the car's engine, shifted into reverse, and backed out of our parking space. "We need to get you back to the bar," he said, "and until we get to the bottom of this thing, you're going to stay there. So am I. I'm not leaving you alone anymore."

I didn't object. To be honest, the idea of having Mal around all the time appealed to me on several levels. Then he complicated things.

"You should call Duncan and let him know what's going on. I imagine he'll want to be staying with you, too."

"That's not going to happen," I said. "I'll be fine." I said this with more conviction than I felt. But in addition to the fear and anxiety rumbling through me, I also felt a strong surge of anger—anger at Suzanne Collier and whoever else was working with her. I was tired of feeling like a puppet in someone else's twisted little show, and I needed to put an end to it.

Mal, wisely, said nothing more during our drive

back to the bar. He was lucky enough to find a parking place right out front as another car was leaving.

"Don't move," he said as he turned off the engine and undid his seat belt. He got out on his side, came around to mine, and opened my door. As I got out, he hovered over me, practically draping his body over mine. He shut the car door and kept me close, one arm draped around my shoulders, as we walked to the bar. I unlocked the door and stepped inside, locking it again behind me.

Mal looked at me with a troubled expression.

"This thing has gotten out of hand," he said. "Given that the letter writer thinks you're working with the police, there's no reason not to do so. I not only think we need to tell Duncan what's going on, regardless of what's happened between the two of you, I also think it's time to bring the full force of the police in on this case."

"I understand why you're worried," I said. "But what good is it going to do to bring the police in at this point? None of the evidence we've collected is usable, so what are they going to do? They can't arrest Suzanne Collier. We don't even know for sure that she's the one behind it. All of the evidence we have is circumstantial, correct?" It was a rhetorical question, and as such, I didn't give Mal time to answer. "And even if we assume we're right about Suzanne, there's still the second person to consider." I shook my head, frowning. "We need a better plan, Mal. We need to figure out a way to expose who's behind this once and for all. And I have an idea about how we may be able to do that."

He eyed me with a mix of worry and skepticism . . . and maybe a hint of hope. "What have you got in mind?"

Chapter 20

As I explained my idea to Mal, we went into my office to drop off our newly acquired evidence and shed our coats. I thought Mal would buy into my idea right away, but he had some reservations. "I don't know, Mack, it seems dangerous. There's so much that could go wrong."

"Have you got any better ideas?"

He didn't, and after a few seconds of pouting, he admitted it. "I think we should run it by Duncan," Mal said. "And update him on this latest note."

"I tried to call him yesterday and got his voice mail. I asked him to call me back, but he hasn't yet. I'm not sure he wants to talk to me."

"Do you want me to call him?"

"Would you?"

He made the call on his cell, using the speakerphone option so I could hear. Duncan answered on the second ring, confirming my suspicion that it was me he didn't want to talk to.

"I've got Mack here with me on speaker," Mal informed Duncan.

"Oh, good. Hey, Mack, I was just about to call you."

I didn't believe him, but his voice tasted sincere, and then he offered up an explanation that seemed reasonable, so I was forced to give him the benefit of the doubt.

"I left my cell phone at home yesterday," he said, "and didn't leave the station until this morning. And then I had to charge it because the battery was dead. I just listened to your message a few minutes ago."

"No harm done," I said, feeling a twinge of relief. Things would no doubt still be strained between us after our last conversation, but at least he hadn't written me off completely.

"Mack and I followed up on another clue today," Mal said. "I'm afraid things have taken a turn with this letter writer. There was no clue this time, just a note saying Mack had broken the rules and would now pay for it."

"Damn," Duncan muttered. "I think it's safe to assume that the letter writer saw the article in the paper. I'm so sorry, Mack."

"I'm not," I said. "I'm tired of being pushed around and bullied by Suzanne Collier and whoever is working with her. We need to bring this situation to a close."

"For what it's worth," Mal said, "our latest clue was buried in the dirt at The Domes. Apparently, they're falling apart, and Suzanne Collier is part of a committee formed to support and save the structures. So we have another connection to her."

"A connection isn't proof," Duncan grumbled. "Did you guys preserve the items for evidentiary processing?"

"As best we could," Mal said. "But I think we all know the odds of finding anything are slim to none. I think it's going to take a different approach to bring some closure to this case, and along those lines, Mack has an idea."

"Lay it on me," Duncan said. "At this point, I'm willing to try anything."

Mal proceeded to fill him in on my plan, with me adding in bits where needed. We also told him about my discussion with the members of the Capone Club and my employees to inform them of the letter writer situation.

"We managed to rule out a couple of people," I said. "But our list of possible secondary suspects is still pretty long, and we're no closer to figuring out who it might be. That's assuming we're right about it being someone from that list. Given the contents of this last letter, I feel like we have to make a move of some sort."

Duncan said, "There are a lot of problems with this plan, but I get why you want to do it, Mack. And it might finally bring things to a close." He paused and sighed heavily. "I say we go ahead with it. I'll take care of things on my end. In the meantime, can you stay there with Mack for now, Mal?"

"Not a problem at all. I already told her I would. And I've also told her she needs to stay in the bar until we can implement this plan."

"That's good," Duncan said, "though she's just stubborn enough not to do what you tell her."

Having the two of them talk about me like I wasn't in the room annoyed me.

"Don't worry. I've got Mack covered," Mal said, finally acknowledging me with a wink. "I'm going to be hanging around here anyway because I've taken on a construction project that we're starting today."

"Yes, Mack told me. You're putting in an elevator. I think it's a great idea."

Mal glanced at his watch. "I've got a bunch of guys I know coming by to help with the demolition this afternoon," he said. "You're welcome to join us. Destruction can be very therapeutic."

"Tempting, but I can't," Duncan said. "Have a good whack at something for me."

"Will do," Mal said.

"Mal, I have one more favor to ask of you," Duncan said.

"Fire away."

"Can you let Mack have your phone, and give us a few minutes of privacy?"

"Sure." He handed me his phone and said, "I'll be out at the bar. Is it okay if I let my guys in when they get here if you're still tied up?"

"Of course."

I waited until Mal was gone and the door had closed behind him. "Okay, I'm alone," I said.

"I want to talk to you about what happened the other day, about our discussion."

"Okay." I said this tentatively, not sure where it was going to go.

"I've given it some thought, and you were right. Courtney is a problem, one I've turned a blind eye to up until now. In fact, I think you may have been on to something when you said we should consider her a suspect. I know she is friends with the Collier family, and she certainly has the motive for specifying me in those letters."

"I agree. So what do we do about it?"

"I will make it very clear to her that she and I are done, and insist that she stop contacting me."

"Thank you."

"But I don't want to do it right away."

I squeezed my eyes closed in frustration.

"I think we should involve her in your plan."

This was an interesting twist, I thought. "How?"

He told me what he had in mind.

"It might work," I admitted. "I can't say I like the idea of being around her, but if it will help clear things up, then I say we go for it."

"Consider it done. Keep your fingers crossed that it will work."

"It has to," I said. "I'm so sick and tired of being manipulated."

There was a moment of silence, and then Duncan said, "Are you and I okay, Mack? I've felt awful about the fight we had. Things have been so stressful between the two of us, between job demands and this damned letter writer thing."

"I think we need to sit down and talk some things through once we get past all this," I said. "But for now, we're okay. Let's focus on resolving this situation once and for all. Then we can pick up the pieces and move on from there."

"Fair enough. In the meantime, stay safe and listen to Mal. Don't go doing anything rash or stupid."

"Are you calling me stupid?" I said in a teasing tone.

"No, I'm just scared to death of something happening to you. You mean the world to me, Mack. I know I haven't been around much lately, and things have been less than ideal, but I want you to know that. I need you to know that."

"Thank you, Duncan. I needed to hear that."

"So we're good?"

"We're good. I'll talk to you soon."

I ended the call and went out to the main part of the bar to find Mal. He was sitting at a table with four other guys, and there was an assortment of pickaxes and sledgehammers on the floor beside them. Mal waved me over.

I handed him back his phone and then took a closer look at his destruction crew. They were dressed in jeans, work boots, and an assortment of shirts, most of which looked grungy. One of the guys was wearing a do-rag on his head; another was covered with tattoos. They were a scary, motley-looking bunch.

"Meet your destruction crew, Mack," Mal said. He went around the table and introduced each of the men to me. "They're ready to go. Shall we?"

They all rose from their seats and grabbed their tools, and Mal led them into the newer section of the bar and toward the basement stairs. He opened the door to the stairs and directed the men below.

As soon as they were all down there, Mal said, "This demolition stuff is fun. Want to try it?"

I gave him a hesitant shake of my head. "I don't know anything about construction," I said.

"This isn't about construction; it's about destruction," he said with a mischievous smile. "Whole different animal. Go on down." I negotiated the stairs carefully and slowly with my crutches. When we reached the bottom, Mal gave a brief outline of what had to come down. Then he pointed toward a cinder-block wall and told the guys to "have at it." Moments later the deafening sound of metal hitting concrete echoed through the basement. Each bang filled my mouth with a metallic taste, not unlike blood.

We watched them go at it for a few minutes, and then Mal steered me over to one end of the wall, where a fellow named Robbie had created a large hole. Mal stepped behind me and slipped his hands beneath my armpits, shoving my crutches away.

"I'm going to hold you up," he said. "Robbie, hand

her your sledgehammer." Robbie did so, and I winced at the weight of the thing. "I'll make sure you don't fall or put too much weight on that bad leg," Mal said. "You swing that thing as hard as you can toward that hole in the wall."

Mal's hands on the sides of my chest felt strong and secure. I gave the hammer a tentative underhand swing toward the wall, just to get a feel for it. It hit the wall and bounced back, sending a resounding jolt up my arm. But it also left a chipped area in the cinder block.

I took a moment to prepare, reviewing all the things in my life of late that had upset or irritated or angered me: my father's death, Ginny's death, the betrayal of someone I had once trusted, the letter writer, Lewis's and Gary's deaths, and the recent issues with Duncan and Courtney. As I mentally ticked off each item, I could feel my frustration and anger build. At the peak of this crescendo, I flexed my arm muscles, braced my shoulders, hoisted the sledgehammer over my head, and brought it down hard into the hole.

This time I was more prepared for the jolt, though I felt it all the way down to my toes. With it, a hazy window of cracked glass appeared around my field of vision. My effort had knocked a satisfyingly large chunk of cinder block loose from the wall, and the piece tumbled out toward me. In an instant, Mal lifted me up and out of the way. He set me back down a couple of feet away, and the chunk of wall plodded to a stop inches from my feet.

I stood and stared at it a moment, feeling a grin start to spread across my face. My body tingled from the jolt of the hammer against the wall, and the cracked glass visual began to shimmer, growing brighter.

"Want to do it again?" Mal's voice was warm in my ear, close and soft.

I nodded and felt his hands tighten their grip as he lifted me again and placed me within striking distance of the wall. Once again, I lofted the hammer and swung it, with the same satisfying results.

Four swings later, my arms were shaking from the effort, my muscles protesting. Over the years, I'd managed to develop some decent biceps and triceps, hauling around heavy liquor cartons, beer kegs, and fountain canisters. But this, fun as it was, was more than my arm muscles were used to. I let the hammer hang at my side, leaning back against Mal.

"I'm done," I said, a bit breathless from my efforts.

"It's a great release, isn't it?" Robbie said with a crooked smile.

"It is," I agreed with a big, tired smile. I held out the hammer to Robbie. "I'll trade you this for my crutches."

Robbie gathered them up from where they had fallen on the floor and held them out to me with one hand while taking the hammer with the other. Once I had my crutches tucked back under my arms where they were supposed to be, Mal let me go. My body felt conspicuously cold where his hands had been, and I was vibrating from the muscle exertions and hammer blows.

I turned and gave Mal an appreciative, grateful smile. "Thank you for letting me do that," I said. "It was surprisingly relaxing in a violent, damaging kind of way."

"It's good to let go every once in a while," he said.

"Indeed," I agreed with a satisfied smile. "I'll leave your guys to their fun now, but let them know they can have whatever they want to eat or drink on the house. Just be careful they don't get drunk and start destroying stuff we need to keep."

Mal arched one roguish eyebrow at me. "We'll try

to contain our enthusiasm," he said with a wink. "And I won't let them have any alcohol until the job is done for the night. Thanks for the offer. I know they'll appreciate it."

"My pleasure."

I started to head up the stairs, but Mal grabbed my arm, halting me. "Listen, Mack," he said, "I would feel a lot better down here if I knew you were safe in your apartment."

"I won't go outside the bar, but I'm not going to hide away in my apartment. The doors are locked for now, and I don't think anyone will try anything in the midst of the bar crowd later."

Mal frowned at this, but nodded, no doubt knowing that further argument would be a waste of his time and breath.

Feeling exhausted yet oddly refreshed mentally, I crutched my way over to the stairs and climbed them back to the first floor. Just before I closed the door after I reached the top, I heard a loud grunt from below accompanied by a resounding crunch. I then recognized Mal's chocolate-flavored voice utter a milky-smooth "Oh, yeah."

The work of the men in the basement was evident not only from the noise they were making, but from the vibrations that could be felt in the floor and walls. I busied myself making signs to post around the bar explaining and apologizing for the noise and mess created by the construction.

My staff showed up between four and five—Debra, Billy, Rich, and Linda. Linda was her usual friendly but mousy self, with no hint of the anger she had expressed during our phone call. I informed her and Rich about the New Year's Eve party plans, and they both said they would be happy to attend. But Linda did express a reservation.

"So I won't be working that night?" she said.

"No."

"I was looking forward to that money."

"Would it help if I told you I have bonuses planned for all of you?" I asked her.

"You do?" she said, her eyes wide.

I nodded. "It should more than make up for any money you lose by not working."

"Then count me in," she said.

We opened the doors at five, and in typical fashion, Cora, Joe, and Frank showed up minutes later. They were eager to sit by the warmth of the fire, so they headed up for the Capone Club room right away. Others trickled in over the next couple of hours, including several members of the club. I wasn't sure who was going to come back after last night's revelations, and wouldn't have been surprised if most of them had stayed away, so I was glad to see several of them had returned.

I avoided the Capone Club room for most of the evening, though I knew who was up there because I had either seen them come in or Cora had texted me to keep me informed. Carter, Sam, Holly, Alicia, Dr. T, Kevin, and Stephen McGregor had all shown up and gone to the room to join the brothers and Cora. Apparently, the letter writer hadn't scared any of them into hiding, but, not surprisingly, Greg and Sonja were both no-shows. And since Nick and Tyrese had worked the night shift, I figured they were sleeping and would come in later.

Cora texted me to let me know she had talked to Tiny about the need to establish an alibi for the time of Lewis's death, and he had told her he was at work pulling overtime and had shown her his paycheck and time card to prove it.

One more name crossed off the list.

Since Dr. T was here and hadn't been the night before, I did head upstairs toward the end of the night to talk to her, feeling I owed her the respect of telling her face to face. Not surprisingly, the others had already clued her in, so I offered her the same apology I'd offered all the others and asked her if she had any questions. She asked if she could speak to me in private.

Curious, I agreed, and the two of us stepped out of the room and went into the other room I had upstairs, one I used for large group rentals on occasion or for overflow seating on busy nights. It had been closed for the past week.

Once inside, she said, "Do you have a suspect in mind for who's behind this letter thing?"

I nodded. "All the evidence we have is circumstantial at this point, and I'm not sure this particular person is the one behind it, though there are a lot of things pointing to it."

"Do you think it's someone from the Capone Club?" she asked.

I gave her a small look of surprise. "Interesting that you asked that," I said. "We have reason to suspect that there are actually two people involved because the primary suspect couldn't have killed Lewis Carmichael. We considered the possibility of a hired gun, of course, but some things have happened that make us think the second person might be someone from the group."

"I assume you have a list of suspects?"

"I do."

"Am I on it?"

I smiled at her. "You are. But if you can give me an alibi for the time of Lewis's death, your name could be crossed off the list."

"What time frame are we talking about? Are you looking at the time around when his body was found?"

"Actually, no. The evidence suggests he was killed before that and dumped in the river sometime during the night before he was found."

I watched as she did the mental calculations in her head. "I'm pretty sure I was working, and I can give you the name of someone who can verify that. But why don't you just ask me if I'm involved? You can tell when people are lying, right?"

"Most of the time," I admitted. "It helps if I have a baseline lie to use."

Dr. T's voice was one of those that came with a visual rather than a taste. I typically saw a billowing whiteness, like a sheet hanging on a clothesline in the wind. The visual manifestations were some of the most distracting ones, so I worked hard to suppress them. As a result, I hadn't paid much attention to my reactions to her voice in the past.

"I killed a patient last night while I was working," she said.

This non sequitur was startling, to say the least. And as soon as she uttered it, the white sheet turned black and crumpled to the ground.

"Good one," I said with a smile. "I'm happy to know all your patients from last night survived. Now tell me, are you involved in this letter writer thing?"

"Absolutely not."

The sheet sprung up as if it had a life of its own and resumed its white color.

"And did you kill Lewis Carmichael?"

"Nope."

The sheet was still white, still hanging, still gently flapping in the breeze. "Thank you," I said. "Now I can cross one more name off the list."

Dr. T's smile was warm and huge. "Thank *you*," she said. "Now, what can I do to help you catch these morons?"

I gave her a warning look. "They are not morons," I said. "In fact, so far they have proven to be quite smart. I think I have things under control for now, but if there's something you can help with, I'll let you know."

"Please do. And don't beat yourself up over this, Mack. It's not your fault, and most of the folks I've talked to understand why you didn't tell us about it sooner. For what it's worth, I think you made the right decision."

"Thanks, Karen."

She gave me a reassuring squeeze on my arm and started to head back to the Capone Club room, but I stopped her. "There might be one thing you can help me with," I said. "Do you have to work on New Year's Eve?"

"I don't," she said.

"Got any plans?"

"My TV and my cat for now. Why?"

"I'm going to close the bar down on New Year's Eve at ten in the evening and hold a private party for some invited guests. That includes the Capone Club. Will you come?"

"Sure," she said with a smile. "I'd be happy to."

We parted ways, and I went back downstairs to attend to some paperwork. After a few hours, Mal came up and tracked me down in my office, where I was busy working on my year-end inventory.

"Hey, Mack," he said. "We have a small problem."

"Typical construction worker," I teased. "Why don't you just dispense with the excuses and skip straight to the money part. What's it going to cost me?"

Mal grinned. "Nothing. One of the guys misunderstood my instructions about what we were taking down tonight, and he started on the wall bordering the stairs. The stairs are going to go eventually, but that wall has to stay because it's load-bearing. It's easy to fix the hole he created, but his hammering caused some shifting of the door frame at the top of the stairs. It's all catawampus, and the door won't close. So I'm going to string some caution tape over it for now. I just want to let you know so you won't try to shut it. And you probably shouldn't let anyone use the basement stairs there, either."

"Okay. The stairs shouldn't be an issue since we never use them. There's nothing in that part of the basement. Everyone uses the stairs by the entrance to my apartment."

"Good. The guys are going to quit around eleven, and I told them they could eat and drink what they want once they're done. We accomplished a lot."

"Good."

"I've got some other help arriving tomorrow, and with the way things are moving along, I expect I'll be ready to put the elevator in place in a couple of weeks. Are you still thinking of going with the one we looked at earlier?"

I nodded.

"Okay, good. I've already ordered some other stuff, building supplies and such, that I'll be needing. But in order to have them delivered, I have to pay for them. I hate to ask, but I need you to front me some money for the job. If I was home in Washington, I could use the family business account and charge all this material, but here I don't have any status or accounts with the suppliers. They want money up front."

"Of course," I told him, opening my desk drawer and removing my business checkbook. "How much do you need?"

He quoted me a number, and I wrote him out a check for that amount.

"Thanks," he said, taking the check, folding it, and stuffing it in his jeans pocket. "The only other thing I wanted to talk to you about was the sleeping arrangements for the next few nights. I'd be perfectly happy sleeping in here on your couch, or down in the basement on a cot, if you have one."

"Nonsense," I said. "You'll sleep upstairs in my apartment just like you did last night. End of discussion."

"Are you sure? I don't want you to feel uncomfortable or create any more awkwardness between you and Duncan."

"Things between me and Duncan are fine. I feel bad that I'm hijacking your life, but I can't deny that having you here makes me feel safer, calmer, and more secure."

"I've already told you I don't have much of a life to speak of outside of work these days," he said. "So don't worry about that."

Reassured of his financial and sleeping arrangements, Mal headed back downstairs to his volunteer workers. And as planned, they all quit around eleven and came upstairs to have some beer and food. They were a fun group, and after an hour or so of winding down, they all left for the night. Tyrese and Nick came in while the guys were still unwinding, and Tyrese eyed them all closely before heading upstairs. It wouldn't surprise me to know he had tagged all of them as cops, too, despite the way they looked.

I made sure to invite the Capone Club members who had shown up to the private New Year's Eve party. Without exception, every one of them accepted.

Mal hung with me until closing time, and we headed upstairs to my apartment together. It wasn't awkward at all. In fact, Mal and I had taken to cohabitation with frightening ease, and after spending a brief time unwinding with a nightcap, we both headed for our respective bedrooms, and I, at least, slept well until morning.

Chapter 21

The following morning, I beat Mal out of bed.
My body had grown used to having only five or six
hours of sleep a night, and when I have the time to
sleep longer than that, I almost never do. On this
occasion, I awoke at eight-thirty, a little earlier than
my usual, and given that we hadn't gone to bed until
well after three, I figured Mal would still be sleeping.
It turned out I was wrong.

My first clue was the open door to my father's bedroom, and my second clue was the hot pot of coffee
waiting for me in the kitchen. I thought Mal might be
in the shower, but that door was open, too, revealing
an empty room. Though I was pretty certain he wasn't
anywhere in the apartment, I called out to him anyway.
Not surprisingly, I didn't get an answer. I poured a
cup of coffee using a travel mug so I could carry it
more easily with my crutches and then headed downstairs, still dressed in my pajamas.

I knew where Mal was, and what he was doing,
when I was halfway down the stairs. I heard the distinctive whining sound of a drill and knew he was
working on the elevator project. When I reached the

door at the top of the stairs, the door that would no longer close, the drill whine had been replaced by the staccato tapping of a hammer. I made my way over to the door and peered down the stairs. Mal was down there using a hammer and chisel to clear away some clinging concrete. He didn't see or hear me; he was facing the wrong way, wearing protective eyewear, and had earplugs in place. After eyeing the stairway closely and noticing the slight tilt to it that hadn't been there before, I decided not to go down. Instead, I turned around and headed back upstairs to the apartment to shower and dress for the day.

The early part of the day was like most others. My day staff showed up between ten and ten-thirty, and precisely at eleven I unlocked the front door. Several of the Capone Club members came in: the brothers, Cora, Carter, and Dr. T, who was enjoying a three-day stretch of time off from working in the ER. Tad showed up for lunch, and I pulled him aside and told him that I had reason to believe the letter writer might be targeting him.

"Targeting me? Why?"

"I don't know," I said. "I quit trying to understand this crazy person a long time ago."

"What makes you think I'm a target?"

"Certain things that were said in the letters," I told him. "Whoever is writing them seems to have a real grudge against people who are well-to-do. That and a few other things make me worried for you. And for Suzanne," I lied. "In fact, if my suspicions are correct, Suzanne might be more at risk than you are."

"Suspicions?" Tad looked intrigued.

"I don't want to say anything just yet, in case I'm wrong," I said. "But thanks to a slipup and some trace evidence we found in one of the letters, I'm fairly certain who's behind this letter writing thing. In fact, I plan to announce it at the private party with all of you and go over the strategy I have planned for exposing them and having them arrested. I'll present the evidence and see if you guys come to the same conclusion I did."

"And if we do?"

"Then we'll get the police involved."

Tad considered this and then nodded his approval. "Sounds like a plan."

"Have you told Suzanne about any of this?" I asked.

He gave me a sheepish look. "I haven't," he admitted. "She's down enough on my coming here. If she knew what was going on and the risks involved, she'd be even more adamant."

"I think you need to let her know. I realize it probably won't help your cause much, but I feel she should know about the letter writer. Now that we are closing in on the culprit, it might result in things getting ramped up. It could be dangerous for both you and her. Do you think she'd come to the private New Year's Eve party?"

"Lord knows, I get dragged along to plenty of functions with her," Tad said, "so I think it's about time she returned the favor. And who knows? Maybe when she gets to meet and know the people here a little better, and see what they do, she won't be so adamant about me not spending time here."

"That's great, Tad," I said. "I hope both of you can make it. Given all that's happened, I suspect being locked in here in the bar with the rest of the group might be the safest place any of us can be."

He thought about this and said, "Good point. I'll do my best to get her here."

"I hope she won't be scared off by the letter writer thing."

Tad scoffed. "That woman isn't afraid of anything. She thinks she's invulnerable." He paused, narrowed his eyes in thought for a moment, and then added, "Although she does have one vulnerability—her fear of losing me."

Yeah, because you're her biggest status symbol.

"I know people think I'm just a trophy husband," Tad said, and for a moment, I was afraid I had voiced my thoughts aloud. "And I confess, there are times when that's how I feel. But I think that deep down inside, Suzanne really cares for me on some level."

I had my doubts, but I kept them to myself.

Tad glanced at his watch—an expensive Rolex, I noted—and said, "I need to get going. I have some client appointments this afternoon, but I'll try to come back later."

As I watched him leave, I felt both a sense of relief and one of dread.

Sam showed up mid-afternoon, as did Greg Nash, Stephen McGregor, and Kevin Baldwin. They hung around for an hour or two, chatting about the letter writer, speculating about motive, comparing whoever was behind it to Sherlock Holmes's nemesis, Professor Moriarty. By inference, it meant they were comparing me to Sherlock Holmes, and I had to admit that I found the analogy a little flattering.

Mal spent the entire day down in the basement, working on the elevator project. But he was no longer working on it alone. Somewhere around one o'clock in the afternoon, a group of four people— three men and one woman—came up to the bar and asked for him. I guessed who they were right away because there was a strong family resemblance.

"You're his family, aren't you?" I said, looking at the foursome. Their abashed grins answered the question for me before they nodded and murmured their assents. "He didn't tell me you were coming," I said. "Does he know?"

"Oh, he knows," said the older of the three men, who was presumably Mal's dad. "He said he had some fun elevator project he was working on here and he could use a hand or two. And since he couldn't be bothered to come back and visit for Christmas, we came here."

Despite the chastising tone of this last sentence, there was a lightheartedness to it that told me no one was really upset.

"He does, indeed, have an elevator project he's working on. Come on, I'll take you to him."

"You mean the project is here, in this bar?" one of the younger men said.

I nodded, and with that, the two younger men did a high five.

I led the group over to the area where Mal was working. The door to the stairway had caution tape across it, and I pulled it loose and opened the door. Mal was off to the side of the stairs down below, hammering away at some sort of wooden structure.

"Mal, there are some people here to see you," I hollered down.

He looked up in surprise, his face lighting up. "You're here already?" he said. "With the holiday traffic, I didn't think you'd get a flight out for days."

"We didn't book commercial," Mal's father said. "Turned out Christian Leech was flying back to Chicago to visit his daughter, and he offered to let us hitch a ride on his plane." Mal's father turned to me and added, "Christian Leech is a friend of ours who happens to own and fly his own planes. He owns a crop-dusting business, among other things."

"Yeah, like half of Yakima," Mal said with a roll of his eyes.

He bounded up the stairs, and his two brothers grabbed him in a giant three-way bear hug, all of them whooping and hollering. When all the back-patting and ear-cuffing was done, Mal turned to the woman in the group, presumably his sister, who had thus far stood by smiling and shaking her head in amused disdain. Mal picked her up in a big bear hug, making her squeal. Once he had put her back down and released her, he turned to me.

"Sorry I didn't tell you they were coming," he said. "I really didn't expect them this soon."

"It's not a problem," I said with a smile. "Although I would appreciate some introductions," I added with a wink.

"Of course," Mal said, slapping himself up side his head. "Mackenzie Dalton, meet the O'Reilly clan, or at least most of them. This is my dad, Connor, my brothers Ryan and Patrick, and my sister, Colleen."

Propping myself on my crutches, I shook hands with each of them. "And Mrs. O'Reilly?" I asked.

"Josephine stayed behind to hold down the fort along with Mal's other sister, Deirdre," Connor said. "Colleen is the master carpenter in the family, and Deirdre is our master plumber. Since this job doesn't involve any plumbing, Deirdre opted to stay home so my wife wouldn't be alone."

I looked at Patrick and Ryan, my eyebrows raised in question.

"Electrician," Patrick said, raising his hand.

"A more masterful carpenter than my sister here," Ryan said.

Colleen slugged him in his arm and muttered, "You wish."

"Anyway," Connor went on, "I should warn you that Jo and Deirdre have threatened to come out here on their own at a later time," he added, arching his eyebrows at Mal.

"That would be great," Mal said.

"Maybe, maybe not," Ryan said. He looked over at me and explained. "My mother is Jewish, and while she isn't particularly religious, she's got that whole Jewish mother guilt thing down pretty good. And Mal not coming home for the holidays is definite fodder for a guilt trip."

All of the O'Reillys chuckled at this, nodding.

"Well, I'm happy to have this much of the O'Reilly clan here," I said. "Mal has talked about you a lot, and it's nice to be able to put some faces to the names."

"He's talked about you quite a bit, too," Colleen said. She shot Mal a sidelong look, and he gave her back a warning one while he blushed up to his roots.

Eager to get off that subject, I said, "Well, while you're here, you're my guests. Food and drinks are on the house. If any of you want anything at any time, just let one of my staff people know, and they'll get it for you."

"Best job site ever!" Ryan said, and then he and his brother once again did a high five.

Mal reached into a pocket of his jeans and took out his keys, handing them to his dad. "I'm sure you're all tired after the flight here. You can take my car over to my place and get settled in."

"We don't need your car," his dad said. "We rented one of our own. And we're fine with getting right to work on this project."

"Besides," Patrick said, "we'll be in a bar for New Year's Eve. It's the perfect setup."

Mal winced and shot me a look. "Mack is closing her bar at ten that night for a private party," he explained. "And I, for various reasons, need to attend. In fact, I'm going to be living here in the bar for the foreseeable future. So you guys will have full use of my house."

"Does that mean we aren't invited to the private party?" Ryan said, looking at me with puppy-dog eyes. "Despite whatever Malachi here might've told you, we're domesticated, and we can behave."

"Of course, you'd be welcome any time under normal circumstances," I said. "But this party is a bit unusual. And it might prove to be dangerous, as well."

"We O'Reillys aren't afraid of danger," Ryan said boastfully.

"It isn't a game," Mal said. "It's actually part of a murder investigation. And just so you know, it's imperative that none of you mention the fact that I'm a cop to anyone. I didn't think you'd be here this soon and hoped this case would be resolved by the time you arrived. Unfortunately, that didn't happen."

"Ooh," Colleen said, her eyes growing big. "A real-life mystery? Can this trip get any better?"

"Hey, you never know," Patrick said with a shrug. "Several fresh pairs of eyes might help you figure out a mystery."

Mal and I exchanged looks. I didn't know what to tell them, so I simply shrugged. "Fill them in on what's going on," I told Mal. "If they want to be at the party, it's fine by me." I shifted my gaze to the rest of the O'Reilly clan. "Have you had anything for lunch yet?" I asked them.

They shook their heads.

"How about I fix you up something to eat then?"

"That would be great, Mack," Connor said. "Thank you very much."

I turned and headed for the kitchen, leaving the O'Reillys to discuss their future plans among themselves.

After explaining to Debra who the new arrivals were, I had her order them sandwiches, fries, a couple of small pizzas, some cheese curds—a Wisconsin specialty—and an assortment of soft drinks. I went with her to deliver them and wasn't too surprised when Mal took me aside and informed me that his family intended to stay for the private New Year's Eve party, despite the risks.

"I tried my best to discourage them," he told me, "but they see it as some big adventure. They're looking forward to it and think it will be fun." He smiled and shook his head woefully. "My family has a unique way of looking at things," he said almost apologetically. "Who knows? Maybe it will help."

I spent the rest of the day decorating the bar for the party and making sure all the other arrangements were in place. It was a quiet, peaceful day, bereft of any drama. I tried to enjoy it, but it was hard to relax. Underlying my every thought and action was an awareness that the letter writer was out there, angry, and threatening.

On the off chance that we were wrong about the person who was working with Suzanne being a member of the Capone Club, I eyed every customer who came in with a wary, inquisitive eye, trying to determine if I'd seen them here before, and if so, what their behavior had been. No one leaped out at me, which was both encouraging and depressing. If the second person wasn't a stranger I didn't know about, it meant someone close to me, someone I trusted, was a coldhearted, scheming killer. The very thought made my heart ache.

Around one in the morning, the O'Reillys called it a night and settled in for some food and drink. They were an entertaining bunch, laughing, teasing one another, and sharing amusing anecdotes about Mal. I adored all of them.

Mal said good night to them when closing time came, and I sent my staff members out the door at the same time, telling them I'd do the closing cleanup stuff. Tyrese and Nick had both come in that evening, and they generously offered to escort people to their cars. While I was comfortable with Tyrese performing this function, I was less so when it came to Nick. But I wasn't sure how to communicate that fact to Tyrese without offending him.

Mal once again came to my rescue, sensing my discomfort and the cause of it, and offering to accompany Nick and the others as they left. When he returned, he helped me finish the closing duties, working at my side and sharing information about this family. It was a relaxing and fun time, and with the two of us safe behind locked and closed doors, I was actually able to forget all the frightening realities for a short while.

But by the time we headed upstairs to my apartment, it all came crashing back in on me. Tomorrow was going to be a big day.

Chapter 22

New Year's Eve day dawned cold but sunny. As the day wore on, however, a cadre of thick, white clouds rimmed in an ominous gray moved in over the city.

I slept until a little after nine, and once again, Mal had beaten me out of bed, leaving a note explaining that his family was due around nine and they would get straight to work on the elevator project.

He'd left me a pot of coffee, but I felt a little disappointed that we wouldn't be sharing one another's company over breakfast. I whipped myself up some scrambled eggs and toast, and feeling festive over the holiday despite the grim circumstances that would be tainting my party later, I decided to celebrate and cooked up four strips of bacon as well.

The end of this horrific year couldn't come soon enough for me. I just hoped the new one would start out on a happy note, with the letter writer issue resolved once and for all.

After a quick shower, I dressed and headed downstairs just before ten. There was no one in the main bar area yet, but I could hear the raucous laughter and construction-related noises of the O'Reilly clan at work down in the basement. I made my way to the top of the basement stairs, where I found the door—still cockeyed and marked off with warning tape that didn't want to stick—ajar. I poked my head through the opening and saw Ryan and Colleen busy at work cutting wood braced on sawhorses, Mal and Patrick hammering away at some lingering concrete in a wall, and Connor sitting on the bottom step, sipping a cup of coffee and looking at the construction plans.

"Good morning," I hollered down.

A chorus of return greetings shot up to me, and everyone stopped working.

"Have you guys had something to eat?"

"We have," Colleen said. "We had breakfast before we came, and we stopped and got some sinful-looking cinnamon buns to have later as part of our motivation."

Connor raised his mug to me. "You have killer coffee," he said.

Probably not the best choice of words, but I took it. "Thanks," I said. "I've got some stuff to do to get the bar ready to open, but holler if you need anything."

"Will do," Connor said.

They went back to work, and I went off to ready the bar.

Debra, Pete, Linda, and Jon showed up between ten and eleven, and we opened on time. Everyone seemed to be in a bright mood, and there was lots of talk of the party later. The usual customers showed up at their usual times: Joe, Frank, and Cora minutes after we unlocked the door, Carter, Sam, and Stephen a short time later. Holly and Alicia came in for lunch, and they were able to stay on since their bank closed at noon for the holiday.

The Capone Club room filled up, and I was glad to

see that none of the members, other than Sonja, Greg, and Tad, were MIA. I knew why Sonja and Greg weren't there, and I hoped that Tad's failure to show didn't mean that he and Suzanne wouldn't show for the party. Dr. T, Nick, and Tyrese all came in at some point during the afternoon, and Kevin Baldwin rolled in around five.

The day stayed busy, and Mal and his family surfaced around two for lunch and joined the Capone Club members. I hung out with them while they were there, listening along with the rest of the club members as the O'Reillys were grilled about themselves and Mal, and shared the requisite family tales, many of which were designed to embarrass Mal. He took it all in stride and with good humor, though there were a few tense moments when his siblings talked about Mal moving to Milwaukee and almost revealed his real occupation. I'm not sure it would have been a horrible revelation—or that it would have surprised anyone, for that matter—at this point. But in the end, the O'Reillys were able to cover their near slips believably and with entertaining, if incomplete, stories about the prodigal son's departure from the family business.

Linda came in to work at noon, and she was in an upbeat mood, so I once again decided not to mention our prior phone conversation. Pete and Jon both went home at five, relieved by Billy and Rich, respectively, with promises they'd be back for the party. Teddy also came in to work at five, and my part-time, upstairs bartender, Curtis Donovan, came in around seven, even though he wasn't scheduled to work. He was decked out in a Father Time costume, complete with scythe (which I relievedly confirmed as fake at one point), a long, fake beard, and a hooded robe.

"I'm getting a head start on the party," he explained. He sat in with the Capone Club members and sipped on a drink for two hours. Apparently, he was pacing himself, at least for now.

I spent part of the afternoon getting out the hats, confetti, and noisemakers I had ordered for the night. I also put dozens of bottles of champagne on ice so they'd be ready to go by ten.

Despite plenty of signage warning customers of the early closing, the bar was still quite full at nine-thirty. I started making the rounds, apologizing for the closure, and informing people they would need to leave. Most people took the bouncing in good stride, but a few grumbled, griped, and made scenes over getting kicked out of a bar this early, on New Year's Eve of all days.

It took some doing, but by a little before ten, the bar was emptied, and I locked the doors. Teddy Bear had graciously offered to play gatekeeper and stay by the door to let in those who were invited to the party. I gave him a list of invitees and told him to ask me if he had any doubts or questions about anyone.

Debra, who had left earlier when Missy came in to work, had gone home to change into something "more festive." She showed up just after ten wearing a fabulous little red dress that hugged her curvy frame in all the right places. She came without her husband or sons. Her boys were having a New Year's Eve party of their own at home with twenty or so of their closest friends, and Debra's husband had generously offered to stay home and play chaperone. I wondered how much of Debra's decision to come alone was based on the perceived danger of my party, and how much was based on the issues she had going on at home. Though, to be honest, I wasn't sure what was more hazardous, my party or one with twenty-plus rowdy, teenage boys.

Missy had brought along a pants outfit with a tight-fitting top that accentuated her generous curves, and she changed into it in the bathroom bar. Like Debra, she had chosen to attend alone. "My parents have the kids because they think I'm working," she said to me when I asked if she had a guest coming. "Being able to party for a change without worrying about the kids is such a treat. Why complicate that by bringing a date?"

Linda hadn't brought anything else to wear and didn't go anywhere to change. She had on her usual black pants and white blouse, though she did don a pair of sparkly glasses with the coming year's date on them. Since she was on my list of suspects, I was actually glad she hadn't left. I had a fear of someone leaving the bar and returning later armed to the teeth and ready to wreak havoc. With her brother in mind, I asked her if anyone was going to join her.

"Nope," she said with a forced smile. "It's just me, as usual."

Joe and Frank Signoriello had gone home around five "to take a nap so we can keep up with you young'uns," Joe had said. They returned at half past ten, the two of them dapperly dressed in matching black suits, though they had parted sartorial ways with the colors of their shirts and ties. Joe was wearing a blue shirt and a lavender and blue striped tie, Frank was wearing a yellow shirt with a solid gray tie.

Mal and his family had quit work on the elevator area an hour before I closed, and his dad and siblings had left to go clean up and change clothes. Mal stayed behind but did borrow my key long enough to go upstairs to my apartment so he could shower and change.

"I'm afraid I might be underdressed for tonight's shindig," he said as I handed him the key.

"There's no dress code, but if you want to jazz yourself up a bit, there are some sports coats and suits hanging in the closet in my dad's room. One of the suits, a gray pinstripe, I think he wore two times in his whole life. You're close to his size, and you're welcome to wear it, or anything else you find in there. One of my New Year's resolutions is to get rid of his clothes and some other stuff, and give it all to Goodwill. So any clothes you take will save me some work."

"That's very kind of you to offer," Mal said. "But won't it bother you seeing someone else wearing your father's clothes?"

"Actually, no," I said. And it was the truth. "My father was the kind of man who hated to see things go to waste, and who would literally give the shirt off his back to someone if it would help. He had a kind and generous spirit, and knowing his stuff has benefited someone else, however minor that benefit may be, feels completely appropriate and fitting."

Mal cocked his head to the side, eyeing me with doubtful suspicion.

"I swear it, Mal," I said with a smile. "Taking some of his clothes would be doing me a favor. It would be as if some small piece of him is still here. I have a sweater he used to wear a lot, and I'm keeping it. It smells like him, and it has some particular memories associated with it. But the rest of it . . ." I shrugged. "Please, take what you want. Knowing some of it ended up with someone like you makes it even better for me."

Mal studied me for another few seconds and must

have deemed me sincere because he nodded. "All right then," he said.

When he came back downstairs forty minutes later, he was wearing his own jeans, a light blue dress shirt, and my father's navy blue sports coat.

"This fits like it was tailor-made for you," I said, running a hand up the left sleeve of the sports coat.

"His stuff does fit me well," he admitted with a grudging nod. "Are you sure you're okay with me wearing it?"

"Positive."

I sent Mal to the door to help Teddy Bear in case there were any issues with people who wanted to come into the bar but weren't part of the group of invitees.

I headed upstairs and changed into a dress, a simple, knee-length, emerald green number with three-quarter-length sleeves that went well with my red hair. After applying a touch of makeup, I headed back downstairs and positioned myself behind the bar, relieving Billy of his duties. Since the bar was directly across from the front door, it gave me the perfect spot for watching to see who was arriving.

A few minutes later, my hired bartender and cook showed up. Their names—Tom Summers and Drew Johnson—were on the list I'd given Teddy, and he directed them to me once they were inside. I eyed both men closely. Summers had a mustache, a bushy beard, a hooked nose, dark brown eyes, and shaggy, brown hair that hung to his shoulders. He was wearing a baseball cap that had HAPPY NEW YEAR emblazoned across the front of it.

Drew Johnson sported strawberry blond hair pulled back into a small ponytail. He, too, had a mustache and beard, though his beard was a goatee. He wore the same baseball cap Summers had on and was also sporting a pair of glasses with a tortoiseshell frame. His build, in contrast to Summer's tall, slim physique, was portly.

I greeted the men, tasting the flavor of their voices, and then directed them to their respective stations, giving each of them a quick orientation. After telling them to let me know if they needed anything, I left them to their duties and went to mingle with my guests.

Over the next half hour, all the members of the Capone Club showed up, except for Sonja and Greg. Cora had verified for me earlier in the day that Greg Nash had indeed bought a ticket to Grand Cayman on a flight that left at four o'clock that afternoon, and while she couldn't promise me that Greg Nash was the person who had used it, someone had boarded that plane using his ticket.

Holly and Alicia arrived together, both of them wearing little black dresses. Holly cozied up to her beau, Carter, right away, whereas Alicia made a beeline for Billy. Alicia had a mad crush on Billy, as did half or more of the women who came into the bar. It wasn't hard to understand why. Billy was tall and handsome, with café au lait skin, green eyes with long lashes, a charming personality, and some serious smarts. I felt torn as I watched Alicia sneak goo-goo eyes at Billy, knowing that Whitney was supposed to be coming. I hoped Whitney would show up because she was key to my plan, but for Alicia's sake I found myself wishing she'd be a no-show.

Unfortunately for Alicia, Whitney did show up, her pert little nose in the air as she entered the bar, as if the place reeked of something terrible. She zeroed in on Billy right away, rushing over to him, looking down her nose at Alicia, and then wrapping herself around Billy's arm. She eyed the other guests with disdain, as if she was afraid someone might touch her and give her cooties.

Tad arrived a little before eleven, and I was relieved to see that my gambit had worked because Suzanne was with him. She was a homely woman, with a long, horsey face, gray eyes that were small and set too close together, and thin, liver-colored lips that she tried to make look plumper with some artful lipstick and lip-liner applications. She was tall and thin, her hair a perfect shade of coppery gold that only accentuated her sallow complexion. Despite physical attributes that might have made other women self-conscious, Suzanne carried herself with authority, regality, and a dash of pompousness. She was obviously a woman of means, someone who knew her way in the world and was used to getting her way in the world—and, if we were right, someone who had no compunction about taking people out of this world.

Tad looked incredibly handsome at her side, dressed in a tailored black suit with a white shirt, though he had added a touch of whimsy with a red, white, and blue star-spangled tie. I assumed the tie was his addition, because Suzanne struck me as the type of person who had no sense of humor, unless creating taunting, deadly scavenger hunts counted. The way Suzanne wrapped a possessive hand around Tad's arm gave me the distinct impression that she considered him another one of her prized possessions, something to show off, and a reflection of how wonderful she was.

Despite her haughty posturing, whenever Suzanne spoke to anyone, she came across as warm, friendly, and polite. I watched her socialize with Joe and Frank, who did a remarkable job of hiding their loathing, and then with Carter and Holly. Both times, she seemed genuine and warm, and she carried the bulk of the conversation, while Tad stood quietly at her side doing his job: looking stunningly handsome.

After chatting with Carter and Holly for a few minutes, Suzanne steered Tad to the bar, where the two of them ordered drinks. Once they had them, they made their way to a table where Cora was seated with Tiny and a frustrated-looking Alicia, who had retreated after falling victim to Whitney's withering glares. Suzanne and Tad settled in, and a moment later, laughter emanated from Cora, Tiny, and Alicia, apparently amused by something Suzanne had said. Their laughter sounded sincere and unaffected, which piqued my curiosity. Granted, Suzanne was a well-practiced socialite who knew how to engage people, but was it possible to come across so warm and genuine if she was a scheming, cold-hearted killer? Was she putting on an act? Or had we figured this thing all wrong?

In sharp contrast to Suzanne, Whitney, who was dressed in a glittery gold-lamé dress that hugged her body and matching gold high heels, had looked out of place and uncomfortable from the moment she set foot in the bar. Billy had introduced her to several people, and the smile she gave each person she met looked pained and forced. Eventually, she steered him off to a corner of the bar near where I was standing, listening in to a discussion between Joe, Frank, and Stephen McGregor about the merits, or lack thereof, of modern educational techniques. The bar TV was on, tuned to a station where we could watch the ball drop at midnight, but the sound was muted for now. Music was playing on the bar's sound system at a volume loud enough to be festive but not drown out conversations. Though Billy and Whitney were standing about six feet away, I was able to overhear their conversation above all the other ruckus.

"I can't believe this is what you're wearing," Whitney said in a side whisper that reeked with disapproval.

Billy had changed out of the jeans and white shirt he'd been wearing behind the bar earlier into black dress pants and a pale green dress shirt that complemented his eyes. The shirt was unbuttoned at the neck and the sleeves were rolled up, revealing his muscular forearms. I thought he looked handsome and hot as hell.

"We have certain standards to maintain," Whitney went on in her hushed but condescending tone. "You're going to have to learn to do better."

Billy's lips grew thin and tight, but he kept his smile on his face and kissed Whitney on the cheek, an action she tolerated.

"You're going to have to learn to love me as I am, Whitney," he said. "Don't try to turn me into your parents. I have my own standards, and I'm quite happy with them."

You go, Billy! I thought.

His tone had been firm but polite, not angry or chastising. At first, Whitney merely stared at him in shocked disbelief. She clearly wasn't used to being put in her place, and eventually her expression morphed into a thundercloud. She stuttered for a few seconds before grabbing Billy's arm in a viselike grip and hauling him off toward the neighboring room in the new addition.

Nick and Tyrese had arrived together, both of them dressed in jeans and polo shirts. Mal's family arrived a little before eleven. All of them were freshly showered and wearing clean, albeit casual clothes. The men had on jeans and pullover sweaters; Colleen was wearing beige slacks and a brown sweater over a white blouse.

So far, it was an interesting mix of people, dress, and conversations. Everyone was mingling and mixing, moving from one table to another or simply circulating in the room. There was an air of expectation, a nervous energy to the crowd that hinted at things to come. That excitation ramped up a notch or two for me when more guests arrived, two of whom weren't on the list of guests I'd given to Teddy.

Chapter 23

I saw Teddy waving at me from over by the door when I was chatting with the Signoriello brothers, and after excusing myself, I got up and went over to see what he needed. He was standing with the door slightly ajar, holding it so it wouldn't open farther.

"What's up, Teddy?" I asked.

"This woman outside said she was invited to come to the party, but her name isn't on the list."

I peered out through the crack of open door and saw Courtney Metcalfe standing there. I hadn't put her name on the list because I wasn't sure she'd show up despite Duncan's plans to invite her. Plus, I wanted to see and greet her when she arrived.

"You're that bartender I've seen on the news, the one who was working with Duncan Albright," she said.

"Actually, I'm the owner of this bar," I said, swallowing down my initial shock. "And you're Courtney, the woman who stood him up at the altar."

Now it was her turn to look shocked. "Ah, I see Duncan has told you about me."

An ironic statement, considering my recent discussions with Duncan on the matter.

"Duncan invited me to come to this party," Courtney said. She leaned to one side and peered past me to the interior of the bar. "Quite a crowd you have already. Is Duncan here yet?"

"Not yet," I said through tight lips.

She let forth with a petulant sigh and looked back at me. "May I come in, please? It's cold out here."

"Sure, come on in." Teddy opened the door to let her in, and then closed and locked it again behind her. "Make yourself at home," I said with a forced smile, and then I crutched away from her, heading for Cora's table.

Courtney stood just inside the door, eyeing the crowd. I settled into a chair, and when Cora leaned over to say something to me, I held up a hand to shush her. I glanced over at the bar and saw Tom Summer staring at Courtney. I turned back and watched Courtney scope out the room, curious to see if there was a hint of recognition on her face.

Whitney got up from the table where she was sitting with Billy and made her way over to Courtney.

"Courtney!" Whitney cooed. The two of them exchanged a brief hug and then did the brushing kiss thing on one another's cheeks. "I didn't know you were coming to this," Whitney said.

"I almost didn't," Courtney said with a tone of disgust. "I don't think that redheaded bartender woman wanted to let me in."

"Well, you're in now, so come over and have a seat."

"First, I need a drink." Courtney removed her coat, draping it over her arm. Then she headed for the bar with Whitney on her tail. I kept shifting my gaze from Courtney to Tom, watching them both closely. She ordered a drink—a cherry-orange sparkler—then turned to Whitney and started talking again.

"I don't see Duncan here," Courtney said.

Tom Summers spilled some of the champagne he was pouring.

"He may show up later," Whitney said. "In the meantime, come and join me and Billy."

Summers finished the drink and slid it across the bar to Courtney, who took it without a second look at him. Then she and Whitney turned and headed back to the table where Billy was seated.

I looked back at Tom Summers, my eyebrows raised. I gave a nod of my head toward the kitchen, and then got up and headed that way. Summers followed.

As soon as the door closed behind us, I said, "I'm surprised she accepted your invitation."

"I'm not," Duncan grumbled, "given how hard she's been hounding me." He scratched irritably at his beard.

"Be careful," I said, nodding toward his chin. "You don't want to loosen that thing."

"It itches like crazy."

"Isabel did her job well with it," I said. "No one has recognized you."

Isabel was a friend of Duncan's family who did theater and stage makeup. At one time, she had worked in Hollywood, but love and a man brought her back to Milwaukee, where she employed her skills for theater groups. She had also employed her skills for me and Duncan a couple of times before so we could get together without anyone being the wiser.

"And not only is Courtney here," I went on, "she's wearing Opium perfume."

Duncan frowned, though it looked rather odd since his eyebrows were fake also. "Courtney may be annoyingly persistent," he said, "and she has her faults, but I honestly don't think she's a killer. A cheater, yes, but not a killer," he added, giving me a hint about what had gone wrong with their wedding plans.

"Who is this Courtney person?" Drew Johnson asked. Only his name wasn't Drew Johnson any more than Duncan's was Tom Summers. Drew Johnson was really Arthur Cook, aka Arty to those who knew him well. He, like Duncan, was a police detective, and a patron of my bar. Having the two of them come here in disguise posing as a hired bartender and cook was part of the night's plan. Since the fact that I was working with the police was now public knowledge, Duncan and I had decided to share the details of the letter writer case with a few of Duncan's trusted coworkers. Arty had been one of them, and since he had worked as a short-order cook when he was younger, it was decided to bring him in as the hired cook. Given that his real last name was Cook, it seemed like fate.

"She's Duncan's ex-fiancée," I explained. "She stood him up at the altar, and apparently, she's been stalking him ever since, trying to get him back."

"Oh," Arty said, his eyes growing big. He bit his lip and went back to his cooking duties, deciding, perhaps wisely, not to engage any further in this particular conversation.

"As long as we're on the topic of surprise guests," Duncan said, "I should probably tell you that Jimmy may show up."

I felt a sudden panic, wondering if he had told Jimmy about the letter writer. But Duncan seemed to read my thoughts.

"Relax, I didn't tell him," he said. "I still think you're barking up the wrong tree with that one, my little bloodhound, but I'm willing to keep an open mind."

I flashed him a smile of gratitude.

"So what's your plan from here on out?" Duncan asked.

"For now, I'm going to let everyone mingle and chat until midnight. After we toast in the New Year, I'm going to initiate a discussion about the letter writer, tell everyone that an arrest is imminent based on some forensic evidence we found in one of the clues. Then we can sit back and see if anyone does or says anything incriminating. I'm curious to see how Suzanne will react. Maybe I can catch her or someone else in a lie."

"Are you going to come right out and ask anyone if they did it?" Duncan said with a curious smile.

I shook my head. "I don't think so. The guilty party is bound to lie, and even if I pick up on that, it's not like my word is enough evidence to convict anyone."

Duncan chuckled.

"What?" I said, feeling a bit offended. "Do you think it's a stupid plan?"

"No, not at all. I'm just amused by how much you sound like a cop."

"Well, I've been hanging around enough of them lately. It's bound to rub off."

"If any cops are going to rub off on you, I want it to be me," Duncan said with more than a hint of salaciousness in his voice. He winked at me, kissed the tip of my nose, and then added, "In the meantime, we best get back out there and stir the pot, don't you think?"

The party was in full swing when we went back out front. Everyone seemed to be having a good time, and the conversations were flowing as freely as the food and drink. One of my beer taps ran dry, and I asked Duncan if he would run down to the basement to replace the empty keg, something he'd learned to do during his undercover time playing bartender.

"I'd do it, but I hate negotiating those basement stairs or those kegs with these crutches," I told him. "I'll tend bar until you get back."

"No problem. Be right back."

As the final hour of the year approached, a few other guests arrived. One of them was Dr. T, who came with a tall, thin man she introduced as Roger. At first I thought he was her date, but Dr. T later explained that he was a cousin of hers, a medical student who was staying with her for a while.

On the heels of Dr. T's arrival, Jimmy Patterson showed up. Based on my conversation with Duncan earlier, I had let Teddy know he might show up and to allow him in. I happened to be standing by the door when he arrived.

"Hey, Mack," Jimmy said, as Teddy let him in and then closed and locked the door behind him. He scanned the room. "Looks like you have a good crowd here."

"Indeed, we do," I said, putting on my best front. "Please make yourself at home. Food and drinks are all on the house. Can I get you something?"

"A club soda with lime would be great," he said.

"No alcohol?"

He shook his head. "No, thanks. But I will have some of that pizza. And I'll get my own drink." He eyed my crutches with a sympathetic look. "You appear to be a bit compromised at the moment." With that, he headed for the food that was spread out on the bar.

I wasn't altogether comfortable with having Jimmy there—a cop as a potential second foe seemed far more dangerous to me—but it served the purpose for the evening. Plus, I was grateful that Duncan was willing to at least consider the possibility of Jimmy's involvement. Given that I knew how much Jimmy disliked me, his presence made me that much more suspicious of him. What other motivation would he have had to come to the party unless he was curious about how much we knew?

I watched Duncan, aka Tom, closely as Jimmy approached the bar. Duncan did nothing to greet Jimmy other than ask him if he could get him a drink. Duncan had been talking to the guests as little as possible and using a fake voice all night to go along with his disguise, dropping his usual Scottish lilt, and speaking a few notes higher than usual. His voice still tasted like chocolate to me, but the flavor was noticeably different, with a saccharine undertone that I'd never tasted before. Duncan served Jimmy his drink and then moved to the far end of the bar while Jimmy helped himself to the food. Once Jimmy had a full plate, he carried it over to a table where Nick and Tyrese were seated and settled in. If Jimmy had recognized Duncan at all, he was covering it well.

The final arrival was my surprise guest of the evening. It was Clay Sanders.

"What on earth are you doing here?" I said to him as he walked up to the bar. "Shouldn't you be home in bed?"

"I had no idea you were having a private party," he said. "Apparently, I wasn't on the guest list," he added with feigned hurt.

"Only because you just got out of the hospital. Of course, you're welcome here any time."

"I had to get out of the house. The walls were closing in on me."

"Well, you picked an interesting time to come. If things go according to plan, I'm hoping to out the letter writer tonight, and whoever is helping her."

"Really?" Clay said, his eyebrows arching with surprise and interest. "Have you winnowed down the potential suspects any?"

"We have," I said, and then I whispered in his ear, giving him the names of the remaining suspects. "They're all here," I concluded.

"Then I guess I better settle in." He eyed the food spread at the bar. "My diet is kind of restricted right now. I don't suppose you have anything mild and soft."

"I have some leftover chicken noodle soup in the fridge. How about I heat some up for you? I can fix you some toast to go with it."

"That would be fantastic," he said with a grateful smile.

He made his way over to a table where Whitney, Courtney, Billy, Tad, and Suzanne had congregated. I suspected his seating choice was intentional, since he knew we suspected Suzanne as the letter writer.

I went into the kitchen, and with a little help from Arty, I made Clay's soup and toast. While the soup was heating, Arty said, "How's it going out there?"

"So far, so good. Everyone seems to be enjoying themselves."

"When are you going to start poking people with your stick?"

"After midnight. Once the toasts are made and the ball has dropped, I'll drop mine."

"I see Jimmy Patterson made it."

I nodded. "Did Duncan tell you what we discovered about him?"

Arty shrugged. "He told me Patterson is moonlighting as a security guard for the Collier warehouses on the waterfront. And he told me that Patterson doesn't like or trust you, and that the feeling is mutual."

"That about sums it up," I said.

"I have to say, I think you're wrong about Patterson," Arty said. I shot him a look of exasperation, and he held up a hand. "But I'm willing to keep an open mind," he added quickly.

"Jimmy doesn't know anything about you and Duncan being here, does he?"

"Not as far as I know. The only people who are in on it are me, Duncan, and Holland."

"Chief Holland knows what's going on?"

Arty nodded. "Duncan wanted to be totally open about it all. Plus, I think he wanted Holland to know about this threat, so he'd understand why you were so upset about that business that appeared in the paper."

I didn't like the fact that Holland was part of this, but I supposed it couldn't be helped. "Thanks for doing this, Arty," I said.

"No problem."

"Can I ask you a favor?"

"Sure."

"Would you carry this soup and toast out to Clay Sanders for me? I can't manage it very well with these crutches."

"Happy to. I was about to go out there and check on the status of the food bar anyway."

I followed Arty to Clay's table, and as Arty set the tray of food down, I grabbed a nearby chair and dragged

it over. Then I sat down, positioning myself between
Suzanne and Whitney.

The sound of saxophone music came through loud
and strong, telling me that both women were wearing
their Opium perfume. I subdued the synesthetic response as best I could and tried to monitor any other
reactions I might have to them. The women were discussing some dress shop—Tad and Billy both looked
bored to tears—and when there was a lull in the conversation, I thanked them all for coming. Then I
dropped my little bombshell about the letter writer by
telling Tad that the cops had found some trace evidence that we felt certain was left accidentally, and
that we hoped to catch the person soon—tonight, in
fact. I watched the reactions of all three women closely
as I said this. Whitney's expression was one of bore-
dom, and irritation that she had to be in this awful
place. I wondered if she knew about the letter writer.
Had Billy clued her in?

Courtney simply looked bemused, though she was
scrutinizing me closely.

Suzanne's interest was piqued immediately, however. "Tad told me about this letter writer thing," she
said. "Some person who is taunting you?" She said
this in a dismissive tone, as if it was no big deal. And I
noticed that her voice triggered a curious reaction
in me. I saw small colored dots raining down, like
hundreds of pieces of colorful confetti. But I also
got a taste of something metallic. Never before had
anyone's voice triggered two reactions at once. Typically, I tasted something—that was always the case with
men—though with some women I got a visual manifestation instead.

"More than just taunting me," I said. "Whoever is
behind it has killed two people, two people who were

part of our crime-solving group here at the bar. One of the victims was an employee of mine."

"Really?" Suzanne said, but rather than shocked, she sounded amused. She looked over at Tad. "You know how I feel about you spending time in this place." She did a quick glance around the room with a look of distaste. "And now I find out that it's not only an inconvenience for me when you come here, but dangerous as well?"

Tad looked annoyed for a second, but he quickly morphed his expression into one of patient tolerance. "You don't understand how it works," he said to Suzanne. "This group, and Mack here with her special talents, are really good at solving crimes. You know how much I enjoy a good mystery," he said in an appealing tone.

"You could just read some mystery novels," Whitney said, sounding bored.

"Special talents?" Courtney said. She arched one brow at me.

"And as busy as you are at work," Suzanne went on to Tad, "you're away from me a lot already." She reached over and put a perfectly manicured hand on his arm. "We have so little time together as it is." Suzanne switched her fawning gaze from her husband to me, flashing me a smile that looked forced and phony. "You understand, don't you, Ms. Dalton?"

Tad looked over at me and rolled his eyes toward his wife, giving me a *see what I have to put up with* look.

"I suppose," I said to Suzanne, not wanting to placate her. If anything, I wanted to rile her. "And please, call me Mack. But I think it's important with any couple that they occasionally do things apart from one another, particularly if they have different, separate interests."

Suzanne's expression turned hard, enough so that I had to fight an urge to rear back away from her.

Courtney stayed silent but continued to stare at me.

"Tad has mentioned to me before that you have some kind of special talent, Ms. Dalton. In fact, he's gone on at length about it," Suzanne said, rolling her eyes. "I confess that I tune him out most of the time, but I do recall him saying you're like a bloodhound, or something like that, though I'm sure he didn't mean to call you a dog." She punctuated this with a brittle, artificial laugh. "So tell me, Ms. Dalton, just what is it that you supposedly do?"

Courtney put her elbows on the table and leaned in closer, still staring.

Suzanne's blatant refusal to use my name as I had requested told me I was getting to her, so despite my annoyance with her and her comments, I pushed on. "I have a disorder of sorts, a neurological thing that both heightens and overlaps my senses," I explained. "So I experience all of my senses in more than one way. For instance, all of you women are wearing Opium perfume. I know this not only because of the smell, but also because I hear a distinctive sound whenever I smell that particular perfume. It's like that with all my senses. Sometimes sounds will come with a taste; sometimes I have a visual manifestation."

I had Suzanne's full attention now, and even Whitney had refocused. Courtney's stare hadn't wavered.

"And just how do you use this to solve crimes?" Suzanne asked, her voice rife with skepticism.

"Mack is really smart and intuitive, and she's like a human lie detector," Tad said. He sounded proud and a little awed when he said this, and it seemed to annoy Suzanne. She squirmed and shifted in her seat and let out a huff of irritation. Then I realized it might not be annoyance, but fear. If Suzanne hadn't been aware of this particular aspect of my synesthesia before, she might be reviewing and second-guessing our entire conversation along about now.

"Yes, yes, Tad," she said with an exasperated sigh. "I've heard you go on before about how wonderful Ms. Dalton is." She uttered this with an exaggeratedly exalted tone that left no doubt how she felt about it.

"Well, I *am* quite intelligent," I said without modesty. "More so than the person sending those letters. And the writer is about to discover just how much smarter I and the police are, because we've found some trace evidence that's going to be critical. The letter writer has been outsmarted." I punctuated this statement with a smug, self-assured smile.

Suzanne leaned back in her chair. If she was worried, it didn't show. She simply looked as if she was deep in thought.

"Little things like perfume, a trace of it, left on a car armrest, might be enough to give someone away," I said.

Suzanne narrowed her eyes at me, and there was a tiny muscle flinch in her cheek.

Whitney said, "So this person you're talking about is sending you letters with clues, or something like that, to see if this disorder you have works?"

"Something like that." I briefly described what some of the letters had said or contained, using adjectives like *ridiculously simple* and *commonplace* to describe some of the clues. "It's really not been much of a challenge," I concluded, and with this, Suzanne shot me a withering look. I decided to push her buttons a little harder. "It's no wonder people like Billy and Tad, smart men with solid morals, are interested in following what's going on. If the letter writer was hoping to break up the Capone Club and the crime-solving tactics we are using, they have failed miserably. It's only served to pique the interest of the participants that much more."

"But this person has killed people?" Whitney said, looking aghast. Her horror seemed genuine, and I now knew that Billy hadn't told her about any of it.

"Yes, and for that this person will pay a very dear price, I promise you." I said this with a high level of conviction, hoping to rattle Suzanne even more. I was moving away from my suspicion that Whitney might also be involved, based on her reactions. Much as I disliked her, I had a strong gut feeling she wasn't a part of it.

Courtney I couldn't gauge. She looked intrigued by the conversation, but also amused.

Suzanne, however, was another story. She was clearly growing uncomfortable with the tack our talk had taken. She was squirming in her seat, her hands wringing in her lap, her face drawn into a tight, angry frown.

"You sound quite sure of yourself," she said. "Such arrogance and conceit are rarely rewarded."

I was about to come back at her with another taunt, but her expression suddenly morphed into one of pleasure and delight. It almost made her pretty. Her gaze shifted, too, as she looked around the room with obvious distaste.

"Have you had enough of this silliness, Tad, dear?" she said. "I think it's time we left." She rose from her seat and shot me a haughty look.

"We can't leave before midnight," Tad said, and for a brief second there was a flint-hard glint in Suzanne's eyes as she looked at him. But it was there and gone in a flash.

"Let me give you the nickel tour," Tad said. "You

should see the Capone Club room. Mack has done a fabulous job with it. It's quite cozy—with intimate seating, a lovely fireplace, and bookshelves filled with books about criminal science and mystery-solving techniques."

Suzanne was clearly not happy with this suggestion, and she opened her mouth, presumably to decline the offer. But before she got a word out, Tad added, "Come on, Suze. Give it a chance. You promised you would." He sweetened this plea by walking over and draping an arm over her shoulders, and then giving her a kiss on her temple. This display of affection appeared to soften her some, though I could still sense the hardness in her just beneath the surface. She glanced at her watch, let out a disdainful sigh, and said, "If you insist."

With a contemptuous sneer of a smile at me, she snaked an arm around Tad's waist and snuggled up against him. He steered the two of them away from the table and toward the newer section of the bar.

Once they were out of earshot, Whitney gave me an intrigued, calculating look. "I do believe Suzanne is jealous of you, Mack," she said, following the comment with a little sniff of derision. "Interesting."

Courtney, still silent, frowned.

While I probably should have been put out by Whitney's belittling behavior, I let it pass. I had bigger fish to fry. "Do you think so?" I said. "That surprises me. Why would a woman of Suzanne's means be jealous of any other women?"

"You're suggesting that men, including Tad, can be bought," Whitney said, a devilish gleam in her eye. "Oh, don't get me wrong, plenty of them can be. Women too. But not all of them. And Tad . . ." She made an equivocal face and waggled her hands. "He's one of those guys who falls somewhere on the fence. He likes Suzanne's money well enough, no doubt about that. But he's a smart guy who I think wants and needs something more, something that Suzanne can't give him. And Suzanne Collier is known for being intolerant of things that don't go her way."

Billy, who had sat through the entire conversation looking embarrassed, said, "Whitney, stop."

"What do you mean?" I said, anxious for her to go on. The more of her true nature Billy saw, the better.

Whitney drew in her lower lip, as if she was trying to suck back the words she was about to say, but I could tell from her expression that she was dying to dish some dirt. She leaned in closer and dropped her voice down to a conspiratorial level. "There are rumors about Suzanne and her temper," she said. "I've seen her go off on people before, and it's a scary sight. Money does that to you, you know."

This struck me as a rare bit of insight for Whitney, and I started to think there might be hope for her, after all. But then she kept going.

"Of course, only weak, stupid people with money have that problem," she clarified in a haughty tone. "There are certain responsibilities and rights that come with that sort of wealth, and if you don't handle it and the people around you with the proper level of discipline and direction, everything can backfire."

Billy suddenly shot his chair back and got up. "I need another drink," he said, and then he hurried off toward the bar.

Whitney watched him leave, sighing heavily. "I've been trying to teach this concept to Billy, to make him understand that wealth puts you on a different plane, but he insists on groveling with all manner of low people." She paused and looked around the room. "I mean, come on, this job he has here. What is up with that? He doesn't need to work here. And mingling with the sort of lowlifes who frequent a place like this will only cast him in an unfavorable light. He needs to start acting and behaving the way his station in life dictates."

I gaped at her, dumbstruck, trying to determine if she was truly so blinded by her classism that she couldn't see how insulting and crass her comments were.

"Billy loves what he does here," I said. "And he's very good at it."

Whitney had taken a sip of her drink, and with my last comment, she nearly spit it out. "Good at it?" she echoed with blatant skepticism. "Good at what? Good at passing out booze to people with no life? Good at chatting up loose women, and begging for tips, and doling out liquid to help people forget how miserable they are. Yeah, right."

"Billy doesn't have to beg for tips," I told her, feeling my ire rise. "In fact, he makes more in tips than any bartender who has ever worked here. His customers love him." And then, after a split second of trying to convince myself not to go there, to stay on the high road, I went wading in the mucky end of the pool, simply because Whitney and her condescending, holier-than-you-and-everyone-else attitude had ticked me off.

"The women customers in particular love him," I went on, and I had the satisfaction of seeing Whitney's patronizing, pompous smile fade a smidge. "They flirt with him unrelentingly, though Billy seems to enjoy it well enough, because he dishes it right back at them. The women just eat it up. Believe me when I tell you that Billy knows how to impress people. And while I'm sure he'll likely make more money once he's done with school and starts working as a lawyer, he does quite well with what he makes here. It's helped to put him through law school."

Whitney looked exasperated, the face of someone who just can't understand why no one gets it. "But he doesn't have to do it that way," she grumbled. "I've told him I can help, but he—"

"He wants to do it on his own," I said, cutting her off. "He's a proud, independent man, Whitney, and you, of all people, should respect and value that in him. If you can't see what a wonderful person he is just the way he is, then you shouldn't be marrying him."

With that, I grabbed my crutches and got up from the table as fast as my casted leg would let me.

Chapter 24

As the final hour of the year wore down, the food and drink kept flowing. Clearly New Year's Eve wasn't about making friends. After ticking off Whitney and Suzanne, and having who knew what effect on Courtney, I moved on to some of the other guests, feeling as if I was poking sticks into the ground of a mine field. I hadn't planned to do this until after midnight, but now that I'd started, I felt unable to stop. I made the rounds, settling in at tables and joining a few standing groups of folks, each time mentioning how we were closing in on the letter writer because some trace evidence had been found that would lead us to the culprit, and how I hoped to expose the suspect later on that evening.

At the table where Sam, Carter, Holly, and Alicia were sitting, my pronouncement was met with badgering pleas to reveal what it was we had found. I told them I didn't want to share the information yet, because I didn't want to say the wrong thing and risk a lawsuit.

Carter gave up begging first, telling me that I had

a knack for creating suspense and should consider trying my hand at writing a mystery novel. Alicia and Holly didn't give in so easily, and they took turns making guesses while I sat there silently, giving them my best Mona Lisa smile.

Sam was by far the most persistent of the group, claiming it was unfair to tease them like this. He even tried using some logical arguments with me about how they as a group might be able to strengthen the evidence by looking at it from their experienced, crime-solving perspective. When I finally got up from their table to move on to the next group, Holly, Carter, and Alicia looked amused and curious. Sam just looked frustrated, and even a little bit angry.

My next quarry was going to be Nick, who was sitting at the bar chatting with Missy, whose face looked like that of a trapped animal. Missy isn't a bright girl, but she's got it all going for her in the looks department, and as such, she attracts a lot of men, most of whom get brushed off rather quickly. Judging from the pained expression on her face, her conversation with Nick wasn't a run-of-the-mill flirtation or she would have dumped him and moved on already.

I eased over in their direction. Nick had his back to me, so he didn't see me coming, allowing me a chance to eavesdrop on their conversation. I heard Duncan's name come up, and then mine.

"He's all wrong for her," Nick was saying. "Mack needs someone who will take care of her, worship her, be there whenever she needs something. This craziness with this letter writer is a classic example. How can Duncan not be here all the time with that going on?"

Nick didn't know that Duncan had arranged for

someone—albeit not himself—to be here as much as possible by setting up the situation with me and Mal.

I cleared my throat as I closed in, and when Nick turned around and saw me, he blushed. I wondered if the color was because he was worried that I had overheard him, or simply because of my presence. I leaned toward the former, only because I hadn't seen Nick blush on other occasions when he was around me.

"Missy," I said, "I wonder if you could do me a favor? The ginger ale soda gun is spitting and needs a new canister hooked up. I'd do it myself, but negotiating those basement stairs is a bit tricky for me these days. Would you mind?"

Missy looked like she not only wouldn't mind, she'd be delighted to do anything I asked of her, as long as it allowed her to escape from Nick. "I'm on it," she said, sliding off her stool. "Can I use your keys?"

"It's not locked. I sent Duncan down there earlier and never locked it back up again."

She nodded and hurried off, looking relieved. I made a mental note to remember that the dead ginger ale canister wasn't really empty and could be hooked back up again later. Then I slid onto the stool Missy had vacated and smiled at Nick.

"Are you having a good time?" I asked him.

"Sure. It was really nice of you to do this, Mack."

"Well, I had an ulterior motive when I planned it."

"Really?" he said with a quizzical smile.

I nodded. "I wanted to provide a safe place for everyone to gather tonight while that lunatic letter writer is still on the loose."

"Lunatic?" Nick echoed. "Do you think the person doing this is crazy?"

"Crazy and careless," I told him. He looked skeptical.

"I mean, come on, you'd have to be crazy to kill people that way, and even though the person writing the letters and coming up with those clues thinks he's being clever, he's made some dumb, stupid mistakes. His days—perhaps his hours—are numbered. I intend to expose the person involved later tonight." I used the male pronoun intentionally. If Nick was involved in the scheme, I wanted him to feel as if I was describing him personally.

"You're playing with fire, Mack," Nick said. He looked troubled. "I don't think you should dismiss this person so easily. It's dangerous to underestimate people."

I gave him a pointed look. "Yes, it is. Me included. And that's where this letter-writing maniac has erred." He frowned and sighed. "As have you," I added.

"Me?"

"Yes. I heard what you said to Missy a moment ago, about how you think I need someone to take care of me. But you're wrong. I'm quite capable of taking care of myself."

"I didn't mean—"

I held up a hand to stop him. "I know what you meant, Nick. And I appreciate your concern. But it's not necessary. I'm fine." And then I made my final parry, driving my sword straight into his heart. "Duncan and I are fine, too," I lied. "In fact, we are better than ever."

Nick said nothing for a moment, his forehead creased. He pulled at his chin. "What about Mal?"

"It was a nice run with him, but my heart belongs to Duncan. We were never really apart anyway. We just pretended we were for the benefit of the letter writer.

Can I get you another drink? I have a great one I call
Sweet Revenge."

After fixing a drink for what appeared to be a
flabbergasted Nick, I moved on to a table where Kevin
Baldwin was sitting—and flirting—with my bartender
Curtis. Linda was with them, as was Dr. T and her
cousin, Roger. Sam had abandoned his earlier table
and had joined this group instead, and they were
listening with rapt attention to something he was telling them. Once again, I came up from behind, giving
myself a chance to eavesdrop.

"And then the guy stripped off all his clothes and
danced across the lawn. And not just any dance, mind
you, but a collection of old style dances from the sixties
that included the Twist, and one you might remember called the Pony."

"I know it," Curtis said.

"Me, too," Kevin chimed in, giving Curtis a warm
smile.

"Well," Sam said with exaggerated anticipation,
"you can just imagine what it looked like. Imagine
what it was like to try to catch him. All the atten-
dants just stood there, watching the guy and shaking
their heads. No one wanted to try to tackle the naked
dancing machine."

Everyone guffawed appropriately, and Dr. T looked
past Sam at me. "Hey, Mack," she said, once she had
her laughter under control. "Sam here was just regal-
ing us with stories of his days working at a mental
health facility. Never a dull moment, it seems."

Linda smiled at me. "Mack, thanks for hosting
this private party. I normally don't even bother with

celebrating New Year's Eve, but this is the perfect way to do it."

"I'm glad you're enjoying it," I said, and as others added their thanks, I settled into an empty chair at their table. "I think it's a great way to kick off the coming year. That, and finally nailing this stupid letter writer."

"Not that again," Sam said irritably.

"Sorry, Sam," I said, winking at him. "I've been informed that some trace evidence we found at Gary Gunderson's murder site, which was his car—has proven to be probative—that's the word the DA used anyway— and the cops have said that an arrest is imminent."

"Really?" Dr. T said, looking doubtful. "That was fast."

"Not really. It's taken more than a week to analyze what we found."

"What exactly did you find?" Linda asked.

I shook my head and winked at them. "It's a secret for now. I've sworn not to tell. But you will all know soon enough—later tonight, I hope. In the meantime, drink up and have a good time."

The next table I hit had Jon, Pete, Debra, and a relieved-looking Missy. I gave them the same spiel about how I hoped to expose the letter writer tonight, and that evidence had been found, but since none of them were on the suspect list, I didn't make any derogatory comments about the letter writer.

The final group to get my spiel was the cop table. Tyrese was there, along with Jimmy and Nick, who had abandoned his spot at the bar to sit with the other two men. It was interesting that Jimmy hadn't so much as acknowledged Suzanne's presence. You'd think he would have at least said hello to her, given that he was working for her and her family. Was his failure to do so because he was trying to hide the fact that he was moonlighting? Or was he trying to hide a more sinister connection?

I fed the cops the same story I had given all the others, and then quickly made an excuse to leave, knowing that this group was likely to be more inquisitive, and knowledgeable, about the evidence issue than the others. And I didn't want to have to dodge their questions.

After leaving the cop table, I went over to a table where Cora—her laptop on the table in front of her as always—the Signoriello brothers, Mal, and Clay were all seated with the O'Reillys. "The stage has been set," I said. "Now we get to sit back and see what happens."

I saw the O'Reilly clan exchange curious looks, but none of them asked for clarification. Apparently, they were willing to sit back and watch whatever happened.

It was about ten minutes before midnight, so I got up to turn the music down and turn the TV volume up. People got up from their tables and started grabbing the hats, confetti, and noisemakers I had set out in anticipation of the midnight celebration. Duncan popped the corks on several bottles of champagne and started pouring glasses. Everyone was up and moving, and I overheard bits and pieces of conversations about the letter writer. The room was abuzz with anticipation.

I made a quick trip to the bathroom to relieve myself and to do a quick primp before heading back out to the bar for the midnight countdown. I had just exited the bathroom when I heard the scream.

Chapter 25

I hurried back out to the main area as fast as my crutches would take me. Everyone was moving toward the newer section of the bar, and I followed, catching Duncan's concerned look as he scurried out from behind the bar. I heard the gasps and exclamations and knew it was going to be bad.

A crowd had gathered around the top of the stairs going down to the basement. The door was wide open behind the loosened caution tape Mal had strung up. Everyone was staring down the stairs, and as I moved closer, people stepped aside to let me through.

Lying on the floor at the base of the stairs, her legs sprawled partway up the steps, her neck angled into an impossible position, was Suzanne Collier. Her lifeless eyes stared up at us. There was a small pool of blood on the floor on one side of her head, dark and menacing-looking. A spilled drink, the glass shattered into pieces, ice scattered and melting, was on the floor a few feet from her body.

"What the hell happened?" I asked.

Dr. T made her way down the stairs, carefully sidestepping Suzanne's splayed legs, and knelt down beside the prostrate form. She carefully palpated along the front side of Suzanne's neck, feeling for a pulse. It was a knee-jerk reaction, I think, because one look at Suzanne's face and neck left no doubt she was dead.

Dr. T confirmed this a moment later. "I suspect she fell down the stairs. Her neck is broken."

"Is she dead?" Courtney said, her eyes wide.

Dr. T nodded solemnly.

There was a loud gasp that came from the top of the stairs leading to the second level, and everyone turned and looked up. Standing on the landing was Tad, his eyes huge, his face a mix of horror and disbelief.

Whitney, who was standing beside the open basement door, a hand clasped over her mouth, took her hand away and pointed at Tad. "Oh my God!" she said. "You pushed her down the stairs, didn't you?"

Tad shook his head, his mouth hanging open. Everyone was staring at him, and he looked pale and shaken. "No, I didn't push her. I was in the bathroom," he said. "We were . . . she was . . . Oh, God." He collapsed to his knees and buried his face in his hands.

From out in the main bar area, I heard the explosions and cheers from the TV as midnight struck.

Hell of a way to start the new year.

Tyrese stepped forward and spread his arms out. "I need everyone to back up," he said. "Until we can prove otherwise, this is a crime scene."

There was a collective gasp, and everyone took a step or two back away from the basement door. Tyrese then went down the stairs. Nick followed, and once he reached Suzanne's body, I carefully crutched my way down to join them. At the top of the stairs, the others crowded in again. This time it was a different voice, one that was no longer disguised, that made the crowd retreat.

"Everyone get back," Duncan said. He pushed his way to the top of the stairs and then turned to look back at the group. "Arty, take everyone out to the main part of the bar and see to it that no one leaves."

"You heard the man," Arty said, corralling the group back away from the door. "Move."

"What the hell is going on?" Holly said.

A cacophony of murmured comments emanated from the top of the stairs, and from what I could hear, I knew that Duncan's real identity had been exposed. One of the voices was less subtle.

"Duncan, is that you?" It was Courtney Metcalfe who spoke, and she sounded surprised, confused, and pleased all at once.

"It's Duncan all right," Carter said.

"Hell of a disguise," I heard Sam say.

The voices gradually faded as the group was herded away. A moment later, Duncan came down the stairs with Mal on his heels.

Nick and Tyrese were staring at Duncan. "Dude, that's one rocking disguise you're wearing," Tyrese said.

"I know someone who does theatrical makeup," he said. Then he refocused everyone. "How the hell did this happen?" He looked over at Dr. Tannenbaum. "Karen, can you tell me anything more?"

She stared down at Suzanne's body. "It looks like one of her arms is broken," she said, "but that's easy enough to explain with the fall. Given the lay of her body, I'd wager she went down the stairs headfirst and with some force, which implies she was either standing at the top of them or going down them when it happened. And I think she was pushed. If she'd simply lost her footing and fallen, her feet would have gone down first, and she likely would have landed with her head on the stairs and her feet on the floor, the opposite of the way she is. But that's just an educated guess."

I looked at Suzanne's extended and broken right arm, the hand open and palm up. "Look at that hand," I said, pointing. "Is that a sliver?"

Dr. T went to reach for the hand, but Duncan stopped her. "Don't touch her anymore until we can get some gloves." He looked over at Mal, who simply nodded and headed back up the stairs.

While he was gone fetching the gloves, we examined what we could see of the hand in question.

"It's a wood sliver all right," Dr. T said, peering at it. "And a big one. It went into her hand in a distal direction."

"Distal?" Duncan said. He was scratching at his beard again.

"Sorry," Dr. T said with a wan smile. "Distal means in a direction away from the center of the body; proximal is the term for closer to the center of the body. So the direction of this sliver is toward Suzanne's fingertips."

Duncan got up and started inching his way up the stairs, examining the old wooden railings on each side of it. He was almost at the top, facing the upper landing, when he pointed to the rail on his right and said, "Here's where it happened. I can see where the sliver ripped off from the wood." He hovered his hand over the spot without touching it. "For the sliver to have come from this railing, and for it to have gone into her hand in the direction it did, she must have been facing the landing at the top of the stairs," he said. "So either she was on her way up the stairs or she had her back to the stairs when she went down."

Mal returned then, carrying two boxes of gloves.

He handed a pair of gloves to Duncan and then brought the boxes down to the rest of us.

"How's it going up there?" I asked him.

"It's pretty intense. Arty is doing a decent job of keeping everyone corralled, with some help from Teddy. But there's a lot of finger-pointing and questioning going on. I told Cora and the brothers to work with Arty at jotting down or remembering what everyone says the best they can."

Duncan came back down the stairs, stepped off to the side, and proceeded to peel off his fake facial hair, stuffing it all in his pants pocket. Nick was watching him, a scowl on his face.

"What's up with the disguise?" Nick finally said. "That's kind of a dirty trick to play on us."

"We felt it was necessary," Duncan said. Nick didn't look the least bit placated by this explanation. "Do me a favor, Nick," Duncan said after a bit. "Go upstairs and help Arty with the crowd up there. Take notes on anything anyone says."

Nick continued to scowl, but he did as Duncan asked. I suspected the reason Duncan had sent Nick away was because Nick was the only member of our group who was still on the suspect list. My suspicion strengthened a moment later.

As soon as Nick was gone, Duncan said, "If we assume Suzanne was pushed, and we're right about her being the letter writer, then whoever did this might be the person who was working with her all this time. Or it might have been Tad."

"I don't think it was Tad," I said. "His shock looked genuine, and I know his voice well enough to know when he's lying. When Whitney accused him of pushing Suzanne, he denied it. And I'm convinced he was telling the truth."

"So that leaves us with our secondary killer," Duncan said.

Dr. T, who had donned gloves by now, was listening to this conversation with a look of intrigue and shock. "Suzanne Collier is the letter writer?" she said.

"We're pretty sure she is," Duncan said. "But all the evidence we had against her was circumstantial, and we don't know who the second person is."

"Wow," Dr. T said. "Who'd a thought it?" She shook her head and then focused in on the pool of blood by Suzanne's head. "For what it's worth, this blood is mostly congealed already," she said. "That means this didn't just happen. Assuming the Collier woman isn't on any sort of blood thinners, normal blood starts to clot after about five or ten minutes."

Duncan, who had also donned gloves, knelt down beside Dr. T and gingerly turned Suzanne's head to one side, away from the pool of blood. "Here's the source," he said, pointing to a gash in Suzanne's scalp that was about an inch long.

"She probably hit her head on the edge of one of the stairs," Dr. T said, and we all turned to look at the steps.

Tyrese saw it first. "There," he said, pointing to a step about halfway up.

On the edge of the step was a tiny smear of red. Duncan got up and climbed the steps to get a closer look. "Yep, there's a hair here caught in the wood," he said. Once again, he looked at Mal. "We need something to collect evidence in. Can you go up to the kitchen and get some plastic and paper bags?"

Mal nodded and climbed the stairs, careful to avoid the bloodstained one.

Duncan came back down to the basement level and looked around the room as we waited for Mal to return.

The sawhorses Colleen and Ryan had been using were set up a few feet away, planks of wood lying across them. Off to the side of the stairs was some wood framing, the start of the elevator shaft. There was sawdust from the wood cutting and concrete dust from the demolition everywhere.

"This construction debris is going to contaminate all our evidence," Duncan grumbled.

He was right. Suzanne had all sorts of debris in her hair and on her clothes already.

"Where does that go to?" he asked, pointing to a door at the back of the large room.

"To another, smaller room. From there you can access the tunnel that connects this part of the basement with mine."

He nodded. Duncan knew about the tunnel because it had played a key role in the murder of Ginny Rifkin, the first murder he had investigated here.

Mal returned with the bags, and Duncan went about retrieving the hair and bagging it. Then he took out his cell phone and started taking pictures of everything.

Tyrese, who looked flustered and frustrated, said, "I'm not much use to you down here, Duncan. Why don't I go upstairs and start questioning everyone, see if we can get a better handle on what happened?"

Duncan shook his head. "I'm almost done here, and I want to be involved in any official questioning." He snapped a few more pictures and then looked around the room again. "Can we get back upstairs by going through that door?" he asked me, nodding toward the exit at the back of the room.

"Sure."

"Then let's go that way rather than contaminate our scene any more than we already have."

"Okay," I said. "I'll turn the lights on." I crutched over to the door and pulled it open. The light in the adjoining room was on, which was odd, but I thought the O'Reillys might have looked in here and left it on. The walls were lined with empty, wooden shelves, most of them supported by bolts drilled into the cinderblock walls. The one exception was a free-standing bookcase on the other side of the room. That bookcase could be moved aside to reveal a tunnel that led into the part of the basement beneath the main bar area. I was about to cross the room to the bookcase when I noticed the floor. Marking a trail from where I stood were a series of spots—small accumulations of cement dust. These spots were evenly spaced about a foot and half apart and led right up to the bookcase.

"Hey, Mal, can you come over here?" I hollered.

He was at my side in a heartbeat. "What's up?"

"Have you or any of your family members been in here?"

"Not that I know of," he said. "But I haven't been with them every second of the day. I suppose it's possible they might have poked their heads in here."

"Did you tell any of them about the bookcase and the tunnel?"

He thought for a second or two and then shook his head. "It hasn't come up. Why?"

"Because there are footprints, fresh ones, going from here to the bookcase."

Mal stared at the floor, narrowing his eyes. Then he squatted and stared some more. "I'm not seeing any footprints," he said.

"Well, I can see them, and I can smell them."

Mal shot me a look and cocked his head. "Okay."

I turned and hollered at Duncan. "We can't go this

way, either," I said, "because our crime scene extends into here and beyond."

Duncan and the rest of the entourage came over to where I stood, gathering behind me.

"Look at the floor," I said to Duncan. "Do you see those spots? I'm pretty sure they're footprints."

Duncan and the others did what Mal had done a moment earlier, and like Mal, none of them could see the footprints.

"Well, they're there," I said when Duncan claimed he had no idea what I was talking about. "I can see and smell them."

"If you say they're there, then I believe you," Duncan said. The others in the group looked skeptical as they continued to stare at the floor, turning their heads first one way, then another. "So you think whoever pushed Suzanne down the stairs made their escape through the tunnel?"

"It makes sense," I said. "Everyone who comes here regularly knows about the tunnel. Hell, even people who have never been here before know about it because it was on the news back when Ginny was murdered. And think about it. If the person who pushed Suzanne wanted to make sure she was dead, they would have come down the stairs to check. And if they went back up the same way, they'd have to reenter the bar from the new area, and someone might see them. But by going through the basement tunnel, they could have come up the stairs on the main bar side and come out through the hall where the bathrooms are."

"That makes sense," Tyrese said.

"It does," Duncan agreed.

"The basement access on the bar side has been unlocked all night," I pointed out. "So whoever did this could have come over here from that direction as well."

"Is there any way to know that?" Tyrese asked.

Duncan thought about it and then shrugged.

I said, "There might be. But I'd have to go through there to know."

Duncan considered this and then nodded. "We need to be careful not to damage any evidence," he said. "But let's give it a try. Mack, since you can see the footprints in here, steer us a path around them." He turned and looked at Tyrese, Dr. T, and Mal. "The fewer of us that traipse through here, the better. You guys stay here and keep an eye on Suzanne's body."

The three of them backed away from the door, and Duncan looked over at me. "Lead the way, Mack."

Chapter 26

I made a wide circuit of the room and led us over to the bookcase. Once there, I hesitated. "There might be fingerprints on this thing. It's on casters, and it rolls sideways, but whoever moved it would have had to grab it."

"We'll make a cop out of you yet," Duncan said. He looked around for something to use to cover his hand with, but there was nothing in the room.

"I have an idea," I said, and then I offered up one of my crutches.

"Brilliant!" Duncan said with a smile. He took the crutch, positioned the foot end of it inside the bookcase, and then used it to push the thing aside. It took some effort to get it started, but once it got going, it rolled easily. The opening behind it was revealed. The tunnel beyond was dark, but there was a light switch built into the wall. I was about to warn Duncan not to touch this, either, but he came up with an alternative solution. After handing me back my crutch, he reached into his pants pocket and removed his key ring. Attached to it was a small LED light. He clicked it on and shone it into the tunnel. Once we were sure it was empty and there were no obstacles in our way, he reached over and used the little flashlight to flip up the switch.

"Don't go in there yet," I said. "Let me look at it first."

Duncan stepped off to one side so I could center myself in the opening. Then I opened up all my senses.

"Smell that?" I said after a moment.

Duncan gave me a quizzical look.

"It's ginger ale. And something else." I sniffed the air with my eyes closed, and then opened them and looked at the floor in the tunnel. "Damp cement," I said. "There are footprints in here, too. Wet ones. Or at least they were wet. Much of it has dried, but there's some lingering dampness I can smell. And I think I know what caused it."

I headed into the tunnel, hugging the wall so as to not mess up the trail the damp footprints had left behind. "The footprints are full," I said to Duncan over my shoulder.

"Meaning?"

"Meaning that they weren't made by anyone wearing heels. They were made by a flat shoe."

"That rules out most of the women on our list," he said. "Whitney and Courtney are both wearing high heels."

"But Linda isn't," I pointed out. "She's wearing her regular, flat-soled work shoes."

We had reached the opposite end of the tunnel. The door on this end was the back side of a worktable that had been my father's. It too was on casters, and when I handed Duncan a crutch again, he easily pushed it open.

I stepped out into the basement and pointed to my right. The drink canisters and gas tanks were located there, with hoses that led up through the floor and to the drink spigots in the bar that dispensed the sodas and draft beer.

"There's the ginger ale," I said, pointing to a puddle on the floor. "I sent Missy down here earlier to change out the canister, telling her it was empty. But it wasn't. I just said that to give her an excuse to leave Nick, because he had her cornered at the bar. Because it wasn't empty, some of the syrup spilled out of the hose when she unhooked it. And whoever came through here walked through it."

"That's all very interesting," Duncan said. "But how does it help us?"

"It helps us a lot," I said, excitedly. "Because now I know how to identify the person who was working with Suzanne."

I told him what I had in mind, and when I was done, I grabbed a rag from the top of the worktable and ran it through the puddle of ginger ale syrup on the floor. Then we headed back to the other end of the basement, closing the tunnel doors behind us. Once we reached the others, Duncan told them that it appeared the killer had entered and exited this room from the other side of the basement.

"Mack has an idea on how we can identify the killer," he concluded. "I need all of you to head back upstairs and wait for us."

Once everyone was gone, I took the rag I had used to mop up the ginger ale and swiped it along a section of the floor over by where the wall had been torn down. Once that was done, I held the rag beneath my nose and inhaled deeply. I experienced a sound I'd never heard before, a sort of tinkling, crunching noise, as if someone were walking over a pile of broken glass.

I looked at Duncan and said, "Let's do this."

We could hear the clamor of voices in the bar as we climbed the stairs, but as soon as we entered the main bar area, everyone grew quiet.

Duncan went over and stood at the middle of the bar. As I passed the table where Cora was sitting with Joe, Frank, the O'Reillys, and Tiny, I leaned over and whispered something into her ear. Then I followed Duncan and stood at his side.

Duncan took the lead. "As most of you know, Mack here has been getting taunting letters for several weeks from a person or persons who we believe are responsible for the deaths of at least two people." He paused, waiting to see if anyone would say anything, and then continued. "We had good reason to believe that the main person behind those letters was Suzanne Collier."

This solicited a low murmur of comments.

"But we don't think Suzanne was working alone. And now we have good reason to believe that the person who was working with her, the person responsible for at least one of those deaths I mentioned, is in this room."

"It's Tad, of course," Whitney spat out. "Everyone knows he only married Suzanne for her money, and by killing her, he now inherits it all."

Tad, who was sitting at the bar with a drink in front of him, forehead resting in one hand, said, "How many times do I have to tell you? I didn't kill her. We went upstairs so I could show her the Capone Club room, and when we were up there she continued to turn up her nose at the whole idea of the club and my participation in it. We had an argument, and she left. I stayed in the Capone Club room for a while to gather my wits, and then I went to the bathroom up there. I was in there for a while. I have irritable bowel syndrome and stress tends to make me, well, loose."

There were some sniggers in the room.

Duncan said, "Who found Suzanne?"

"I did," Whitney said. "She and Tad had been gone for a long time, so I went to check on them to see if she needed rescuing. I didn't see anyone in the other room or upstairs, so I started to come back out here when I saw that open door to the basement. I walked over there and looked and . . . well, you know the rest."

"So the scream we heard, that was you?" I said.

"Yeah," she said, looking at me like I was an imbecile. "It's not every day I run across a dead body, especially of someone I know."

Duncan looked at Arty, who had also removed all of his fake facial hair, revealing his bald head, which I could see still had traces of whatever glue Isabel had used to secure his wig. "It's likely Suzanne was pushed down those stairs anywhere from five to fifteen minutes before Whitney found her," Duncan said to Arty. "Have you figured out who was where in the time before she was found?"

Arty shook his head. "I haven't asked anyone anything specific. I've just been keeping track of everyone and listening in on their conversations. But your friends over there said no one went into that other section of the bar except for the victim and her husband until that lady went in and found the victim." He pointed toward Cora and the others at her table; they were seated closest to the new addition.

"That's because the killer didn't go through there," Duncan said. "He, or she, went through the basement from this side of the bar."

I was watching the faces of the people who were still active suspects—Nick, Sam, Stephen, Jimmy, and Linda—looking for reactions. But the most I saw was mild interest. Nick and Jimmy were the ones who had the most in the way of motive and a reason for wanting Duncan out of my life. And with his known connection to Suzanne, Jimmy was still at the top of my list. Part of me was disappointed that I'd ruled out both Courtney and Whitney. I disliked both women immensely.

I was tired of speculation; it was time for action. I nudged Duncan with my arm, and he said, "Go ahead."

I approached Jimmy first. He was sitting at a table with Clay Sanders, and I walked up to him and said, "Can you please take off your shoes and give them to me?"

Jimmy gave me a look that suggested he thought I'd lost my mind.

"Do it, Jimmy," Duncan said, his tone brooking no objections.

Clearly irritated, Jimmy bent over and removed his shoes, which he then handed to me. One at a time, I raised them to my face and sniffed. I gave myself a moment to process the smell and then sniffed again to be sure.

I turned and looked at Duncan. "It's not him," I said, the disappointment I felt audible in my voice. I handed Jimmy back his shoes and moved on to Nick. He was standing at the end of the bar near the kitchen.

"Nick, your shoes, please."

He rolled his eyes and gave me an irritated look. But he voiced no objection. He settled onto a nearby barstool, removed his shoes, and handed them to me. I repeated the same actions I had carried out with Jimmy's shoes.

Once again, I turned to Duncan and shook my head. "He's clear."

I turned back to look at the room. Everyone's eyes were on me. The TV had been turned off at some point, and the room was so quiet you could have heard a pin drop. I considered the people I had left: Stephen, Linda, and Sam.

First, I went to Stephen, who was standing over near the door. "Stephen, please remove your shoes." He took a nearby seat, doffed his shoes, and handed them to me without hesitation. I sniffed and handed them back, shaking my head at Duncan.

I moved in on Linda, who was sitting at a table with some of my other staff: Debra, Pete, Jon, and Missy.

"Linda?" I said, looking down at her. "You're next."

Linda's reaction was a shrug. She took off her shoes and handed them to me. I sniffed them three times, unwilling to accept what I was finding. With a heavy sadness in my heart, I handed them back to her, looked at Duncan, and again shook my head.

Carter and Sam were sitting at a table with Holly and Alicia. As I approached them, my legs felt more leaden than usual, the crutches more cumbersome. I stopped between the two men, looked at Sam and did a gimme gesture.

"I don't know what this is about, Mack," Sam said, bending over to remove his shoes. As he took his shoes off, he stared back at me, and there was something in his expression, in the darkness of his eyes, that gave him away. We held our gaze for what seemed like an eternity, and I saw small beads of sweat break out on his forehead.

"Here you go," Sam said, handing me his shoes.

I sniffed them without taking my eyes off him.

"Why, Sam?" I asked, feeling the sting of betrayal as a sharp pain between my shoulder blades. It was as if he had figuratively and literally stabbed me in the back.

I don't know what response I expected from him, but it wasn't the one I got. In the blink of an eye, he bolted up from his chair, ramming into me, and knocking me to the ground. Then he took off running.

The fall stymied me momentarily. I was aware of gasps, grunts, and shrieks from around the room. I saw Duncan and Arty both take off after Sam as he ran down the hallway that led to my apartment door, the basement door, and the alley door. Seconds later, I heard the alarm on the alley door go off and shouts that emanated from down the hallway.

Hands gripped me under my arms and pulled me up. A chair was shoved beneath my butt, and I sank into it. Then I heard Carter's voice say, "Are you okay, Mack?"

I nodded. And then everyone's attention shifted to the near end of the hallway, where Duncan and Arty were dragging Sam Warner back into the room. Sam was handcuffed, and the two cops shoved him into a chair, and then stood on either side of him.

Carter walked over to them, his face a mask of hurt and incredulity. He stopped in front of Sam and looked down at him. "Sam, did you really do this?"

Sam glared up at him and said nothing.

"I've known you since we were kids," Carter said. "I thought we were friends. You're like a brother to me. How could you do something like this?"

"I never wanted to be your brother," Sam said, tight-lipped. "And I did it for you. Don't you see? Mack is one of a kind, a crime-solving machine. I've given you the story of a lifetime, that big break you've been waiting for all your life. I did it for you, Carter. All for you."

Carter gaped at him, shaking his head. "Why?"

"Because I love you, man. Are you really that blind? I've loved you since I've known you. I just needed to show you how much. And after that time at the shore when we went to that party, I knew you loved me, too."

Carter took a step back, a hand clamped over his mouth. His face flushed red, and he looked around the room with an embarrassed expression.

"Get him out of here," I said to Duncan. "I can't stand to look at him anymore."

Duncan and Arty hoisted Sam out of his chair and steered him toward the front door. Carter collapsed onto a barstool, his eyes closed, tears rolling down his cheeks. After rounding up a coat to throw over Sam's shoulders, Duncan and Arty escorted him out of the bar.

I turned to look at the rest of the crowd. They were all dumbstruck. I looked over at Cora. "Did you get it?" I asked her.

"Every move and every word," she said, turning her laptop around so it was facing her. When I had whispered to her after coming back into the bar from the basement, I had asked her to record what was about to happen. Fortunately, she had obliged.

I looked at Tyrese. "Can you see to it that Suzanne's body is taken care of?"

He nodded and took out his cell phone.

To the rest of the group, I said, "Happy New Year, everyone. Mack's Bar is now closed."

Chapter 27

The bar remained closed the following day, while cops and technicians came in and out throughout the day, searching for evidence, shooting pictures, and questioning me. Somewhere around nine in the evening, they finally all left. I sat at my bar alone, listening to the silence, ruminating over everything that had happened, sipping on a drink I called a Bittersweet. It seemed appropriate.

My cell phone rang, and I saw it was Duncan. I almost didn't answer it, not wanting any intrusions. But in the end I took his call.

"Hey, Duncan."

"Hey, Mack. I'm out front. Can I come in?"

I debated my answer for a few seconds, but in the end my curiosity won out over my desire for seclusion. "Be right there."

I disconnected the call and crutched over to the front door, unlocking it. Duncan stepped inside, and I closed and locked the door behind him. When I turned around, Duncan pulled me into his arms and held me in a tight bear hug. We stayed that way for a good minute or more. When he finally released me, he held me by my shoulders and looked down at me.

"Are you doing okay?"

"As well as can be expected," I said. "I'm still struggling over how someone so close to me could betray me that way, and wondering how it was that I couldn't see it. He totally fooled me."

"He fooled everyone," Duncan said.

"Have you talked to Carter today?"

Duncan nodded. "He's having a rough time of it. Given that he and Sam were childhood friends, you can imagine how betrayed he feels."

I could, and my heart went out to him.

"He had no idea Sam felt that way about him," Duncan went on. "Though in retrospect he said there were signs he should have picked up on. He said Sam kept trying to convince him to break up with Holly, claiming she wasn't good for him, that she stifled his inner artist or some such garbage."

"I need to sit down," I said, feeling my arms aching as I held myself up with my crutches. We made our way back to the bar, and I offered Duncan a drink.

"I'll take you up on that offer, but let me make it myself," he said. He went behind the bar and started pouring. "We went to Suzanne Collier's place and found enough evidence to verify that she was behind the letters," he said as he worked. "We found the paper, and the calligraphy tools and ink, and she even kept a diary of her clues that included the names of the people she used to deliver them, the dates and times, and pages upon pages of disturbing rants and trains of thought that make it clear she wasn't right in the head. The shrink she was seeing said she was a classic sociopath and a narcissist, incapable of empathy. Her parents identified issues with her when she was very young and started her seeing shrinks when she was a little girl. Apparently, they made access to the family money conditional upon her ongoing cooperation. They thought she was doing fine. So did her shrink, for that matter."

He had finished making his drink, one called Crazy Broad, which seemed doubly apropos given our topic of conversation, and the fact that it included ginger ale.

"I knew something was off with her," I said. "Even her voice showed it. I had two different responses to it, and that's never happened before."

"Well, that makes sense in a way. Sociopaths are able to adopt personalities that suit their situations. You were probably picking up on the real Suzanne as well as whatever persona she was putting forth for you."

"I think Clay knew more than he let on," I said. "When I mentioned to him that I thought Suzanne had some serious mental health issues, he didn't react or ask me any other questions about it. That's so unlike him. It should have clued me in."

"He probably wouldn't have said anything anyway," Duncan said. "My guess is he heard the rumors about her but had no real firsthand knowledge."

"How on earth did Suzanne get hooked up with Sam?"

"He met her while doing his graduate work. He spent time doing clinicals for a shrink here in town, and it happened to be the same one Suzanne was seeing. In fact, he was allowed to oversee some of her sessions. They took a liking to one another—birds of a feather, I suspect, because one of the shrinks I talked to said Sam displays sociopathic behaviors too. Suzanne invited him to come to her house for some of the sessions, an effort to avoid the paparazzi, and the two of them started talking about their mutual dissatisfactions in life, including the inattention they were getting from their respective love interests and, in Sam's case, his financial woes."

"Financial woes?"

Duncan nodded. He came around and slid onto the barstool beside me before continuing. "Sam was paying for his education on his own. His parents don't have much money, and his father suffers from some mental disorders that caused him to lose jobs and get committed a time or two. The family finances suffered as a result. Sam was pretty broke when he started counseling Suzanne, and she offered to help him out with an under-the-table scholarship of sorts. In return, he had to do some things for her, one of which was falsify her medical record about their sessions.

"When Sam followed Carter to your Capone Club group, Sam and Suzanne started plotting out how to commit the perfect crime. They came up with a 'strangers on a train' plan wherein each of them had to kill someone, both to provide them with some security and trust in one another, and to confuse the authorities. The plan to involve you and start writing the letters came about as a result of the two of them trying to find a way to kill two birds with one stone—pardon the pun—and not only prove their superior intellect, but provide a means of getting more attention from their love interests. Suzanne hoped the killings would scare Tad into staying away from the bar—based on what she had written in her diary, she was jealous of you and fearful that Tad had a crush on you—and Sam hoped to give Carter a best-selling true-crime novel to write, one Sam could later take credit for to prove how devoted he was."

"Why were you excluded from helping me?"

"According to Sam, you were the crux of the story, you and your abilities. That's what he was convinced would sell. Assistance from the cops would have weakened that, and in his mind, it would have also weakened the story. He knew he couldn't do much to keep the cops who were part of the club from participating, but he felt that excluding them from the letter project would be easy enough."

"I'm surprised Suzanne went along with it if she was jealous of me. Having you around would have reassured her, I would think."

"You're right. And she did, in fact, argue the point with Sam, according to him. But he was insistent on no police being involved, and when you hooked up with Mal, Suzanne seemed to be satisfied that you had an alternative love interest."

There was a period of silence while we both digested the many ironies of this. After a sip or two, I asked Duncan, "So, did Sam kill Lewis?"

Duncan nodded. "And he said Suzanne did kill Gary. The rest of it was a joint effort. Suzanne collected a lot of the clues and identified the people who were targeted to deliver them to you. And she put up the money that motivated those people, of course. But she had Sam drop off the letters to the deliverers. He also advised her on how to make sure there was no forensic evidence that would lead back to either of them."

"So all this time, while Sam was part of the Capone Club, we were teaching him how to do what he and

Suzanne did in a way that would let them get away with it," I said, shaking my head.

"Ironic, eh?" Duncan said, and we both took a drink.

"Sam advised Suzanne on the wording in the letters," Duncan went on, "doing it in a way that he thought would wreak psychological havoc on you, ramping up the threats and the terror for a bit, and then dialing it down a little before ramping it up again."

"Well, he did a top-notch job of it," I said. "The fact that he was part of this isn't going to help my case with Holland when it comes time to work with him. He and Dixon were both resistant to including the Capone Club, and now they'll be even more against it."

"Maybe. Maybe not," Duncan said.

I looked over at him with an apologetic smile. "I'm sorry I was so insistent on the topic of Jimmy. I really thought he was the one."

"I get it," Duncan said. "And for what it's worth, he's been suspended for the time being until they can look into his work for the Colliers and make sure he had nothing to do with this."

"He won't lose his job, will he?"

Duncan made an equivocal face. "Nah, assuming they clear him of the letter writer thing. He'll get his hands slapped for the moonlighting, but he'll keep his job."

There was another period of contemplative silence while we both sipped our drinks. Then I broached a question that had been bugging me ever since the big revelation.

"Why did Sam think Carter might reciprocate his feelings for him? What was he referring to when he mentioned something in their past?"

Duncan coughed and wiped his mouth with his

hand. "It seems there was this one night when the two of them were seniors in high school. They went to a party and got pretty wasted, drinking and smoking pot. At one point, they drove out to the lake and went skinny-dipping. It was an isolated spot they'd been to before, but this time when they came out of the water, they collapsed on the shore and then smoked some more weed. One thing led to another, and they indulged in a . . . shall we say . . . a mutual satisfaction session. No intercourse, but apparently they, um, helped one another reach their goal. It was hands only, according to Carter, and he was embarrassed about the whole thing afterward and wanted to forget it had ever happened. But apparently it was enough to fuel Sam's fire."

"Wow," I said, shaking my head. "Carter must be devastated."

"He's quite distraught over the whole thing, but I think he'll be okay in the long run."

"So what happened between Sam and Suzanne? Why did he push her down the stairs?"

"Apparently, you got Suzanne spooked when you started talking about evidence and perfume on a car armrest. She thought we had her, and she panicked. Sam overheard that part of your conversation with her and sensed that she was getting worried, so he went through the basement after Suzanne and Tad had disappeared into the new section. He came up the stairs and listened in on the two of them. He heard their argument, and when Suzanne came down from the Capone Club room by herself, he summoned her over to the stairs. We'll never know for sure what happened, because we only have Sam's version of things, but he said that Suzanne got upset with him and threatened to cut him off and turn him in. He said she taunted him, telling him how they'd never believe him over her, and even if she was arrested and tried, she had the money to hire the best lawyers in the country. Sam got pissed and shoved her. He claims he was only trying to scare her, not kill her. But I don't believe that. There's a side to Sam that he hid well from us, a very scary side."

He had that right.

I drained the last of my drink and then turned to face him. "Can we talk about Courtney?"

Duncan cleared his throat and took a long tug on his drink before he answered. "Yeah, about that. I spoke to her earlier this morning and made it crystal clear to her that not only were we done as a couple, but if she continued to try to contact me, I'd take out a restraining order on her."

"That seems clear," I said, with a smile.

"Yeah, well, the restraining order was an empty threat, because she hasn't done anything to justify it. No one would grant it to me at this point. But I'm counting on her not knowing that. I can't promise you what she will do, but I can promise you what I will do. Unfortunately, she is friends with Whitney, and if she mentions my threat of the restraining order to her, Whitney is likely to tell her it's an empty threat." He paused and shrugged. "We'll just have to wait and see what happens, I guess."

"Well, thank you for talking to her," I said. "And speaking of Whitney, when I spoke with Billy on the phone, to let him know the bar would be closed today, he informed me he has put things on hold with Whitney for now. That's good news as far as I'm concerned. Whitney wasn't the right match for him. But I suspect the wrath of Whitney and Courtney combined could be considerable. We may be in for some fireworks."

"If we are, we are. We can handle it together."

I liked the sound of that.

"Speaking of together, there's no longer a need for you and Mal to pretend to be a couple. But given that we don't want anyone to know what he really does for a living, the two of you might need to stage a breakup. Assuming that's what you want, that is."

Was it? My feelings for Mal ran deep, but my feelings for Duncan ran deeper.

"I adore Mal," I told him. "But my feelings for him are more brotherly than romantic. I don't want to hurt him, but I don't know that I can avoid that. Besides, he's going to be around for a while yet building my elevator."

"He really cares about you," Duncan said, a hint of worry in his voice.

"I know he does. And I care for him. Just not in the same way I care for you." I gave him a warm, hopeful smile.

"That's a good thing, I think. Given your new working relationship with Holland and Dixon, you and I are going to be spending a lot of time together." He winked at me, and then he leaned over and kissed me. It was a very nice kiss that sparked all sorts of synesthetic reactions.

When we finally pulled apart, I said, "I guess I'm going to have to let Mal down easy. And keep it amicable. Otherwise I'll end up with an unfinished construction project in my cellar."

Duncan downed the last of his drink, set his glass on the bar, and slid off his stool. Then he extended a hand to me. "Any chance we can continue this conversation upstairs in your apartment?" There was a deliciously wicked gleam in his eye.

"Can do," I said, grabbing my crutches.

And as we headed upstairs, I felt good about the future for the first time in a long while, confident that the coming year would be a happy one.

Look for the next Mack's Bar Mystery
in August 2018!

Now, turn the page
for some enjoyable drinks recipes
from Mack's Bar!

Recipes

Bloody Bubbles

1½ ounces silver tequila
5 ounces pineapple juice, chilled
½ ounce simple syrup
3 ounces champagne, chilled
½ ounce grenadine

Mix tequila, pineapple juice, and simple syrup together in a tall glass. Stir and add the champagne. Top off with grenadine.

Sweet Revenge

½ ounce lime juice or ½ lime
flavored sugar (optional)
1 strawberry (plus one for a garnish if desired)
¼ ounce simple syrup
2 ounces Sweet Revenge Wild Strawberry Sour
    Mash Whiskey
3 ounces dry champagne, chilled

If desired, wet the rim of a tall glass with lime juice and then dip in flavored or plain sugar. Muddle one strawberry and the lime juice or lime in the bottom of a shaker along with the simple syrup. Then add ice and the Sweet Revenge whiskey. Shake and strain into a tall glass. Add champagne. Garnish with a strawberry on the side of the glass if desired.

Super Mimosa

1 ounce of vodka
1½ ounces of Red Bull
1½ ounces of orange juice
3 ounces of dry champagne, chilled

Pour vodka, Red Bull, and orange juice into a shaker
filled with ice. Shake and strain into a tall glass. Add
champagne. Stir gently.

Chocolate Tootsie Roll Pop
(with a cherry option)

1½ ounces light rum
1½ ounces coffee liqueur
1½ ounces Amaretto
3 ounces of cola
½ ounce cherry liqueur (optional)

Pour rum, coffee liqueur, and Amaretto in a tall glass
filled with ice, add cola, and stir. For a cherry Tootsie
Roll Pop flavor, add the cherry liqueur and stir to mix.

Root of All Evil

1 ounce scotch whiskey
½ ounce of light rum
½ ounce of gold tequila
3 ounces root beer

Pour all ingredients into a highball glass with ice. Stir
and enjoy.